WILLIAM MARSHALL

TO THE END

THE YELLOWTHREAD STREET MYSTERIES

To the End
Nightmare Syndrome
Inches
Out of Nowhere
Frogmouth
Head First
Roadshow
The Far Away Man
War Machine
Perfect End
Sci Fi
Skulduggery
Thin Air
Gelignite
The Hatchet Man
Yellowthread Street

THE NEW YORK DETECTIVE MYSTERIES

The New York Detective
Faces in the Crowd

THE MANILA BAY MYSTERIES

Manila Bay
Whisper

ALSO BY WILLIAM MARSHALL

The Fire Circle
The Age of Death
The Middle Kingdom
Shanghai

new M MAR

WILLIAM MARSHALL

TO THE END

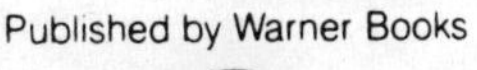

Published by Warner Books

A Time Warner Company

Mysterious Press books are published by Warner Books, Inc.,
1271 Avenue of the Americas, New York, NY 10020.

Visit our Website at http://warnerbooks.com

A Time Warner Company

Printed in the United States of America
First printing: August 1998

10 9 8 7 6 5 4 3 2 1

Library of Congress Cataloging-in-Publication Data

Marshall, William Leonard
To the end / William Marshall.
p. cm.
ISBN 0-89296-575-4
I. Title.
PR9619.3.M275T6 1998
823—DC21

97-39159
CIP

This is—forever and always—
For Mary

The Hong Bay District of Hong Kong
is fictitious, as are the people who,
for one reason or another, inhabit it.

WILLIAM MARSHALL

TO THE END

Wei shan tse liu fang pai shih . . .
The odor of virtuous conduct lasts a thousand generations . . .

—Hankow Province Proverb

METHOD

June 1, 1997: one month exactly before, after one hundred and fifty-six years of British colonial rule, the Chinese People's Republic came in to take back the island of Hong Kong and the old British-ruled areas of Kowloon and the New Territories on the mainland around it.

5:56 A.M., and in the lobby of the sixteen-story Pearl Gardens Government Apartment Building on Icehouse Street, the night janitor, Chester Cheng, standing under the light and gazing at his own reflection in the glass of the main doors to the street, said firmly from the steely and determined depths of his soul, "No, you can do it!"

The steely and determined depths of his soul had the power and strength and youth and sinew-hard leanness of a greyhound, of a whippet.

The reflection staring back at him from the glass didn't.

The reflection staring back at him from the glass had the fatigue and bent-over shoulders of a fifty-five-year-old man staring at himself in a glass door trying to convince himself he was a greyhound or a whippet. And a balding head that seemed to sit at a funny angle on the neck.

But such was Art, such was transformation. Rolling the sleeve of his khaki work shirt back a little from his wrist and stabbing a boney finger at the old Cheng in the glass, the new Cheng, putting a bit of iron into the reflected man's spine, said in the harsh-syllabled street Cantonese that people normally reserved for rabid dogs and teenage daughters, "What's the matter with you? I can't just bring all this up from the depths of my soul! I need a little physical help from you too!" Cheng said, in case his body—that dumb bastard—hadn't quite gotten the message his mind—that glittering repository of all things brilliant—was trying to send it, "You're involved in this too, you know! So pull yourself together and look like someone appealing, someone lovable—someone an audience is going to identify with!"

Outside in the street, behind the reflection in the doors, it was still a few minutes before dawn, and out there, with nothing moving, it was the sort of dark, miserable, misty morning where, if you were a body, all you wanted to do was stagger off to the bathroom and relieve yourself, and then—relieved—crawl back into a nice warm bed and go to sleep.

Cheng, gazing at his body and hating it, ordered, "Wake up! Get that I-don't-care—all-I-want-to-do-is-sleep look out of your eyes and get with the program!" Cheng said, as an afterthought, "And don't look so *old!*"

But he did. He looked ancient.

He thought of other great actors like himself.

He thought of other great actors with funny-looking bodies.

He thought of Dustin Hoffman.

Cheng said to the reflection, "Think of Dustin Hoffman! Think of the world's greatest actor! Think of a man who can do anything, play any part!" Cheng screamed, "Do you think

Dustin Hoffman has to beg his body to look right for the part? No! All Dustin Hoffman has to do is *think* himself into the part and he *is* the part—*and his body automatically transforms itself into whoever he wants to be and does what it's supposed to do!*"

The body standing there staring back at him in the reflection looked like all it wanted to do was sleep.

And he could have taken it by the scruff of the neck and throttled it.

Cheng shrieked, "Great! Terrific! *Thank you!* Here's the big moment—here's my last day on the job! Here's the one day all the fucking rich Europeans up here are going to finally stop and shake my hand and wish me well—because they're all going home, see!—and the one time—*the one time!*—I can be the Eternal Chinese full of suffering facing an uncertain future under the cruel Commies and especially in need of a few last dollars, what do you do? You don't do anything! What do you say? You don't say anything! You don't say *suffering!* You don't shriek pain and terror and deprivation from every pore of your body! You don't cry out silently *Help me!* from the deepest, sunken-socket canyon of your eyes—*all you say with your rotten, stupid, miserable body and your dopey-looking eyes is 'Oh, yeah, good-bye. Who cares? Get lost and let me go to sleep'!*"

Cheng said coldly, "I hate you. I hate you because, inside you, there's a great body trying to get out and it can't."

It was a body that, all his life, had done nothing except carry his mind around.

Cheng, glancing for a moment at his watch and seeing his entire life ending not with a pile of cash but a snore, said vehemently, "I have the mind and the soul of a great actor—of a Dustin Hoffman, of a Jackie Chan—and what do you give me?—you give me the body of a nothing, of a shadow, of an invisible man—of a *janitor!*"

At the end of his last day, he was going to get nothing from the rich Europeans, not even a handshake. After almost thirty years on the job, no one was even going to notice he was gone. Cheng shrieked at his body in the glass, "So thank you! Thank you very much! Thank you for that—*you bastard!*"

He was a man who, all his life, had had nothing. He was a man who had never married, never had children. He was a man with a bland, unremarkable face who, never once, had seen anyone pause in the street even for an instant and notice him.

He was a man who, with a body and a face that registered no emotion, all his life had dreamed his dreams and sung his songs in silence.

He was like a plain, fat, homely-bodied girl no one ever asked to dance, a girl with the soul inside her of an angel.

No one would notice him.

No one would shake his hand.

No one, not even this once when it was his last day on the job and his future was uncertain, would notice the suffering on his face—real or created—or even care.

He could have, if he had had the body and face for it, been a great actor.

He could have been someone.

He was nothing.

He was just someone there on the face of the earth talking to his own reflection in the glass.

He was no one.

Behind him, the center elevator door opened with a hiss, and Cheng, with the tears rolling down his face, said to his body a moment before he turned to see who it was, "What are you waiting for? *Why don't you just kill me now and have done with it?*"

And in that instant, as the two full loads of double-oh buckshot travelling at almost twelve hundred feet per second hit him in the chest with the force of an express train and almost cut him in half, his body did exactly what it was told, and in the storm of blood that enveloped him, he could not believe his mind had not seen it coming, and all he could get out as he fell were the words, "Bastard . . . Bastard! . . ." and wonder why, after his body had thought of nothing but itself all these years, why, why now it had done it.

Hong Kong is an island of some thirty square miles under British administration in the South China Sea facing Kowloon and the New Territories areas of continental China. Kowloon and the New Territories are also British administered, surrounded by the Communist Chinese province of Kwantung. The climate is generally subtropical, with hot, humid summers and heavy rainfall. The population of Hong Kong and the surrounding areas at any one time, including tourists and visitors, is in excess of six and a half million people.

The New Territories are leased from the Chinese. The lease has an expiry date of June 30, 1997, at which time the officials of the Chinese People's Republic of China involved in the planning, promise that Hong Kong will become a special, independent region of the People's Republic with a peaceful blending of British parliamentary rule of law and the Chinese Communist People's Army to enforce it—and if, a month before it was all due to happen, if you believed that was all going to happen peacefully, you were the sort of person who would believe just about anything.

In the lobby, as, after a moment, the center elevator door automatically shut again, all there was, was a hiss.

All there was, was silence.

Hong Bay is on the southern side of the island, and the tourist brochures advise you not to go there after dark.

* * *

All there was, broken and bloody and dead, on the floor of the lobby, reflected in the big glass doors of the main entrance, was the empty and forever soul-silenced body of a janitor, the name of whom, when they were questioned, not one of the one hundred and eighty residents still remaining in the sixteen-story apartment block even knew.

1.

The sign on his desk read:

Detective Senior Inspector Christopher Kwan O'Yee
Royal Hong Kong Police

No, it didn't.

It read, *"Vermin."*

It read, *"Vermin Here."*

It read, *"Aim Here For The Vermin!"*

7:35 A.M., and in the Detectives' Room of the Yellowthread Street Police Station, Hong Bay, just within the last fifteen minutes everyone else had been called out on cases and left him to face the entire horde of Fiends In Human Form due to descend on them all by himself.

The Fiends In Human Form were the advance guard of the liaison section of the Chinese Communist People's Police down from across the border in Canton to begin the first stage of the final process of transition before the Communist People's Republic took over and instituted a new-order Reign of Terror in Hong Kong that was going to make the old order look like a nice, calm, balmy day the Almighty had only dreamt up as a joke before He tossed the Great Flood down to earth and drowned everyone and everything in sight.

In the empty room, trying not to panic, Detective Senior Inspector Christopher O'Yee said in a panic, "Oh God! Oh God! Oh God!"

No good. God had dozed off for a while. You could tell that because, that morning on the news, China State Television had kindly supplied some footage of last night's big final Canton-Peking soccer match and, just in case anyone in the place had a few lingering doubts about the promised coming era of peace and tranquility, thrown in an extra pregame reel of the Canton Police taking a busload of criminals to the match in the comfort of air-conditioned buses to the very best standing-room spots in the stadium, behind the home goalposts.

And then shooting them.

And then going off in their buses again for another load for halftime.

And then—

In the Detectives' Room, O'Yee, trying another line of reasoning other than saying, "Oh God!" and trying another emotion other than panic, said in a panic, "Oh, God! Oh, God! Oh, God!"

He was a Eurasian, half Chinese. He had thought, up until about sixteen minutes ago, that he might stay on in Hong Kong after the takeover and keep a low profile and maybe start up a small business in the construction or export line.

The son of a San Francisco Chinese father and an Irish mother, he thought maybe, if he had any sense, he should get on the phone now to Bums Of America, West Coast Branch, and see if they had a nice job selling pencils on the street he could apply for before the only construction business he got involved in was holding up goalposts with his dead body and exporting film of bits of his blown-off body parts hanging in the netting.

All he knew was Hong Kong. He knew nothing about China. All he knew about China was that the moment the Communists had taken over in 1949 his father had fled the place with everything he had, settled in San Francisco, married an Irish-American girl, and, when he was born, made sure that O'Yee went to a Chinese-speaking school so that he was totally unfit for life in modern-day America, barred from ever entering China as the son of his father, and, on his mother's side, was going to have one hell of a job fitting in with his Chinese eyes and American accent if he ever decided he wanted to live in Ireland and be an Irishman.

He was no one.

He was Number One on their List of Vermin.

Once they spotted him—and, by God, they were going to spot him real quick if he was the only one there to be spotted—he was going to be first up at the old Hong Kong soccer ground even before the goalpost erectors got there to erect the goalposts.

He was doomed.

Oh, and had he mentioned that for the past two decades he had been working in Hong Kong for the British—*who had stolen the entire place from the Chinese in the first place*—as a *cop?*

He was doubly doomed.

He was doomed beyond measure.

He was doomed so deep in doom that, after they shot him before the game, they were going to shoot him again at halftime in the game, and then, after the game was over, they were all going to have a really nice, instructive time for the masses and shoot him again.

And again.

Know thyself.

Words of a very famous English poet whose name in that moment he had completely forgotten, and in his mind he had no room to remember.

He did know himself.

He knew exactly who he was.

7:46 A.M.

In the Detectives' Room, starting to walk around and around in little circles, O'Yee yelled, "I'm scum! I'm garbage! I'm nothing! I'm the son of a treasonous, deserting-rat traitor who fled his ancestral home with all the booty and loot wrenched from the bosoms of the poor he could carry! I'm no one! I'm a nothing! I'm a mongrel cur half-breed running-dog armed oppressor of the people with nowhere to go and nothing to look forward to except maybe a nice view of the setting sun at the other end of the soccer field before it finally sets on me! I'm a cipher! I'm a man without a country! —And I'm doomed! Doomed! *Doomed!*"

"Oh." It was someone standing at the open door: a pleasant-looking northern Chinese man in his fifties wearing an expensive lightweight charcoal-gray suit and matching gray-silk tie with tiny clusters of little silver rings embroidered on it and carrying a black leather bag in his hand.

The man, cocking his head to one side and touching at the tie with a long, carefully and professionally manicured-nailed finger, said softly in what sounded like Parisian-French-accented English, "Oh, I'm very sorry to hear that."

He smiled a sympathetic smile.

It was a very nice smile.

O'Yee said, "Thank you."

The man, still smiling his nice smile, said pleasantly, "Um . . . Mr. . . . O'Yee?"

"Yes."

"Ah." The nice man said, still pleasantly, "Ah." He tapped at his tie: "Colonel Kong, Chinese People's Police. Forgive me for being a little early, would you?"

Sure.

He would.

If he could.

He had all the words, but, like the name of that poet, he just couldn't remember any of the names of them or what they sounded like.

But he said something.

Stimulated by that little touch of human companionship, that wee smidgeon of civilized company, that nice smile, that mellifluous accent, O'Yee, standing facing the man in the center of the empty room like the only player in the only game in town, said, saying it all, "*—AAARRGHHH!!!*"

At the corner of Icehouse Street and the Jasmine Steps, as Detective Chief Inspector Harry Feiffer sat doing nothing but waiting inconspicuously in his unmarked car in the midst of a honking, hooting, screaming, shouting traffic jam of cars and trucks and wagons and pedestrians ignoring the traffic lights completely, someone on the other side of the street—a huge, sweaty, bald-headed southern Chinese man driving a rice truck—decided he didn't like the look of him, and, getting out of his cab onto the running board and cursing at him, hurled a tire iron that bounced off the roof and hit the car behind.

And then the man in the car behind—an otherwise perfectly sane-looking small man in a business suit—went berserk, got out of his car, and, with a stream of invective, threw the tire iron back and took out the truck window with a crash.

And that was all it took. The woman in the car behind the truck—an ancient-looking crone Feiffer knew as one of the lower-grade madams from the red-light district—decided that

that was no way to treat a lady and, in a ladylike fashion, came out of her car and, with even more invective than the businessman had been able to muster—and even more colorful—drew an enormous crescent-bladed beheading knife from her purse and, using both hands on the hilt, stabbed both the truck's back tires and stood there waiting for the truck driver so she could stab him too.

Then things really got nasty, and in a melee of honking and revving and smoke and diesel fuels and screaming, an army of street bums and beggars appeared out of nowhere to relieve the fighting and the fallen of any excess weight of jewelry or coin that might hamper them in their battle, and as the fighting and the fallen turned on them, all Feiffer could do was sit in his car and, in the absence of uniformed cops anywhere in the street, clip his detective's shield to the top pocket of his coat and hope that if at least it didn't say, BEWARE! THIS MAN IS A SWORN OFFICER OF THE LAW, at least it said, BEWARE! THIS MAN HAS A *GUN*—and everywhere, on all the streets all over the Colony, everything was starting to become unglued, and, and even if he had wanted to, there was nothing he could do about any of it.

The glue was gone. It had only ever been applied anyway by what the Chinese had called the *gweilos*: the ghost white people, and now, as they left, as they fled back to England or Australia or America or Canada or wherever they had come from, they were not even ghosts anymore, not even dust—they were not even memories.

What the hell did it matter if you beat the hell out of someone on the street and parked your car in a no-parking zone, or even burned down half the city? Who was going to arrest you? The European *gweilo* cops who weren't there anymore? The uniformed local Hong Kong Chinese cops who were deserting en masse and doing everything to hide the fact that they had ever been cops? The Communists when they came in because you had done something that the old, imperialist, anti-Communist regime thought was wrong?

In his car, Feiffer ducked as something came flying out of the smoke and fumes and ricocheted off his front windshield—and no one, no one was going to do anything except, if they were like him and from a family whose life had been tied up with China and the Chinese now for four generations, do what they could and wonder what the hell was going to happen next and, after the takeover, what they might even be allowed to do then, if anything.

Signs and symbols. Flags and banners and the passing of the last days of the old order before the first day of the new.

Soon, in the nights, there would be the sounds of gunshots as old scores were paid off, as people jockeyed for position and power and influence, and as, in the chaos, everything moved and heaved and became unstable before, the last day, in the new order, like a huge land mass locking back into position, men with power and laws and armies and ideologies came back in and it all stabilized and became still again.

Signs and symbols, flags and banners . . . In the English-language *South China Morning Post* newspaper—a newspaper full of eulogies for its own almost one-hundred-and-twenty-year history and self-pity for its own undoubted imminent demise—it said that it had been reported that somewhere in the Colony, Sun Yaoting, the last eunuch in China—a ninety-five-year-old man who had lived through the last Imperial dynasty, the Nationalist uprising, the Second World War and the Japanese Occupation, and then the Communist Revolution, was either dying or dead—and everywhere, everything was changing, and it was all over and there was no going back on any of it.

In the smoke and the battle, someone shrieked at the top of his voice, *"Sut ne go tao!!* I'll cut your head off!!" and as the truck driver suddenly decided that, flat tires or no, it was time to leave, there was a roar of diesel power and a terrible crashing of gears, and as he blasted his way forward and got onto the sidewalk and mowed down a line of street stalls, there was a break in the jam and Feiffer managed to get through.

He got through to the end of Icehouse Street where, behind a double glass door covered in blood, there was a dead janitor named Cheng lying in two pieces in the lobby with only a single uniformed European traffic policeman and two uniformed Chinese constables there to guard him.

There was a tape cordon run around the entrance to the building to show that it was a crime scene, but it was not an official police three-inch-wide self-adhesive yellow departmental tape marked *Police Line. Do Not Cross Under Penalty Of Law.*

There was none of that left.

No one was making that stuff anymore.

It was a long red length of streamer tape printed along its full length with red stars and a long patriotic message welcoming in the coming Communists.

It was all they had been able to borrow.

Probably, they had not even borrowed it at all.

Probably, when one of them went to get it from the nearest shop or street stall back where the traffic jam was, standing there at the counter in his soon-to-be-history, comic-cop colonial Hong Kong Police uniform, he had been made to *buy* it . . .

At the door, Colonel Kong waited politely to be asked to come in.

At his desk in the Detectives' Room, O'Yee said, "Um . . . Um . . ."

Well, he knew a few words with a French accent too. O'Yee, using both of them, said, "Um . . . Um . . . *Ent-rez.*"

Colonel Kong said with an even wider smile, *"Ah. Si gentil.*

Merci. Merci bien." He could tell exactly from the French accent just how many words with a French accent O'Yee knew.

Colonel Kong said politely in English, "Thank you. Thank you very much."

And came in.

As he came in from the street to the front lobby where the body was, Feiffer had no idea why the uniformed European Inspector in charge or his two uniformed local Chinese cops were still there in the Colony, still working, and, like the rest of the cops in the Colony—even most of Uniformed at his own Station—hadn't fled into anonymity.

Ducking quickly under the red ribbon that roped off the area of the lobby where, everywhere, everywhere, there was blood and viscera and chunks of blown-off human flesh, and where everywhere there was still the smell of cordite and human excreta and urine, the European Inspector, a thin, bloodless-looking man in his thirties, said briskly, "Inspector Burtenshaw, Headquarters Accounts and Planning Section, on temporary fill-in six-week assignment to Traffic and General Duties," and, taking his hand for the brief moment Burtenshaw held it out, Feiffer knew exactly why he was still there.

He was an accountant, a man whose entire life had been spent making sure all the numbers matched, and if the number of days he was required to work to finish out his tour added up to six weeks—to the very brink of the takeover, by God, he was going to work each and every one of them until he reached the full total.

The two uniformed Chinese cops were his clerks. They were going to work too, and then, again, if, by God—by the great God of Numbers—one of them had had to buy the length of nonstandard crime-scene cordon from the private marketplace, then, by God, he had better come back with a receipt.

"Harry Feiffer." It was all pointless. None of it was going to matter anyway. He glanced down at the body. "What happened?"

He looked like a man who, in lieu of life and passion, probably collected clocks. He had almost no accent at all, but if there was one there, to Feiffer's ear it sounded vaguely Australian.

Looking down at the body of the dead man not at all, Burtenshaw said briskly, "According to the ID papers in his pocket, the dead man is one Chester Cheng, aka Cheng Hsioa-ju, age fifty-five, employed as a janitor here in the Pearl Gardens Apartments for the past twenty years or so, and—" He furrowed his brow slightly as if it were something that for a moment didn't seem to have a place in the world but should be put in the remarks column anyway—"And according to an ancient out-of-date Actors' Union card, some sort of part-time unemployed actor who"—he looked down at the twisted, blown-apart creature with a slight pursed-lip disapproval—"Who, according to what looks like part of some sort of newspaper review pasted to the back of it, was once the lead in a revival of some Chinese play or other called *The Return of Uncle Yen* and who the reviewer described as 'bland and lifeless.' "

He was bland and lifeless now. Lying there on the carpet midway between the elevators and the double glass doors to the street, all he was was a dead, waxen-faced man staring forever out at his own reflection in the glass. Burtenshaw said, "Clearly, what happened was that the shooter exited the center elevator there to make a getaway, saw him standing here in the lobby, and in order to avoid identification shot him dead on the spot."

He glanced back to the center elevator. It was open.

Burtenshaw said, "Again, clearly, the weapon involved was a shotgun. Judging by the absence of any ejected shell cases anywhere in the area, probably double-barrelled." Numbers were important. Burtenshaw said as if it were not already obvious,

"The dead man has been shot twice—once dead center in the heart and once in the lower-left side."

He had it all down, all worked out, all tabulated.

"Clearly, the first shot was the one to the side as the man was turning around towards the elevator, which may or may not have been instantaneously fatal, and the second, the one to the chest, which, judging from the extreme major-organ damage, undoubtedly was."

What he meant was that the second shot, tearing through flesh and bone and sinew and soft tissue like a scythe, had blasted his heart and lungs to ribbons.

Feiffer said softly, "I see." It was good, professional police work done by the numbers, but the man didn't need to be told that: he knew it was. Feiffer asked, "What have you done about witnesses?" He glanced at the two silent Chinese cops and saw one of them, almost imperceptibly, smile at the suggestion.

"No witnesses." Burtenshaw said quickly as if he did not quite understand why the Chinese cop was smiling, "My two officers here door-knocked a sampling of all the apartments within earshot on the first and second and third floors—primarily to inform the residents that they should use the rear entrances on their way to work this morning—and no one responded about seeing or hearing anything."

It didn't matter to him: it had nothing to do with his part of the job. Burtenshaw said, to finish at least that part of his report, "The ambulance-transport people are on their way, and I've had Despatch contact the appropriate person at the Government Housing Agency to make a disposition in relation to the cleaning and reopening of the main entrance of the building for the evening use of the tenants, but with the traffic jams and the general chaos outside, I wouldn't expect them to arrive for at least another half hour or so."

"What about Scientific and Forensic?"

Burtenshaw said, "They're already here, on the fourteenth floor."

"Why? Why are they on the fourteenth?" Feiffer said in sudden alarm, "Why are Scientific and Forensic up on the fourteenth floor?" It was so obvious—if his brain had been working. It was so obvious the armed man, firing across the lobby with the shotgun already out in his hands, had come from somewhere else, and done something else *before*. Feiffer demanded, "Why? What the hell happened up there before this did?"

Everything had to be done in order. Obviously, one thing led to another. Obviously, though, there was no point in getting ahead of yourself with a second entry before you had fully dealt with the first. Obviously, the world, like clocks, worked one tick at a time. Obviously, they didn't tick out of order, or instead of going tick-tock they would have gone tock-tick and been useless.

Feiffer demanded, *"Well?"*

He shrugged. Burtenshaw said, "Well, obviously—" It was clear to him, even just on a basic statistical level, that you would hardly have been prepared to shoot a fellow human being dead to avoid identification if you hadn't done something else at least on the same numerical level of risk just a few minutes before. "Well, obviously, there's another body up there—the prime target." He permitted himself a little show of warmth and humanity: "A fellow countryman of mine, I believe, although I didn't know him personally."

He had no idea about anything in the real world at all. To him, all numbers and ticks of the clock were identical, all nothing more than numbers and ticks of the clock all the same, all identical, and neutral and bloodless, all proceeding regularly and in order, all exactly the same.

Burtenshaw said with no tone in his voice at all, merely imparting information, "A Detective Chief Superintendent from, I think, the Anti-Triad Unit. A man in his late forties or early fifties named Charlie Porter."

Numbers. He understood numbers. He looked for the first time directly into Feiffer's face and calculated his age.

Burtenshaw said with no notion of what the hell he was really saying at all, a man who never had any notion of what the hell he was really saying and who could never understand why sometimes people reacted so violently to him and why he had never, never been promoted, "A man about your age. Someone you knew personally, maybe?"

He was a Fiend: you could tell.

Colonel Kong, not sitting before being invited, but standing in front of O'Yee's desk, said in that polite way that all Fiends had, "But, of course, you are wondering, sir, just who is this man? What exactly is his title? How does his existence impinge on mine? How do I address him? And does he have sufficient breeding to know how to address me? What is his role? What does he do? What, in the great ebb and flow of life, does this meeting with him mean to me—if anything—in my own, great, eternal quest for the perfection of my soul?"

No, he wasn't. He was wondering whether the bus ride to goalpost central was free or whether you had to work to pay for your own ticket, or, if you couldn't work because your brain couldn't get your body to move, they just yanked a few gold teeth out of your head with pliers and sold them off—and if, like him, you didn't have any gold teeth, what other part of you they were going to take instead.

O'Yee said, "Yes." He was going to be great under torture. He was the sort of man who wasn't going to tell them a thing until they asked.

Kong said, "Special goalpost shooting section. Mass murder a speciality."

No, he didn't.

Kong said, "Kwantung Provincial Police, Societal Reeducation, Rehabilitation and Civil Rectification Unit, Canton City Division."

Oh, what a relief. He wasn't in the section that took people out to the goalposts and shot them—he was in the unit that turned their brains to Jell-o and then, when they were zombies, ordered someone else to take them out to the goalposts and shoot them. O'Yee said, "Oh."

Colonel Kong, still smiling, said pleasantly, "Yes, I find my earlier background as a monk suits me well for the position."

Funny. For a moment there, he thought he had said *monk*. Obviously, what he had said was *punk*. O'Yee said, "Oh."

"Yes."

"In fact, up until recently, I commanded that unit."

Oh, well, if you were going to go, you might as well go from the top.

O'Yee, still holding up well, said, "Oh."

"Yes." He smiled again, a very nice smile. Obviously, he was enjoying the interplay of rapier-sharp wits and the pleasure of the cut and thrust of rich and far-ranging philosophies very much.

Colonel Kong, touching at the little rings on his tie (garrottes? nooses? empty brainpans?), said happily, "Mr. O'Yee, sir, I cannot tell you how delighted I am to at last make your acquaintance, and with what pleasure I look forward to talking with you!"

He did seem happy. He smiled yet again.

For a Fiend, it was a very nice smile.

Colonel Kong said, still smiling, really not like a Fiend at all, "Please, it would give me such a feeling of warmth and friendship and mutual understanding . . ."

Colonel Kong said, "Please . . ."

He glanced for a moment at the nameplate on O'Yee's desk.

Colonel Kong said, "'Christopher,' isn't it?"

Colonel Kong said, "Please . . . Call me 'Claude.'"

Yes, Charlie Porter was a man he had known personally. He was a man Feiffer had known almost ten years, a man he had—

In the elevator as the light above the door came on for the fourteenth floor, Feiffer said with sudden fear in his voice, "Where's his wife? Where's Annie? *Where's his wife?*"

The elevator door opened and, as it did, all he could see in front of him was Porter's apartment with the door swung back, and everywhere, moving around just inside the main room, people in protective coveralls and face masks working carefully around the body of a man who had taken a full shotgun blast in the face and, for a head, had only a blasted-away and blackened mass of blood and bone and brain and viscera.

He saw Annie, still in her nightdress and robe, sitting directly opposite it all, staring down at the blood with eyes that saw nothing, holding her hands clasped together in front of her like a little girl and slowly rocking back and forth, back and forth.

Burtenshaw, still talking, still computing, said tonelessly to explain the entry in the column, "Statistically, in violent deaths occurring in the home setting, typically the surviving wife or husband runs a better than eighty-five percent chance of being either the perpetrator or co-conspirator, and I deemed it best to keep her on the scene rather than let her run off loose without adequate supervision," and in that moment Feiffer could have turned and taken the man by the throat and, so quickly he would not have even known it happened, strangled the life out of him.

But he didn't.

He had no more time for that, no more time for him. All he had time to get out was to roar at the top of his voice into the man's stupid, dumb, bland, smug accountant's face, "Are you *crazy?* Are you completely out of your fucking *mind?*" before he shoved his way into the apartment past all the coveralled and gloved and masked people, past the awful dead thing on the floor, and, taking her by the shoulders at once, got Annie to her feet and propelled her out of the room down the corridor and away from it all to safety.

Maybe he wasn't a Fiend at all, maybe he was just a—

Or was he?

Suddenly, on Claude's face the smile was gone.

Suddenly, in Claude's eyes, something seemed to harden, become darker.

Leaning a little forward in his chair, Claude said softly, not exactly just one old chum to another, but in a suddenly colder, more businesslike, more Fiendish tone of voice, "Now Christopher, I know where you are, and I know, because I heard the call on the police radio on my way over here, where Detective Chief Inspector Feiffer is . . ."

". . . But the other two members of your squad, your other two detectives—Detective Inspector Spencer and Detective Inspector Auden. Exactly where are they? Do you know? And exactly what are they doing at 7:45 A.M. on this first day of the last month before, after over a hundred and fifty years of vicious, cruel, and oppressive imperialism on the part of the British rulers and all the running dogs who serve them, the forces of the great Chinese People's Republic of China come in to make everything in what was once the truly despised and evil British Crown Colony of Hong Kong right and fair and legal, and, above all, morally incorruptible and *pure* again?"

2.

Where were Detective Inspectors Auden and Spencer, and what were they doing?

Well, on a rise just above the waterfront, they were standing stopped at the glorious, coffin-crowded corner of Wooden Box Street and Dire Fortune Road having a little conversation.

It was a very little conversation. It was one word.

It was Auden's word.

That word was, "*No!*"

Auden, shaking his head to make it a little clearer to knucklehead, and then waggling his finger to make it even clearer, said, standing his ground, "No. No. No. No. *No!*" It was his last day on the job: maybe knucklehead had forgotten that. Auden, taking a step backwards, said, "No, it's my last day on the job and I'm not fooling with that stuff the way Old-Whatever-His-Name-Was fooled with the Mummy's Curse in Egypt and spent the rest of his life coming out in scabs and warts and buttons!"

"You won't come out in scabs and warts and—" Detective Inspector Spencer said, "Buttons?" Spencer asked, "Do you mean Howard Carter and the tomb of Tutankhamen?"

Auden said, "Whatever." (Forget the buttons. That was a mistake. That was a family affliction anyway and the less said about that the better.) Auden said, "I read all about that sort of stuff in a magazine once in a dentist's office when I was a kid about Old-Whatever-His-Name-Was. He went into a place like that once and after that everyone who ever touched the thing died, or came out in scabs and warts and . . . and died a horrible death!"

"What thing?"

"Whatever the thing was he got from the Mummy's Tomb!"

He hated it when people got things wrong. Spencer said as a matter of information, "Carter didn't get anything from the Mummy's Tomb in Egypt! That was the Hope Diamond, and someone else got that from the eye of a stone idol named Rama-Sita in India!"

Aha! Even closer to home! Auden, taking yet another step backwards, said with his face set, "No! No! No!" It was a very full dentist's-office magazine story. "It's all the same stuff. You start fucking with any of that stuff and even if you don't come out in warts and Christ only knows what else, they—"

Who were They? The Mummies? The Rama-Sitas?

"And they find a way to get you and they sneak into the library of your castle at night and they get their poison blowguns and they—"

He had spent a lot of time in dentists' offices.

The dentists had obviously had very cheap taste in reading material.

Auden said, "And they—they get you!"

They were heading for the Geomancers' Union Building on Tiger-Dragon Square, two blocks away. (Well, one of them was anyway.)

Spencer, shaking his head and trying to be reasonable, said firmly, "Chinese geomancy—Chinese earth magic—*feng shui*—is not the same as the Mummy's Tomb or the Curse of the Hope Diamond! *Feng shui* isn't all about getting bad luck—it's all about changing bad luck into good luck!"

It was like reading a Peter Rabbit book to an inattentive child: every line or two you had to stop to discuss the color of Peter's ears.

Spencer said, "The Geomancers' Union is Good Luck Central! It's where the geomancers think day and night about how they're going to get rid of people's bad luck and, instead, bring them good luck!" Peter's ears were snow white. Spencer, reaching out to pat the man on the shoulder, asked with a smile, "Okay?"

Not okay. How old did he think he was? Six?

Auden said in intellectual triumph, "Oh, yeah? And where the hell do they keep all the bad luck after they've gotten rid of it?"

He'd seen *Ghostbusters*, both of them—his information wasn't just restricted to what he read in dentists' offices.

Auden roared, "I'll tell you what they do with it—they take it back down there to their union building—to home base—and they put it there on shelves or in cupboards so some poor mutt can walk in there, brush up against it, and then spend the rest of his life—" Auden said, "No! No, I'm not going down there! Not for anything!" Auden said suddenly, "And anyway, what the hell do they want us for anyway?" Aha! The master stroke! "If they're so great at bringing a little bit of good luck to everyone else, they must have put it aside for themselves by the ton!" Physician, cure thyself. Auden roared, "So why the hell would they need a couple of cops to bring them anymore?" He was getting into the swing of things here: he could feel the great Auden brain firing on all cylinders. *"Obviously, they—"*

"They weren't the one who called! Someone else called!"

Auden demanded, "Who?"

He didn't want to say. Spencer said, "Um—"

"Aha!"

Spencer said, "The Duke!"

John Wayne? Things were that bad? Auden said, "Who?"

He just didn't want to say. Spencer said softly, shrugging it off, "The— Someone else . . ." It was in Mandarin. He knew Auden didn't speak Mandarin. After today, when he went back to England, he was taking up an appointment, first as a part-time tutor in classical Chinese at Oxford, and then, if things worked out, as a full-time don. Spencer said donnishly, "The Yen Sheng Kung!"

"Oh." Someone big? After today, when he went back to England, with all the other ex–Hong Kong cops over there all looking for exactly the same sort of work, he was going to be lucky if he got an appointment as a kids' balloon seller in Hyde Park. Auden said, "A local? Someone . . . important? With influence?"

You could say that. He said that. Spencer said, "Yes, you could say that." He saw the little piggy eyes gleam. Spencer said, "It was a call from none other than the Yen Sheng Kung himself and he asked for both of us to do him a little favor and go to Tiger-Dragon Square personally for a little while until he could get there and—" Spencer said, "See! It's got nothing to do with the Geomancers' Union at all! The Yen Sheng Kung isn't even a geomancer! He's a— He's a—" He gave him both barrels. Spencer said, "I've only ever read about him, but he's a—" Spencer said, barely able to control his excitement, "Phil, he's the Duke Of Extended Holiness, the Sage Of All Sages, the *k'o*—the Imperial Guest—a person of such learning and influence and importance that for as long as Chinese history has been recorded, not one member of his family has ever—*ever!*—had to bend his knee to anyone—not even the *emperor!*"

"Really?" That big. Auden said, in spite of himself, "Wow!"

"Yes!" Spencer said, "And I'd give anything just to be able to say I once met him . . ." It made him tingle all over. "Just to be able to say I once stood in the presence of someone like that—in the presence of everything that's *China* and all the thousands of years and millennia of Chinese learning and culture and civilization and—"

"Well, yeah. Yeah, I can see that, Bill. But—"

"It'd mean a lot to me, Phil."

"Yeah." Well, he could see that. Auden said, nodding, with both his brain and his voice box working in unison, "Yeah. I can see that . . ."

Gold! Riches beyond the dreams of avarice!

Auden, starting to nod, said, kind and thoughtful and ever-fast friend that he was, "Well, I can see that would be pretty important to you, Bill. I mean, after all, I guess there's not much to think about at Oxford and places like that, and a few nice memories . . ."

Spencer said, "Exactly!" Spencer said, throwing his hands away in the air as if it were just . . . just something for nothing, a mere trifle, a bagatelle, "And it's just such a little favor—something men like us could do with a mere flick of our wrists, something . . ."

"Sure." He was going, wavering. The eyes nothing more than tiny little glittering points of light. After all, whatever else was happening in the world, he was still a man of strength and power and muscle. And heavily armed. Auden said, "What is it anyway? What is it he wants us to do down there?"

He put his hand on Auden's shoulder and gave him a hearty and harmless encouraging little pat. "Nothing! A mere nothing!" He was so excited by the prospect he could hardly keep himself from falling down onto his knees and shouting up humbly to the heavens to thank them for the chance. Spencer said, "He just wants a little pro-active police work, that's all. He just wants us to toddle over to Tiger-Dragon Square—you know, the confluence of *ch'i*, the life-giving energy, and yin and yang, the opposing forces of good and bad and dark and light and earth and heaven, and . . ."

Spencer said in a rush, "And because everything there has gone wrong and everything is in flux and heaving and exploding and full of demons starting to fly off from the center, stop the entire universe and all human life that inhabits it from destroying itself in one huge cosmic explosion of total desolation and evil until he can get there!" Spencer said brightly, "Okay?"

There was a terrible silence.

Spencer said, still brightly, ". . . Okay?"

Spencer said, "Okay, Phil?"

He hoped very much that Auden would say, "Okay."

He didn't. He didn't say that at all.

Auden said, "What?"

Scabs, warts, buttons: somehow, standing there, they seemed like things hardly even worth mentioning anymore.

Auden said, *"What?"*

He kept trying to get past that one word, but couldn't. Auden roared, *"What?"* and then, with a mind honed razor-sharp by the steady whetting of the emery stone of a childhood spent exposed to all the best intellectual challenges dentists all over London had had to offer, got past it in one great elegant insight that encapsulated everything in a single word.

Auden said again, *"What?"*

And then the elegance.

Auden roared, "No! No! No! *NO!!*"

* * *

The little nameplate on his desk didn't say *Chief Number One Blabbermouth*, it said *Detective Senior Inspector* . . . um, someone or other.

There was a point beyond which no man should go, even tho' it cost him his life.

Leaning back in his chair and stiffening his back, O'Yee said formally, "I'm sorry, but I regret to have to tell you that in the light of the current legal and political situation presently obtaining in what is still, at least for another month, the British Crown Colony of Hong Kong, I am unable to satisfy your curiosity concerning the present whereabouts of either Detective Inspector Spencer or Detective Inspector Auden, or, indeed, what they may or may not be doing there at this time."

It seemed to please him. Colonel said with a beam, "Ah, an honest man!"

He was. O'Yee said, "I am." It was the truth. He wasn't in a position to tell anyone where Auden and Spencer were for the simple reason that all he knew about where Auden and Spencer were was that ten seconds after Harry Feiffer had taken off to the Pearl Gardens Apartments on a homicide call, Spencer had gotten a phone call, screamed something that sounded like, "Oh my God! The Mother Lode!" and then, taking Auden in his wake as he went, rushed out the door of the Detectives' Room like a complete madman, and, like everyone else, *gone off and left poor Mutthead still sitting at his desk to face the Fiend from Hell alone!*

O'Yee said, "I am." He was. O'Yee said, "I am!"

"Ah, the rewards of virtue are too numerous for an honest man to count."

"They are?" They were. O'Yee said, "They are!" He thought things were going a little better. He thought things were going so much better he would pull open the top drawer of his desk and get a cigarette. O'Yee said happily, "Yes!"

He pulled open his drawer and pointed in to tell old Claude that if he felt like a quick puff too, then—

The drawer was full of money and gold and gold coins and more money and—

O'Yee said, "Oh, shit!"

It was Informers' Day, the day when all the police informers came in to get their payoffs. O'Yee said so quickly it all came out as one word, "Um, um, um . . . Um, *it's Informers' Day! It's the day when all the police informers come in to get their payoffs!"*

He moved not a muscle. Claude said pleasantly, still smiling, "Of course it is."

"And any moment the phone will start ringing and the first of them will check that the coast is clear and then he'll come in for his payoff, and then, when he's gone, the next one will ring and check that the first one has gone and then he'll come in for his payoff and then—" He looked down at the money.

It was a lot of money. And gold. And gold coins, and—

Claude said pleasantly, "Of course." He looked down again at the loot and smiled.

"The phone will ring!"

"Yes." Claude said again, "The rewards of virtue are too numerous for an honest man to count." He leaned forward a little and glanced into the drawer to count them.

"It'll ring!"

"Yes."

"It will!"

"Of course."

"It will!" O'Yee said desperately, "It'll ring! Any moment now, it'll ring!—*Honest!"*

Spencer's turn for a few "No's."

Putting his hand on Auden's shoulder to try to drag him

around the coffin-packed corner of Wooden Box Street into Unfinished Coffin Lane where there were even more coffins, Spencer said, "No, the Yen Sheng Kung—the Duke Of Extended Holiness—is not the traffic cop directing people straight down the highroad to hell, he's a nice person! He's a good person! He's a person full of—"

He thought he was talking to a moron! He thought he was talking to the sort of vile, cursed, wart-faced moron who sold balloons in the park, and—when people like Spencer and his Oxford buddies came strolling along with their wives named Titania and their brats named Tarquin and bought a balloon from him—said, "Arrgg! Arrggg! Thankee, kind Master," and nodded droolingly as said buddies and their buddies gave their brats little liberal lectures about always being consistently kind to poor creatures like Quasimodo.

Spencer said, "He's a, and a . . ." Maybe the holy thing had put him off a little; God and holiness and hell and all that sort of stuff.

Spencer said, still dragging, making a little headway, "The actual title in full, Yen Sheng Kung, maybe doesn't actually mean Duke Of Extended *Holiness* because in ancient Mandarin it's possible that 'holiness' has a significance—at least to Western ears—that wasn't originally intended way back then in—Way back then, two and half thousand years ago, and, certainly, from my own reading, the term would fall closer to the meaning of 'sagehood' rather than holiness for the simple reason that, as a Confucian title, it would necessarily be part of a more religiously neutral and purely pragmatic philosophical stance than one that the translation of the term 'holiness' might imply, and—"

He was nuts. He was crazy. He was raving.

Auden, de-dragging, said firmly, wrenching the man's arm off his shoulder and planting himself like a rock, "No, I'm not going into Fang and Fire Square—"

Spencer said pettishly, "Tiger-Dragon Square!"

"Or whatever the hell you call it and get turned into some sort of toad by some sort of evil fucking Demon or Mummy or what-the-hell it is on the say-so of some lunatic who should be locked up in a rubber room and fed through a rubber tube—and that's all there is to it!"

"The Duke Of Extended Holiness isn't some lunatic who should be locked up in a rubber room and fed through a tube! He's—"

He hadn't meant the Duke. He had meant Spencer. Auden, starting to take a step backwards from whence he had come and to whither he intended to go at the speed of fucking light, said to make it clear to the Mad Hatter of Hong Bay that somewhere out there there was a real world, "No! No! No! I'm not going to Fang and Fire Square or Snap and Snarl Square or—"

Spencer said, "Tiger-Dragon Square."

"—or whatever the hell you want to call it, and that's the end of it—and certainly not on the say-so of some Duke Of Extended Whatever, who, for all I know, is some sort of evil spirit himself trying to lure me into the Mummy's Tomb or across to India to the idol of fucking Raving-Sitar or whatever the hell it is, and that's the end of it!"

"It's not Raving Sitar, it's *Rama-Sita!*"

"Whatever!"

It was the end of it. He turned to go.

All right. He was going to keep this for a little surprise, but now—now he gave him both barrels at once. Talking to Auden's back, Spencer said in a voice suddenly full of strength, "He isn't an evil spirit, and, no, you're right, he isn't anyone very important in the 'big' sense, in the sense of money and commerce and manna and—" He was snarling. Spencer said, "You're right! He is a lunatic! He's out of his mind, and he's no one! He's no one either of us should ever spend a moment of our time going out of our way to meet! He's a nothing, a zero, a cipher—in the real, hard world—in the world of today—a joke—in the hard, commercial, money-grubbing, live-for-the moment, me-generation, a no one! A joke! *A Nothing!*" He was almost in tears. Spencer said suddenly angrily, "Go! Go then! Go then on thy way and—" Spencer yelled, "You fool! You moron! You, you—" Balloon seller? "You unlucky man! Don't you know who he is? Don't you *know?* Don't you know who it was who called me and asked for our help? It was the Yen Sheng Kung! It was the Duke Of Extended Sagehood! It was, in an unbroken line for two and a half thousand years of Chinese history, the authentic and direct descendant of *Confucius!*"

Oh.

Oh, *him?*

Spencer said quietly, "And I would die a thousand deaths and a thousand more after that for the mere privilege of even seeing him as he passed by me."

Well, so would anyone. Turning back from whither to whence, Auden said, "Yeah, well . . . Well, so would anyone . . ."

Spencer said in a voice that strongly resembled Gregory Peck doing Douglas MacArthur, "It's your last day on the job and, in His greatness, God has sent an old soldier one final great battle to wage, one last Titanic struggle with the forces of Good and Evil to fight, one crowning—" Spencer quoth ringingly, "But, no! Go if you will!—

> He who hath no stomach to this fight,
> Let him depart; his passport shall be made,
> And crowns for his convoy put into his purse;

We would not die in that man's company
That fears his fellowship to die with us.
This day is called the feast of Crispian;
He that outlives this day and comes safe home,
Will stand a tip-toe when this day is nam'd,
And rouse him at the name of Crispian.
He that shall live this day, and see old age.
Will yearly on the vigil feast his neighbours,
And say, "Tomorrow is Saint Crispian:"
And then will he strip his sleeve and show his scars,
And say, "These wounds I had on Crispin's day."
Old men forget: yet, all shall be forgot,
But he'll remember what feats he did that day.
This story shall the good man teach his son;
And Crispin Crispian shall n'er go by.
From this day to the ending of the world,
But we in it shall be remembered!

Wow. He had a way with words. He made warts and scabs and buttons and balloon selling seem like nothing more than just—just a mere blink of the eye of Eternity. He could just make stuff like this up on the spur of the moment that left people like Auden feeling, suddenly, so . . . unworthy.

He wasn't finished.

Coming forward and clasping Auden hard by the shoulder and making the poor old chap blink back a tear, Spencer said as his friend, as his better part, as his *pal:*

We few, we happy few, we band of brothers;
For he today that sheds his blood with me
Shall be my brother; be he ne'er so vile
This day shall gentle his condition;

And gentlemen in England now a-bed
Shall think themselves accurs'd they were not here,
And hold their manhoods cheap whiles any speaks
That fought with us upon Saint Crispian's Day!

Auden said, "... Gulp!"

Spencer said brightly with a little reassuring smile, "And really, Phil, just how bad can Tiger-Dragon Square be anyway? I mean, it's not as if it's like something from another world or anything— Is it?"

In the Detectives' Room, O'Yee, trying to think of something intelligent to say, said, "Um ..."

He looked at the phone, and the phone, exactly on time, right on the button—

... Didn't ring.

Yes, it was.

It was exactly like something from another world.

Reached via a series of side streets and alleys and lanes, Tiger-Dragon Square was not a square at all, but a huge, octagonal cobblestone- and sett-paved open plaza lined on all sides by wonderful stone temples and pagodas with sloping tile roofs and red-lacquered walls with icons and idols at their doors, and, hidden away from plain sight in the canyon formed by the huge, peeling, windowless rear walls of the eight-story-high tenement buildings that rose above it on all sides—in the midst of the noisiest, most densely populated city on the face of the earth—as if it had been hit by something so evil everything that had lived in it had been overwhelmed in an instant, sepulchrally silent and still and empty, and utterly, completely *deserted.*

3.

Death was silence. On the fourteenth floor of the Pearl Gardens Apartment Building, death was only the steady humming of the air-conditioning outlet by the corner corridor window.

Standing to one side of her as she stared out that window, Feiffer asked quietly, "What happened, Annie? Do you know?" She was a tall, fine-featured northern Chinese in her forties, still dressed in her nightclothes and a hastily thrown-on robe with her hair uncombed and dishevelled. Feiffer asked, "Annie? . . ."

And then had no idea on earth what to say to her next, and although he wanted to reach out and put his hand on her shoulder or take her in his arms to comfort her, did not, could not, and, with a sudden, sick feeling of pure helplessness, realized he did not know anything about her at all, had never known anything about her as a separate person at all, and had never once, not even at her wedding, kissed her on the cheek, or—except for maybe accidentally brushing against her at dinner or a party—ever touched her at all.

She was Charlie Porter's wife, and when Feiffer and his wife had gone to eat with them, which they did on a regular basis, it was to eat with Charlie, at Charlie's apartment, to eat Charlie's food, to hear what Charlie had been up to, and all she had ever been was an appendage, always polite, always charming, and always Charlie's—and he had never once, and he could not understand why, ever spoken to her about anything that did not have something to do either directly or indirectly with Charlie.

Feiffer said again softly, "Annie—" but then, when she did not turn around, did not know what to say to her next.

Like all northern Chinese, she was tall—even in her bare feet almost as tall as him—but the only thought that automatically came to mind was that he had never realized how tall Charlie must have been to have made her look so small and insignificant when they were together.

Next to Charlie, everybody looked insignificant, everybody sounded insignificant.

A big, bluff Irish-Australian with both a bulldog head and a bulldog manner, and a way of telling stories that made them sound as if they were the authentic views of God and a habit of ending them with a booming, "You'd agree, Harry?" and then to Feiffer's wife—usually at that stage reduced to tears of laughter—"Then you'd agree, too, Nicola?" everyone paled in comparison to Charlie. And he missed him already.

"You'd agree, Annie?"

But he had never once heard Charlie say that.

"Annie? . . ."

And in the apartment, in Charlie's apartment, Charlie lay on the floor with his entire head blown away, and everywhere, everywhere in Charlie's apartment, all there was was blood and bone and viscera. All there was in there now, booming away, was nothing.

Reaching out and taking her by the shoulder, he brought her

around to him, but her eyes were blank and he was not even sure she knew who he was.

Feiffer said softly, "It's Harry. It's Harry Feiffer," but in the eyes, the name meant nothing to her.

Feiffer said, still looking hard into her face, "Annie, another man was killed downstairs after it happened—a janitor here, a man named Cheng—" but if she knew who that was nothing registered. "What happened? Did someone come to the door to see Charlie and—"

He had been fully dressed, in his standard light-gray summer suit and plain tie. He was with Intelligence: he met people at all sorts of hours. "Did someone come to the door and—" But she didn't know, it wasn't there. "Did you hear anything? Apart from the shot, did you hear anything at all? Did you hear anything before the sound of the shot?"

Annie said softly, politely, as she had always been all her life with Charlie, soft and polite, "Charlie's dead, Harry . . ." and it hadn't been the sound of a shot. It had been the sound of all her world coming to an end in a single instant, and then, when she had automatically grabbed her robe and thrown it hastily over her shoulders and thought it was Charlie doing something stupid with a gun or some sort of noisemaker and gone through into the other room and seen Charlie with nothing where his head should have been but a bloody, still blood-pumping pulp, and his legs kicking and twitching on the carpet in his death throes, all her world had stopped, seized, and everything, everything in her life was over.

He thought it was a brief window and he had to use it quickly before it closed again: "Do you know why, Annie? Do you know what happened? Do you have any idea who might have done it, or why? Do you know what Charlie might have been—"

But it was no window at all.

Annie said incredulously, "Charlie's *dead!* He's dead, Harry!"

and in that moment, he realized that she knew nothing about Charlie, that he had never talked to her about what he did or how he did it, or how they lived, or how he paid for it—that he had never spoken to her about anything except in generalities.

Annie said incredulously, "We were staying on, Harry. Charlie said we were staying on and that made me so happy because I thought Charlie would want to go back to Australia— But we were staying on, Harry. Charlie said he had something—a sure way of staying on, and I wasn't to worry because . . . we were staying on and I could—" She sounded like a little girl promised a wonderful birthday gift for being so good all year—"And I could—once the border went—I could go back on trips to Shanghai to see my family and Charlie could come too, and we could—"

She was Charlie's. She was something Charlie owned, something delicate and shy, like a flower, something Charlie tended.

Her hands had no blood on them at all. She had not touched Charlie, but instead, after she had called the police (because Charlie was a policeman and had told her she should always do it if she was in trouble), she had merely gone and sat on the sofa opposite Charlie, and, because he had always known what to do, waited for him to do something.

And then the blood and the kicking had stopped and all there was in the apartment then, as there was now in the corridor, was the steady and unvarying hum of the air-conditioning.

It broke his heart to see her standing there alone.

He wanted to touch her, to take her in his arms and hold her, but she was not his to do it—she was Charlie's, and all he could get out was, "Annie . . . I'm so sorry . . ."

But there was nothing anyone could do except Charlie, and, as something suddenly changed in her eyes, suddenly she began shaking like a leaf and Charlie was gone, and all Feiffer could do for her was grasp her hard in his arms and shout down the corridor to order either Burtenshaw or one of his constables or whoever was still there to call down for an ambulanceman to come up and give her something to calm her down, and then, traffic jams or not, get her away as fast as possible to somewhere safe.

Somewhere away from here.

Somewhere away from Charlie.

Somewhere, away from here and from Charlie.

Somewhere alone.

. . . Somewhere in hell.

Okay.

Okay, well, if they weren't going to call him, he was going to call them.

In the Detectives' Room, taking charge, O'Yee said firmly, "Okay, well they're a little late this morning, and since I have a lot of more important things to do, I'll just call up the people this money is for and tell them to come in and collect it."

That sounded pretty good. He looked down into the drawer.

Money. Filthy stuff, very unhygienic, glad to get it out of the way.

O'Yee, sighing, said with a flick of his head, cop to cop, "Informers, huh? Just can't trust them at all . . ."

Well, actually, these ones you could.

O'Yee said quickly, "Well, no, these ones you can. These ones are good. These ones are worth their money. These ones are—" *What the hell were these ones—goddamned heavy sleepers?* O'Yee said, "I'll just give them a quick call to come in and collect their loot. Shall I?"

O'Yee said, "Not loot! Earned income! Taxable! Taxable earned income for services rendered!" O'Yee, dialing a number at top speed, said, "First one up. Can't tell you the name though, of course, for—for the reason I already explained because, um—" O'Yee said on the phone in Cantonese, "Ah, Mrs. Ung. Christopher O'Yee. Let me speak to your son Aquarius, would you?"

O'Yee, suddenly looking up and seeing Claude's still-smiling face, said in horror, "*. . . Oops!*"

There was a pause, then, on the phone, Aquarius Ung said, "Who?"

Aha! He put the phone on speaker and nodded hard at Claude, who, still smiling, nodded back. O'Yee said, "O'Yee."

There was another pause.

O'Yee said formally, just to make sure Claude got every word, "Detective Senior Inspector Christopher O'Yee, Yellowthread Street Police Station, Hong Bay." O'Yee said, "Money due."

There was another pause. Aquarius Ung said, "How much?"

He had a little list. It was on a scrap of paper to one side of the gold coins. O'Yee said, "Ten thousand in Hong Kong dollars, eight hundred and fifty-five in US dollars, and two ounces of gold in South African Krugerrands, and in silver, two Chinese taels."

There was another pause.

Leaning back a little in his chair, Claude reached down and opened his bag and brought out a thermos of hot Chinese tea and two tiny enamelled Chinese cups.

Aquarius Ung said in Cantonese on the speaker phone, "When?"

O'Yee said in Cantonese on the speaker phone, "Now."

Aquarius Ung said in Cantonese, "All right!"

O'Yee said in Cantonese, "Good!"

Claude, holding up the thermos with a smile, asked in English, "May a humble colonel of the Chinese People's Police offer you a cup of tea, Mr. O'Yee?"

Aquarius Ung, changing to English, shrieked at the other end of the line, *"What?"*

Ung, obviously thinking at the speed of sound, shrieked at the top of his voice, "All right! All right! You've got it! God only knows how a poor, honest, hardworking, mother-sole-supporting, decent, closet-Communist, ordinary person like myself is going to get it, but, yes, you filthy blood-sucking corrupt example of everything that's wrong with the whole filthy world of scum-sucking evil-colonial-oppressors-of-the-masses bastard, I'll get it together somehow and send it around to you as soon as I can!" And then, with a Bang! hung up.

It was nice tea.

Always best to drink nice tea in silence.

He drank two cups.

Nice tea.

He . . .

O'Yee said to Claude, "Nice tea." He thought the tea was what made him suddenly have an overwhelming urge to rush into the men's room at the back of the Detectives' Room and throw up, but it probably wasn't. It was probably something else.

It was probably the next thing Claude pulled out of his bag: a file, a dossier.

The one with O'Yee's name written across its cover in large letters.

In black.

The one he made a little note in.

—In red.

All there was on the carpet of the main room where Porter lay was blood; like some awful subhuman creature dredged up from a bog, he was drenched in it, drowned in it, on the once-white carpet of the floor, sinking back into it.

Kneeling on a rubber mat next to Porter's blood-soaked, flung-out left arm and doing something with a pair of forceps inside the empty and faceless helmet of Porter's head, the Government Medical Officer, Doctor Macarthur, said professionally and unhurriedly, "Cause of death was a single massive shotgun wound to the face fired at close range using, I speculate, a full charge of double-oh buckshot."

He had something in the jaw of the forceps that he held up for a moment before depositing in a metal tray next to the mat—"Like this one. Double-oh? Is it?"

Standing above him, looking down at what was left of the head and trying not to connect it to the man it had once been, Feiffer said with a nod, "Yes." It was a round ball of about thirty-two caliber, one of the at least ten or twelve that had blasted everything that had looked like Charlie Porter's face to vapor, then, continuing on through muscle and sinew and eyes and nerves, had turned everything behind them to pulp, and then, finally, hitting the back of the skull and skewing back, spun around and around inside what was left of the skull and—

Feiffer, looking away, said, "Yes, it's buckshot."

Macarthur said, "Probably from the same weapon used on the dead man downstairs in the lobby." That one, unlike this one, hadn't had his head almost literally blown off his shoulders—that one had been hit in the body and been almost cut in two.

"Probably."

He reached in again with the forceps with a corkscrewing motion that made a coring sound that almost turned Feiffer's stomach on the spot. "What happened, do you think?"

He looked down at the chest. "This one's fully dressed and I don't see any signs of forced entry on the door—do you think this one opened the door to someone, got shot, and then whoever it was, shot the other one on his way out . . . um . . . making his escape?"

He liked to play detective. He glanced around the room.

Macarthur said, in case his efforts at detection weren't welcome, "Makes a change these days to be in a place that isn't full of packing crates—I guess this one was staying on after the takeover, huh?"

Yes, he was. There, dead and with everything that had ever been him blasted into nothingness, this one was staying on forever, going nowhere, making no more memories, never saying again, "You'd agree, Harry?" never again booming with laughter, never . . . never maybe loving Annie gently, never tending her, never protecting her from what he thought she needed to be protected from, never . . .

"Yes. So it seems." He tried to keep his eyes on the body, but they kept straying around the room to everything that Charlie had been—to everything that Charlie had owned or been proud of, to everything that had been Charlie's life: to souvenirs and trophies on the bookshelves, to Charlie's corner table desk with Charlie's favorite wine decanter and glasses set out on it, to the line of Charlie's awards and commendations and certificates of appreciation on the wall above it, to the photograph of Charlie and Feiffer and Annie and Feiffer's wife, Nicola, all standing together on the deck of the boat that Charlie had rented one summer, grinning and mugging for the camera.

He looked over at the picture too. Macarthur said professionally, "In cases like this—in the death of a police officer—I have to make sure all weapons and police identification are taken in charge on the scene by the—" Macarthur said, "I've checked the body and he doesn't appear to be armed or—"

Charlie's gun was where Charlie always kept his gun: way up out of easy reach on the top of a bookcase. His badge would be there too.

Feiffer said, "That's okay." Next to where he always kept that, too, was an ancient stuffed child's kangaroo with the words "Hop It!" written on it in ink for the moment in the evening when, drunk as a skunk and ready for bed, Charlie had had enough of company and wanted everybody to go home. Feiffer said with a nod, "I'll take care of it later."

"He was a Detective Chief Superintendent, wasn't he?"

"Yes."

He stopped probing inside the head for a moment—"I didn't know him. The uniformed guy outside, Burtenshaw, said he was with Intelligence and the Anti-Triad Squad. Is that right?"

"Yes."

"Do you think one of the Triad people—someone from one of the gangs—killed him?"

"I don't know. He didn't talk much about what he did." *And in that moment, he could not take his eyes off the stupid kangaroo and he could not get the sound of laughter and Charlie's booming voice ordering everyone out and raving about reporting everyone for private drunkenness and Annie tugging at Charlie's sleeve in concern and everyone but Annie knowing it was all a joke and then, the next day, Annie calling everyone up to apologize for Charlie and everyone telling her gently that they knew it was all just a joke and—*

Feiffer said suddenly, "I don't know! I don't know anything about him!" He had known the man for over ten years, and apart from boats and kangaroos and booze and laughter, he knew nothing about him at all. And in all those years, he had never known anything about Annie either. Feiffer said, standing there above the dead and bloody creature that had once been Charlie, "I don't know anything about him at all!"

He opened his mouth to say something conciliatory. Macarthur said—

He was a cop. It was a crime scene. He was a cop and it was a crime scene and the medical examiner was in attendance and there was a routine to be observed, and, to save himself, Feiffer observed it.

Feiffer said, with a quick jab of his finger to indicate the tape recorder in the side pocket of Macarthur's bag, and with a rapid twirl of his hand to order the man to turn it on, "Crime Scene. Homicide. Date and time as on hard copy to follow. Body of European male discovered in apartment, fourteenth floor Pearl Gardens Apartment Building, Icehouse Street, identified as that of Detective Chief Superintendent Charles Porter, Anti-Triad Unit, Hong Bay. Identified in situ by DCI Feiffer, Yellowthread Street Station." He looked hard at Macarthur: "Preliminary cause of death—"

"Gunshot wound to the head." He looked down at the recorder for a moment to check it was running: "The subject, found lying on his back as per attached photographs to be supplied by Forensics, is fully dressed. Stainless-steel Rolex Air King Date watch. No other jewelry. Height approximately—"

He was an inch taller than Feiffer or an inch shorter than Feiffer, depending on who, standing back to back, had craned higher one night when—much to Annie's horror—Charlie had advanced a theory about height and sexual endowment based on a series of medical and sociological data he had made up on the spur of the moment that had sent everyone else in the room into howls of laughter.

Feiffer said with no tone in his voice, "Five-eleven."

"Age approximately—"

He was fifty-one.

Feiffer said, "Fifty-one."

"Weight—"

It was Macarthur's call.

Macarthur said, "Approximately one hundred and eighty pounds." Macarthur asked, "Was he staying on?"

If he was, it was the first he had heard of it. He had never really said. Like Feiffer himself, even though time was running out fast, it was as if he had never decided, never been sure, never wanted to be sure. "I don't know." But he was. According to Annie, something wonderful had happened, and he was. Feiffer said again, "I don't know." He looked down at the body and then, looking up again, asked suddenly, "Are you?"

"Oh, yes. Sure." Death was death, and in his job he had nothing to fear from anyone. Macarthur said brightly, "Sure. I'll be here. Same church, just different pew." He looked down at what was left of the head and almost leant forward and patted it like a pet. Macarthur said with a faint smile, "All things come and go and all the affairs of men rise and fall, but Death and I, we go on forever . . ."

He was a man who in all the years Feiffer had worked with him had never been anything but professional and polite and always eager to please, and when it came out of nowhere in a snarl, it surprised even Feiffer himself with its vitriol.

Feiffer said with all the frustration and pent-up violence welling up in him all at once, "Good! Then after the fucking Communists take over in a month and all this doesn't mean shit to anyone you can send me a postcard to wherever the hell I am in the world and tell me what the hell really happened here and why!"

And who, maybe, his friend of ten years, who good old Charlie Porter, really was.

Feiffer demanded, "Okay? Can you do that?"

He wished, seeing the sudden look on Macarthur's face, he could stop himself from saying anymore, but he could not.

Feiffer said, "Thanks! Thanks a lot! *Much appreciated!*"

In the Detectives' Room, O'Yee said in a voice so soft Claude had to lean forward in his chair to hear, "Um . . . um . . . I thought . . . I thought, maybe after the takeover . . . I thought maybe my family and I might stay on . . ."

Claude said, "Really?"

He seemed to think that was an extremely interesting notion.

He put his cup carefully down on the edge of O'Yee's desk and made a second note in O'Yee's dossier.

In red.

4.

Something awful was going to happen.

There wasn't a pigeon or a rat or even a goddamned cockroach moving anywhere in the entire place!

And it smelled bad. It smelled of dust, and sweat. It smelled vile and ancient, and *old.*

At the far end of Tiger-Dragon Square, peering out cautiously from behind what looked like some sort of horrible, man-eating bronze griffin, Auden shouted to Spencer, happily trotting off towards what looked like an even bigger bronze man-eating thing at the other end of the square, "Don't touch anything! Don't move anything! Don't go near anything! *Don't even breathe on anything!*"

Auden shrieked as Spencer, obviously having been informed as a mere wee bairn by Mumsy as she fed him from a silver spoon that he was immortal, suddenly stopped dead center in the middle of the place, "Don't stop! Don't call me over! Don't—"

He called him over. Spencer, hopping up and down and

pointing down at what was undoubtedly the stain on the cobbles of the last dumb bastard who had been called over, yelled, "Look at this! It all revolves from here!"

He waited until Auden came over. (It seemed to take a long time.)

Spencer yelled, pointing down at something set into the bricks of the square in bronze, "Look! It's the yin and yang symbol: the bisected circle—the very center of the Chinese world! The symbol of all the great waning and fluxing forces in the universe, the very apotheosis of the Middle Kingdom notion of Creation, the great symbol of four thousand years of Chinese history and thought and cosmology!" He flung his arm in a great circle around the huge pattern of laid-out setts and cobbles surrounding it: "And look! On each of the eight sides of the octagon surrounding it, the eight great trigrams!"

He stabbed a finger at the man-eating bronze creature at the south end of the street—"And look! The tiger!"

And then back in the other direction—"And there where you were just standing—the dragon, the great backbone and spine that holds all the World together!"

There was no stopping him stabbing his finger.

He stabbed it now to the trigram to the north: "And look! The symbol for Earth—three broken yang lines laid parallel to each other, called in Chinese *k'un*! And, facing them—" He spun completely around and pointed in the other direction to the south: "—the symbol for Sky: three unbroken yin lines called in Chinese *ch'ien*! And then, to the east, the parallel two unbroken yang lines and the one broken yin line to the west for the symbol for the Moon, for Darkness, of *k'an*! And then, next to that—"

He was so happy. He was at least as happy as old Whatshisname had been before he had opened the Mummy's Tomb and immediately became one giant walking boil.

Spencer, counting them off one by one, yelled in his joy, "And, next to that, the yin-yang symbol for Mountains—*ken*! And, southeast of that, *tui* for Water and Lakes! And the two unbroken yang lines and one broken yin line symbol for Wind, *sun*! All arranged at each point of the compass surrounding the central circle of yin-yang!" He was beside himself with happiness. "And there, to the east, from whence the sun rises and all life renews itself each day, the two unbroken lines of yang with the one broken line of yin between them for sun and lightning and all life itself, *li*!"

Great. Yeah. Very interesting. Nice bricklaying. Terrible stink.

Auden, glancing up at the blank walls on all the tenements and wondering why they didn't have any windows in them, said, "Yeah, I know. Good luck–bad luck. All that. Great. Very interesting. Can we go now?"

No, they couldn't. Spencer, exhaling a long nostalgic breath and gazing happily at all the wonderful lines of the architecture of all the temples and pagodas that surrounded the place the way old Mr. Chips must have gazed on the ancient and ivied masonry of the old school of Snobton-on-Superiority, or whatever the hell it was called, said, sighing, "And at each of the eight points, a temple, a place of contemplation and peace anchoring each of the eight elements that hold the cosmos firmly into place. And there! Just where it should be, built as a great protecting keep, the castle of the Geomancers' Union at the place of the dawning of the sun, of *li*, to the east!"

Good. Well, fine. Jolly good. Phew! That was a close-run thing. But, false alarms happen, and, well, time to go now and—

Spencer, gripping his hands into fists and shaking them in the air, yelled, "Perfect! *Perfect!*"

"Exactly!" Auden said, "And very interesting too! Good work! Most enjoyable! Great little explanation!"

But now, time to catch a jet for the next hemisphere.

Auden, starting to go, said happily, "Well, Bill, after all the hard work you've put in over the years here, and all the books you've read, you certainly deserve an extra little treat right at the end and I'm glad you got it, but now, unfortunately, life goes on, and—"

Spencer yelled, "Phil! Don't you know where you are? This isn't Tiger-Dragon Square in Hong Bay! This isn't even Geomancers' Square in all of Hong Kong! Not even—not even—" He looked around and clasped his hands to the sides of his head as if he still could not quite believe it—"Don't you know where this is? This is the *center*, the *ideal*, of *everything!* This, this great pivot, this great balancing point, this fulcrum, this sceptered isle, set in a sea of chaos, this is . . . this is—"

Spencer said humbly, almost unable to believe his own luck to have been allowed to approach even its farthest, most remote frontier, "This is the anteroom of Chinese *Heaven!* And I cannot think in all my life what I might have done that was so worthy as to be even allowed to enter here even for a second!"

He turned to Auden. Spencer asked, one privileged soul to another, "Can you, Phil?"

. . . No.

No.

No, he couldn't. It was just after eight o'clock in the morning and if he could just live through another six or seven hours, the entire world of park balloon selling was out there waiting for him in the real world with all its thrills and adventure and rich returns.

Auden said with a shrug, "Nope. Sorry. Beats me completely. But I'm glad you got the opportunity to see it all, and I'm very happy for you." And to commemorate the occasion, he had a little plastic yin-yang disc thing on a silver chain one of his old girlfriends had given him once, and if Spencer felt like driving back to Auden's apartment—*or to anywhere on the entire face of the fucking earth except here*—why, he was going to wrap it up in a little piece of tissue paper and give it to him as a souvenir.

Auden said in a rush as, from out of nowhere—from out under the claw of the man-eating bronze dragon thing to the north—a lone pigeon came out, and in a mad flapping went like hell for parts unknown, "But, well, unfortunately, it's time to go now and we just don't have the leisure to think about it now, because, you know, life's a-calling and—" He glanced up in horror as the pigeon didn't fly off into parts unknown, but instead flew straight into a tenement wall and fell down dead—*"And it's time to go!"*

"Well, I wonder . . ."

Don't wonder, just do it!

Auden, reaching out and laying his hand gently on the man's shoulder, said, trying to sound calm, "Always a mistake to try to think about things too much, Bill. Nice you got here. Nice you had a little chat with the Duke of Whatever, but now, well—Well, gosh, I guess you're just going to have to say to yourself, Well, that was really a nice little visit I had down here in heaven, and I wish I had more time to spend down here thinking about it, but I haven't and so—"

Funny about that pigeon. After it had hit, it didn't even twitch: it just fell down dead almost as if it was glad to go.

Auden said brightly, clutching Spencer a little more firmly preparatory to, if he had to, clubbing the man unconscious with his gun butt and dragging his limp body out of there by the heels, "So, off we go, old son, and what a good time we had while we were here even though it was just nothing more than a false alarm!"

God, the place stank! It stank of sweat and feet and a smell he couldn't identify that smelled like burned pigeon.

Auden said merrily, "Well, so much for all that, aye? Just another funny old false alarm. What a disappointment." He looked over to where it had fallen and couldn't see the dead pigeon anywhere.

He still had the same stupid, faraway, funny look on his face. Spencer, twisting slightly out of Auden's grip to face the man full-on, asked donnishly, "Ah, but was it a false alarm?"

"Yes, it fucking was!" If he didn't go down with the first club, then, by God, he was going to shoot him, but one or the other, he was leaving! Auden snarled, "Yes! It was a false alarm! Don't read the fucking footnotes! Read the fucking *text!* It was a false alarm!"

Time to tell little Willy that there wasn't any Santa Claus.

"All that stuff about the cosmos falling to bits and all life on earth as we know it being destroyed wasn't true, see? It was a lie! It was a little fib! It was all *made up!* And the Duke of All Enlightenment or All Holiness or whatever the hell he said he was, wasn't the real Duke at all! It was just someone playing a little game with you! It was all just Pretend!"

Auden roared, glancing quickly up at the blank walls of Avian Collision Central, "For all I know, it was someone who just wanted to lure the pair of us in here so he could shoot us both dead like dogs and leave our rotting, dead carcasses out here on the square for the fucking pigeons!"

What pigeons? Even the fucking pigeons who ate the rotting dead carcasses were rotting dead carcasses. Auden said slowly so (a) Dumbo could get it through his head, and (b) Auden could get his hand under his coat for the Colt, "None of it's true! It's a little trick! It was a false alarm! It was just someone being *naughty!*"

"Then where is everybody?" He looked around. "Certainly, everything appears to be in order, and the flow of the life-giving force of *ch'i* unbroken, and the dragon, and the tiger that devours it, safety kept apart by the power of all the forces separating them, but—"

Okay. It was the bullet in the head.

Okay. Putting his hand deep under his coat, Auden reached for his Colt Python.

"Or maybe I got it wrong! Maybe I misunderstood. Maybe my Mandarin isn't classical enough and some of the nuances are still a little lost on me!" Aha, that was it! "Maybe what the Duke said wasn't that the cosmos was falling apart *at the moment*—" He wondered what Auden was looking for under his coat— "Maybe I got my tenses wrong! Maybe he didn't say—present tense—it was falling apart *now*, because, obviously, if it was, he would have been down here himself—maybe what he said was—future conditional categorical imperative—*keep* it from falling apart until he got there! So obviously it hasn't fallen apart *yet* and all this is the debris! Obviously it's *going* to fall apart and all this is just the calm before the storm! So obviously—"

He was a moment from being clubbed and shot, killed, dragged and dismembered.

Spencer said in triumph, "Ah-ha! That's it! That's why there's no one and nothing around, not even a pigeon, or a rat, or even a fly or an insect!" He looked over at Auden gazing at him in admiration with his hand under his coat to stop his heart beating in excitement at the discovery: "It isn't that something awful has happened here—it's that something awful is *going* to happen here!"

He glanced over to the Geomancers' Union Building—"And why that place over there is all locked and shuttered! And—"

He heard the sound of humming, like two giant swarms of angry hornets way off converging fast from opposite directions directly towards him.

Or felt the ground beneath his feet tremble.

Spencer said happily, with all his classical Mandarin tense changes falling into place at once, "See? *See?* I was right!"

Reaching out and trying to turn Auden in his direction from where the man stood staring openmouthed with his half-drawn gun frozen in his hand and a look of absolute, utter horror on his face, Spencer yelled in triumph a moment before everything in the cosmos seemed to fly apart at once in a roar as a massive volley of rock-salt-loaded cannonfire fired from all the windows of the castle at once blasted him to his knees and filled the entire place with smoke, "See! I was right! The cosmos is just starting to fall apart *now!*"

Well, so much for Ung. Time for Ong.

On the phone in the Detectives' Room, switching the receiver to speaker the moment the phone was picked up at the other end so Claude could hear every word, O'Yee said briskly, "Ah! Ong!"

Ong said briskly back, "Ah! um—?"

O'Yee said, "O'Yee."

Ong said, "Ah! O'Yee!"

O'Yee said, "Yes."

Ong said in horror, *"O'Yee?"*

O'Yee said, "Yes."

Ong said in English, "Oh God!" Ong said in utter, absolute terror, "No! No! *No!*" Ong said in a lather of terror, thinking fast, "Oh, Ong? No! Sorry! No, honest to God, Detective Senior Inspector, this isn't Ong, this is—"

Ong said a moment before he slammed the phone down and, presumably, rushed out to find a hole somewhere to hide in, "No! Wrong number! No! This isn't Ong! This is . . . um . . . um . . . This is *Ung!*"

Eng.

On the phone, O'Yee said so quickly the next lying, venal bastard on the list didn't even have time to blink an eyelid, let alone gather his wits, "Ah! This is O'Yee and I have a pile of money for you you earned from all your filthy and godless and immoral and degenerate and disgusting, low-life, filthy, whoring work as a fat filthy rat and a pimp and the lowest of the low and it's your money and all you have to do is tell me where to dump it and I'll dump it and you can use every cent of it for all I care doing whatever disgusting and revolting and nauseating and immoral thing you feel like doing, but it isn't my money, it's your money, and you can have it all anytime you want it!"

O'Yee demanded, *"Okay?!"*

He looked at Claude and nodded.

Claude said politely, with absolutely no tone in his voice at all, "Hmm."

O'Yee said, "Yeah!"

The voice at the other end of the phone, speaking in English, said, a little confused, "Um, Mother Teresa Orphanage, Sister Mary Immaculata speaking. I'm sorry, I didn't quite catch what came after 'filthy and godless and immoral and degenerate and disgusting, low-life, fat whoring pimp.' Would you mind repeating it so I can write it all down, please?"

She sounded very nice.

She was very nice.

She sounded like a nice convent-educated Chinese girl who didn't have much English, but tried hard.

Sister Mary, making sure she had it all right, said nicely, "Mr. O'Yee, was it? No hurry, Mr. O'Yee. I'll wait."

Um . . .

On the phone, calling his own home number, O'Yee said desperately, "Emily, it's me!"

"Hi, this is Emily . . ."

O'Yee said, "Please! All you have to tell someone is that I'm a good—"

She was another nice person.

Emily said nicely, "There's no one here at the moment to take your call, but if you'd like to leave your name and number . . ."

"Oh! . . ."

". . . someone will get back to you as soon as possible."

Or, maybe even sooner.

In the dossier, Claude, with a sigh, made yet another note.

In red.

Just one little problem with the equation.

In Tiger-Dragon Square, Spencer, coughing back smoke, asked Auden who, fortunately, was very close by him and actually reaching out with both hands to help him up, "Phil, coming straight towards us from both ends of the street at once, who are all those people?"

Poor fellow, in the smoke he couldn't quite get his aim right and instead of grasping Spencer helpfully by both shoulders, grabbed him rather painfully around the neck.

Spencer said, gasping it out to make sure the man heard him, "All those people dressed in black making that humming noise—the ones with the sticks and the clubs and the swords coming from either end of the street straight for us . . . Just who are they, and what do they represent, do you think?"

* * *

In the Detectives' Room, Claude said with a smile, "More tea?"

In the Detectives' Room, taking glazed silence for consent, the Fiend in Human Form said with a nod in a perfect, upper-class English accent, "Yes? Oh, good. I'll be Mother then, and pour. Shall I?"

In Tiger-Dragon Square, screaming simultaneously from either end, the black-clad people, carrying sticks and clubs and swords, had but a single word to say to explain who they were and what they represented.

That word, in Cantonese, screamed at full volume, was:

—*"DEMONS!!!"*

And then, two huge unstoppable forces meeting two very small, very movable objects in the exact center of the place, they charged.

5.

At the other end of the phone in the night janitor's tiny living and eating alcove off the main lobby of the Pearl Gardens Apartment Building, the Commander said softly, regretfully, "I'm sorry, Harry, and I'm particularly sorry to hear about Porter, but there's just nothing I can do anymore, and, so far as I can see at the moment, there's no one else in a clear enough position of authority to do it in my place."

His place, now, was nowhere. His place, now, in the last few hours of his career was clearing out the last few personal effects from his office.

The Commander with no sound of anyone in his office helping him, working alone, said to put an end to it, "I just don't have any power anymore, and there doesn't appear to be anyone here who does."

He sounded suddenly very old. "I'm sorry, Harry—but it's all over, finished. All the uniforms and badges and insignia of rank and power don't mean anything anymore, and all the guns and the papers and the warrants and the court orders have all been put into crates to be shipped out or shredded, and there's just nothing left, and no one left in any of the places where they were once kept except ghosts—people like me, just cleaning out the last traces of it all before it's all ancient history."

He wanted a moment to reflect. After he went back to England and a pension and the rest of his life of God knew what, he was going to have time to do nothing but reflect, but here, now, while he was still at least temporarily in the place he had devoted his life to, he wanted to reflect with someone who at least knew what the hell he was talking about, who understood the loss.

He was a good, decent man. He had been a good, decent man all his life. Which meant he was going home poor. Which meant he needed to know that morality was important.

The Commander said, "I think we did a good job, Harry—the cops. I think, considering we all worked in probably the most corrupt city on the face of the earth, we did a good job. Well, some of us anyway. I think some of us can be proud of what we did. I think some of us, particularly those of us who tried to live a Christian life . . . I don't think we disgraced ourselves."

He was all there was. There was no one else he could ask. Feiffer said softly, insistently, "Neal, Porter worked for the intelligence-gathering section of the Anti-Triad Unit. It's a secured unit. I can't even get in there to talk to anyone without an authorization from at least Division level—"

And got one. The Commander, sounding weary and old and sad, said, "It's over, Harry. Oh, all the flags haven't been run down yet and all the new ones run up in their place, but it's over. Looking out of my window, I can see the old naval shore station, and all the people there are lined up in their best dress whites for the final decommissioning, and out there in the harbor I can see ships ready to take them all away, and it's all over. Everything is running down like an old clock, and everything—all the joy and the pride and the adventure of it all—is going with it."

It was everything his entire adult life had been: over thirty years. "And I'll miss it all. I'll miss it all very much. I'll miss the colors and the smells and the wonderment of it all, and I'll miss—" The Commander said almost with surprise, as if the very center of it had never occurred to him before, "I'll miss working and living in a place none of us ever really quite understood, and I'll miss the joy and the surprise and the curiosity of it all. I'll miss, when I know exactly how every day is going to begin and how every day is going to end—I'll miss waking up in the morning and wondering just how the fuck I'm ever going to get through the day without doing something wrong or stupid or just plain inept! I'll miss the teeming, noisy, impossible, wonderful and joyous and always optimistic *life* of it all!"

In the lobby, Burtenshaw and his people were supervising the removal of Cheng's body out through the main glass doors and into an ambulance. They were supervising it—with absolutely no onlookers, no crowd anywhere to be seen—by the numbers.

The Commander said, almost to counterpoint the absence of that crowd, "Everything that's happening now is happening below the surface—maybe it always did—but it's happening now where no one can see it."

He finally answered Feiffer's question about the Anti-Triad Unit: "Even if you get into Anti-Triad, you wouldn't find anything, because, now, there's nothing to be found. Even the Triads—the gangs—aren't behaving the old way—like gangs—anymore, they're all behaving like businessmen, achieving status, worming their way into the workings of what will be the new regime, and even if there was anything there in the Unit that connected Porter's death with any of them, someone—probably one of the local Chinese officers worried about his own position in the future—would have taken it away and given it free of charge to whoever he thinks will have the power after the takeover to keep him and his family alive and prosperous and in a good position."

Maybe the janitor, Cheng, had wanted to be alive and prosperous too.

He wasn't.

A bloody mound zipped up in a coroner's black body bag, all he was was dead.

And, in the street, where normally there would have been a huge crowd of the ghoulish, there was no one. *And if all the remaining tenants, under Burtenshaw's direction, had been able to use the rear freight elevators to leave the building without going through the lobby, why the hell hadn't the killer?*

Feiffer said, to bring the man back to the here and now, "Neal, I think whoever killed Charlie Porter up there in his apartment came down in the elevator to the main lobby on purpose. I think he killed Cheng on purpose. I think, if Cheng hadn't been where he was found, by the door, the killer would have sought him out and killed him and left him there! I think he killed him out there in plain sight as a warning sign, as a *message.*"

"To who?"

"To whoever— To whoever else was jockeying for position! To whoever Porter was going to do business with!" Feiffer said curtly, to keep the man on track, "According to his wife, he'd found a way to stay on and—"

"Had he?" It was a faint, unrealistic hope, but nevertheless it was a hope. The Commander asked, "Doing what?"

"I don't know, and neither did she, but apparently, sometime in the last two or three days, something changed and he did a deal with someone, or something changed, and suddenly, even though he'd been telling me for the last few months that he was arranging to go home to Australia a month or so after the takeover, suddenly he tells her that they're staying on permanently, and then, just as suddenly—"

"He's dead."

"That's right! And so is some poor bastard nobody even seems to know around here, nobody even noticed! So is one of the people who made up all the joyous and curious life of this place you enjoyed so much all your life! So is a poor, fucking harmless human being named Cheng!"

There was a silence, then the Commander's voice said very softly and quietly, "You're not going, are you, Harry? You haven't arranged anything for yourself after the takeover, have you?" The Commander asked suddenly urgently, "Harry, where are Nicola and— Where are your wife and son?"

"They're in Manila, staying with friends."

"Until what?"

He didn't want to think about it. Feiffer said tersely, "Neal, whatever happened with Porter happened suddenly. Whatever happened is still happening now—and I need to talk to the people who worked with Porter and look through his papers and files to find out what it is!"

"Oh, God!" He had forgotten for the moment who Feiffer was. He had forgotten that he had lived in Hong Kong all his life, that his family had lived there all their lives, and that— On the line, the Commander said in horror, "Oh, my God, Harry, you haven't got anywhere else to go, have you?"

"Give me the authorization, Neal."

"I can't give it to you!"

"Call them. Call the Anti-Triad Unit and—"

"There's probably no one in charge there either!"

"Good! Then the only person you'll need to convince is the uniformed constable guarding the entrance!"

"If there is even one anymore. I haven't got any more uniformed constables on duty over here. Have you?"

"No, they've all gone. There's only O'Yee at the Station with the Chinese People's Police liaison officer, and Auden and Spencer—and they're both on their last day, so there's no one—"

"Except you."

"And you."

The voice was quiet. The Commander, afraid of what Feiffer might say next, said slowly, exploratorily, "No one cares, Harry, do they? No one cares about any of it anymore . . . do they?"

"I do! I care! It's important! Two men are dead and even if nobody else cares about them, *I* do! *I care!*"

And it was the answer he had not wanted to hear.

He had been a good and decent man all his life, and all he had to show for it at the end was only—and today, for the first time, he had begun to wonder whether it had even been worth it—was only the firm and unwavering belief that he had behaved towards others in a good and moral and Christian way.

And suddenly, at the other end of the line, the thought of it all reduced him to tears.

Everything was gone. Everything. At the other end of the line, the Commander said suddenly, "Harry, please! There has to be something else for you after this! Don't! At least for the sake of your wife and family, right at the end—don't— Don't do this! *Don't get yourself killed!*"

"Will you give me the authorization?"

God only really knew what morality was. All any man could do was just the best he could.

Maybe it could even mean his pension.

The joy, the wonder, the privilege of a life spent in a place full of light and colors and movement and smells and people and—

And decency: the feeling of a job well done with no shame. That was worth it. That was worth anything.

On the line, suddenly full of authority again, full of power, the Commander said as if it were a fact already accomplished, "—*Yes!*"

In the Detectives' Room, the Fiend asked in that open, straightforward way Fiends always did, "Christopher, you seem to think that being recognized as an honest man will somehow keep you from some dreadful future fate that only you know of." He beetled his brow. "Personally, in the world as it is today, I would have thought the contrary was true. So tell me, what would be the value of such an honest man in such a world? In the world as it is today? In your opinion?"

Ah-hah! Ah-hah-*hah!* Got you, you Commie-scum dirtbag! Got you, you Marx- and Engels-reading, closed-minded, pragmatic, essentials only, up from the masses, unaware of four thousand years of Chinese history clod! O'Yee, ready for that one, said to change the name of the game from victim to victimizer, "One honest man is worth more than a hundred dishonest ones!" He even knew the Mandarin for it: *"Yi cheng ya pai hsieh!"*

Well, you could see that one stopped him.

Claude said, "Hmm." He beetled his brow. (He didn't have any beetles. If anything looked like it might cause him a little beetle, he took it down to the old football field and had it shot on the spot.) Claude said, "Ah. Yes . . ." With his poor, unclassical mind, he thought about it for a moment. Claude said, "But of course, *'Hao k'an nan tso, 'hao 'han nan tso*—Pretty things and honest men are difficult to make."

All right . . . *"Hsien wei kuo chia chih pao!*—Honest men are a kingdom's treasure!"

"Good men."

"What?"

Claude said, " 'Good men.' The actual translation is, 'Good men are a kingdom's treasure.' "

"Same thing."

"Is it?"

Oh, ho, ho, ho. He knew that one. He'd read *1984.* Right now, he was supposed to fall into that old trap and ask, "Well, isn't it?" O'Yee said, "Yes, it is."

"An honest man is the same thing as a good one?"

"Yes!" Was it? O'Yee said, not too sure, "Isn't it?"

"Yes."

Well . . . good. Time to put in something a little more personal. O'Yee, glancing at the phone and explaining it all away, said with a nod, "Good men get cheated; as good horses get ridden—*Jen san pei*—" and had a humdinger: "*Ch'ih te k'uei shih 'hao 'han!*—He is a good fellow who can endure wrong!" And another. (Thank God for Father's useless education.) "*Hao jen to mo nan!* Good men suffer much!"

"Good men are perhaps, as you say, one in a hundred."

"A good man fears nothing!" O'Yee said, *"Hin ni wu leng ping, na p'a ch'ih hsi kau!"* (Actually, what it meant literally was, "He who is free from fever fears not to eat watermelons," but he could tell from Claude's nod that he got the general idea.)

"But is there such a thing as a good, or an honest, man?" He raised his finger and waggled it in the air: "Perhaps—perhaps *Yu liang 'hao jen, yi ko ssu liao, yi ko wei sheng*—There are only two good men in the world—one dead, the other unborn."

"Right! And—um . . ." And, oh God, he'd run out! That was it. He didn't know any more. O'Yee, desperately dredging with his deepest dredge, said quickly, "Socrates said that all men are liars!"

He finished the quotation for him: "And Socrates was a man."

"Right!" He nodded.

He shouldn't have nodded.

Claude said, smiling, "Ah, the celebrated paradox, quoted by the famous Greek, Aristotle, 384 to 322 B.C.—"

Move on, move on! O'Yee said quickly, "*You can't cheat an honest man!*" He could see that one threw him—"The famous movie star, W. C. Fields, 1939!"

"There's a sucker born every minute!—the celebrated line attributed to the equally famous circus owner, P. T. Barnum, circa 1878!"

"At dawn we die"—the famous . . . um, well, perhaps not. O'Yee said in a burst, "I'm no good at being noble, but it's easy to see that the problems of three little people don't amount to a hill of beans in this crazy world . . ."

Claude said, "*Casablanca,* 1942! The airport scene between Rick and Ilsa just before the plane takes off!"

"Right!" O'Yee, drawing back his top lip, said in his best Humphrey Bogart accent, "Major Stroesser, I was willing to shoot Captain Renault, and I'm willing to shoot you!"

Claude said, "I love that movie." He pointed his finger at the invisible Nazi about to phone for reinforcements, "Now, get away from that phone! . . ."

"Play it again, Sam!"

"Bogart never said that in the movie!"

"I know that!" He waggled a finger too. O'Yee said, "What he really said was—"

They said it together, "*Play it, Sam! You played it for her and you can play it for me! —Play it!*"

Claude said, " 'As Time Goes By.' Hoagy Carmichael. What a

great song. And only too true—for it does go by: time. Doesn't it?"

"Yeah."

He sniffed back a sniff. Claude said with a shake of his head:

Ah, 'Tis all naught but a Chequer-board of Nights and Days
Where Destiny with Men for Pieces plays;
Hither and thither moves, and mates, and slays,
And then, one by one, back in the Closet lays . . .

O'Yee said, "Omar Khayyám, *The Rubaiyat,* um—"

Claude said—"1453. Translated, so it is said, by Edward Fitzgerald, 1859. But possibly not. Possibly a complete fabrication entirely of Fitzgerald's own making."

"Really?"

"So it is said."

"Really?" O'Yee said, impressed, "I didn't know that." O'Yee said, "Wow!"

"Sure." Claude said, "I checked up on it in the manuscript section of the British Museum the last time I was over there."

"Really?"

"Wonderful place. Do you know it?"

"No." British Museum . . . O'Yee said brightly, "Isn't that where Karl Marx wrote *Das Kapital* and all that?"

"The very place!" He leaned forward a little and dropped his voice: "And, just a few feet away from where he sat, they have the Obscene Collections Room where you may only read with a guard in attendance and both your hands clearly laid flat out in front of you on the table at all times . . ."

Now, that was a thought. "You don't think that . . ."

He didn't. Claude said, "No . . ." Well, maybe. Claude said, "Well, as you said, Socrates was a man, so . . ."

"Oh, my God!" O'Yee said, "Is that true?"

"Would I lie?"

"No, of course not!"

"Why not?"

"Well, because—"

It seemed to perturb him too. Leaning forward a little in his chair, Claude asked intimately, "What is an honest man? Do you really think?"

"I don't know." He didn't. He had never known. He had just never known who he was at all. O'Yee said softly, sadly, "I don't know. Not really—"

He was a Commie-scum dirtbag, a shooter of men, everything that old J. Edgar Hoover had ever warned all the army of junior G-men about on the radio and the backs of cereal packets—the Filth of the Earth.

But he was all there was, and he certainly seemed to be a very intelligent and well-read man.

O'Yee, taking off his glasses and laying them down on his desk by the telephone, rubbing at his chin to try to nut it all out, said softly, "I don't know."

He looked hard at Claude with his unbeetled brow and ever-smiling face.

O'Yee said, genuinely perplexed, "I don't know really." O'Yee said, "Tell me— What do *you* think?"

Here am I! See me!

At the end of Kite Makers' Street, as Feiffer sat for a moment in his parked car gazing down at it, everywhere in Hop Pei Park, all the way down to the harborfront, the kites were up at the end of their hundred-foot test strings, bobbing and fluttering and straining and trembling in the air, shimmering with color, all in the shapes of great birds or dragons or moths or fabulous blue and gold and yellow half-men, and creatures with no name—anything that might attract the attention of the gods—all to be sold to ordinary men and women—all to the Chinese—all calling out the same thing to sometimes deaf heaven: *"Here I am! See me! Protect me! Help me!"* and, in a nation of almost one billion human beings and four thousand years of history, in the final analysis, that was all any ordinary man or woman could do to be seen or to be helped or be protected.

To people like the Commander, it had all been a puzzle all his life—China and the Chinese—but if you knew the key, it was no puzzle at all: it was not a puzzle because, having no solution, there was no answer to it, no finality, and it did not, like a puzzle put away in its box at night, *cease.*

Anathema to the Western mind, like a river, China and the Chinese did not admit of a beginning and a middle and an end, but instead, went on into a sea, and then into an ocean, and then, in the fullness of time—time measured in millennia—came back to where it had all begun and, with no ending to it all, flowed back again.

China was time not measured in decades or centuries, it was time unmeasured, and if some tiny, insignificant event came to briefly halt its progress, it was of no great moment, and the movement and the flow paused only for an instant and then, swallowing it up, moved on.

And life was short, and, in the end, all there was for the insignificant event that was an individual human life was a kite flying up to the gods, not to attract their attention for some great change in that life, but merely, simply, humbly to beg that no great change take place and things not become bad or, if they were already bad, become even worse.

It was the plea of Old Hundred Names: the eternal Chinese—the coolie who had striven in the fields of the most ancient and legendary Hsia dynasty that ended fifteen hundred years before the birth of Christ and had begun the-gods-only-knew when, and of the serf of the Chou, and the conscript of the Ch'in, alone and afraid at night on guard duty on the Great Wall of China, and the desperate, starving farmer of the Han, and the generations of farmers and coolies and desperate men with families that followed him, and all the generations that had followed them down to the present, and, inevitably, like a river, would continue to flow when they were dead.

Taoism, Buddhism, Confucianism, Communism, Christianity—the Chinese, desperate for anything that might mean help to a man's life, had embraced them all, embraced them, not because it might mean joy and pleasure in the next life, but, simply, because it might mean peace from fear in this one, and if the Eternal Chinese—ever the optimist—found one religion or belief wanting, he would simply embrace another. And, almost unbelievably, still ever the optimist, would fly that kite optimistically into the heavens.

"Here I am! See me! Protect me! Help me!"

All they had, in the end, were the gods.

There were too many of them, too many people: too many striving and working for what little there was to share, and in the end, if through a life of toil, they had prospered enough to live, all they wanted was the luck and the fortune to be able to keep it and pass it on to their children.

In the morning paper, it had said that the president of the United States had warned the Chinese that any curbs on the right of free speech in the new Hong Kong in the few months after the takeover were going to incur a serious reaction from the West; but in the great flow of the river that was China and the Chinese, that was not even a momentary pebble—that was a joke.

But, almost totally incomprehensible to the Western mind that framed the threat, the notion of the first few months was not the joke, nor the threat itself—nor indeed, that in no more than another four or eight years at the most, any president of the United States would probably no longer be president anyway—the joke was that, in a mere blink of time, as it had been only two hundred years before, the United States of America itself would probably no longer exist, and, as the river flowed, maybe become something else—maybe, for all anyone could tell from the standpoint of the eternity of four thousand years of Chinese history—maybe even a part of *Cuba.*

All any man could do was work hard, and work hard to be a good man, and . . . and fly his tiny kite up into the heavens and hope.

Like Robinson Crusoe, the Chinese were people lost in a huge, unfriendly, and harsh universe, each of them with only what he or she had or could build or could create or could believe in or could hope for to sustain them—ever cheerful, ever hoping, ever *toiling*—and he thought, sitting there in his car watching them, that he liked them very much and, the third generation of his family to live among them, could not imagine living anywhere else or among anyone else.

And suddenly, catching sight of his own reflection in the windshield of his car, as for a moment an entire squadron of the diving and looping kites blocked out the morning sun, he could not stay among them, and, because of who he was and what his face looked like, he was going to have to go and live among people somewhere else he knew nothing of and, like the Chinese, did not understand at all.

And, sitting there, the thought upset him very much.

The office of the Anti-Triad Unit was just ahead of him to his left at the corner of Kite Makers' Street and Hop Pei Park

Road, on the third floor, and, as Feiffer got out of his car to walk to take the elevator up and try to explain to the bevy of armed guards who would be there just who he was and what business he had with them, he had to look away from the kites and the sun to stop his eyes blurring with tears, and his soul, like one of those lost, frightened Chinese over four thousand years crying out as the kites cried out: *"Here I am! See me!* Protect me! Help me! *Tell me how I can keep the one thing I've worked all my life to have—my own tiny place in the world—intact!"*

He was never going to know what Claude or anyone else thought—he was going to be driven insane by fucking Ong or Ung or Ong-Ung, or Ung-Ong, or—

Stabbing down the speaker button on the phone even before the first ring stopped, O'Yee snarled, "What? *What? WHAT?"*

There was a sizzling sound at the other end of the phone, and then, in a welter of hacking and coughing and groaning, one of them—Ong or Ung—yelled in English in a voice full of animus and pure, utter, animal hatred, "*—IGER!!"*

O'Yee yelled back, "SCUMBAG!"

More hacking and coughing and sizzling. "*—RAGON!!*" It was a very bad line, full of static, like a cell phone full of salt.

O'Yee yelled back, "RAT FINK BASTARD, LYING *TURD!"*

"*—UARE!!*" More static.

O'Yee yelled back, *"Ong?"*

"—MADMAN—!!"

"Ung?"

The voice yelled back in a terrible roar, "—END OF THE ENTIRE FUCKING *WORLD!!"*

Funny, he didn't recall that Ong or Ung spoke English with an East London accent . . .

. . . or that either of them had such a deep voice . . .

. . . or that . . .

O'Yee said warily, "Um . . ."

"—IGER! —RAGON! —QUARE! END OF . . . *MADMAN!!*"

O'Yee said pleasantly, "Um . . . Ong?"

There was an utter silence.

O'Yee said, "Ung?"

And then, in the midst of the sizzling sound, there was a roar like a wounded bull about to charge someone or something and kill it stone-dead on the spot.

In the Detectives' Room, O'Yee said, *"—Auden?"*

Um . . .

In the Detectives' Room, a moment before the line, with a sudden, even louder sizzle, went utterly and instantly dead, O'Yee yelled desperately at the phone in horror, "Um . . . Um . . . . . . *PHIL?"*

6.

There was no armed guard at the security post facing the elevator blocking any further access through onto the third floor, none either outside or inside the steel door leading to the Anti-Triad Unit rooms down the long corridor behind it, and, as Feiffer walked straight through, no need to show any identification or authorization to anyone.

Everyone who had been part of the Anti-Triad Unit was gone, and, trembling with the roar of a line of paper and document shredders going full blast and blasting mounds and piles of paper out like confetti onto the floor, and the hiss of hand-held gas cutters as little groups of coveralled men burned open safes and cabinets along the wall, the only people left at all the desks and work consoles were plainclothes clerks and white-coated computer technicians erasing files, and then, when they had erased them, unscrewing the hard drives from the machines and tossing them down beside them on the floor to be sliced in half by even more men with gas cutters.

Someone carrying something had hit a line of sprinkler nozzles on the ceiling, or the wax caps had melted from the heat of one of the torches, and the entire bank of them was leaking water and forming huge, muddy, paper-sodden puddles on the floor and then hitting cats' cradles of electrical flex and wire and making them spark.

It was no longer the huge, heavily organized office of the Anti-Triad Unit—it was the desperate and chaotic headquarters of a retreating army destroying everything that could be destroyed before the enemy came and overran them. At the end of the room where a bank of gas incinerators burned with white-hot flame ready to vaporize it all, there was a huge mound of broken pinboards and organizers still with papers and notes stuck on them, and blackboards with schematics of Triad organizations still on them in chalk, and—pulled down from the lines of steel shelves and bookcases that lined the room—books and pamphlets and files and paper and documents, and, in more mounds and piles, safes and desk drawers, other objects: guns, and knives, and bits and pieces of jade or soapstone or ivory carved with some sort of Triad lodge insignia: things seized, taken in, collected, or just found God-only-knew when or how, and shoved away in a drawer and forgotten about, forgotten about for so long even the key to the drawer had been lost—some things so arcane Feiffer, glancing at them, did not even know what they were.

Everywhere in the huge, windowless room, there was the smell of heat and sodden papers and burning.

Everywhere, there was the smell of defeat.

Suddenly appearing out from behind a bookcase with his eyes on the fate of a huge pile of brown-covered dossiers as one of his people carried it in the direction of the incinerator for instant and total destruction, His Honor, Mr. Justice Herbert Ang of the Independent Commission Against Corruption, said with a nod to acknowledge his presence and to give him his permission to remain there, "Detective Chief Inspector Feiffer . . ." and then, glancing quickly away again, watched like an eagle as the entire bundle of dossiers went into the open door of the incinerator and was instantly consumed by the flames. A coveralled man carrying a video camera, coming out of nowhere, videotaped their destruction for posterity.

They were videotaping everything.

Everywhere, as Feiffer glanced around the huge room, there were cameras set up on tripods, and on the ceiling and on desks, and where those cameras could not cover everything that was happening, other men in coveralls were taping the contents of each individual drawer or cabinet with hand-held cameras as it was burned open and the contents pulled out, and then, other coveralled men were videotaping what was picked up from the pile and then, videotaping the things all the way to the incinerators and their total and utter destruction.

They were destroying everything. There, in that room, carefully and painstakingly gathered together over years, was enough information and innuendo and intelligence to sink half the people in the entire Colony—enough to keep an entire army of blackmailers and extortionists fully employed for the next twenty years.

All the Anti-Triad Unit people had gone because not one of them could be trusted enough not to at least read one or two of the files before they left the Colony—everything was being videotaped twice because with the power of the things that were in that room, not even one of the coveralled men from Ang's own staff could be trusted.

Nodding at the completion of the burning and then nodding to the coveralled man to go back to the bookcase for other, maybe less sensitive material, Mr. Justice Ang said in case Feiffer wondered about it, "It's all going—everything."

A short, balding man in his fifties wearing an expensive lightweight brown suit and a tightly knotted plain silk tie, somehow, in all the mess and filth, as clean and untouched as if he had just dressed, he was the head of the Independent Commission Against Corruption—the extragovernmental authority that investigated complaints against the police and the civil service. In its brief twenty-year existence it had jailed at least three hundred and fifty Chinese and European cops and at least twice as many Chinese and European middle- and top-level officials from Tax and Licensing and Trade and anywhere else where money had changed hands in return for influence and favor.

"Fiat Justitia et ruant coeli"—"Let Justice be done though the heavens fall." It was ICAC's motto from Watson's *A Decacordon of Ten Quodlibeticall Questions Concerning Religion and State* from 1602.

It was his motto. A man with no vices, he was Impartiality. He was Fairness. He was the *Law.*

Mr. Justice Ang, standing like a rock in the midst of the chaos, overseeing it all—missing nothing—said as a statement from God, "It was agreed that nothing here should pass on to either the old administration in London or the new one from Peking. It was agreed—" and it had probably been agreed because *he* had said it had to be agreed that way—"that everything here, irrespective of which side it might benefit, should be destroyed sight unseen and therefore benefit no one."

A tape of the destruction was going to go to the Communists and to the British.

"It was agreed that, all things considered, the British should leave with no advantage to themselves for later use, and the Chinese People's Republic enter on the same basis."

He nodded.

That was settled.

Mr. Justice Ang, for the first time looking fully into Feiffer's face, said formally, "I was sorry to hear about the death of Detective Chief Superintendent Porter, by the way." He nodded in the direction of a corridor leading off the far end of the room where, presumably, Porter's office was: "I worked with him here briefly during the past few months and he was always extremely courteous and helpful to me." From somewhere behind one of the metal bookcases there was a sudden sharp crack as one of the coveralled men must have blown the lock off a cabinet with a small charge of plastic explosive, and he glanced behind him to check it. "I gather from the Commander that he was a friend of yours." He was totally noncommittal. If he knew anything about Porter, it did not show.

"Yes, he was."

"Hmm." He glanced back again to see that the contents of the blown-open cabinet were being taped.

He could hardly believe what the coveralled men were taking out of the cabinets and from the bookshelves. Judging by the file names written in ink across the fronts of some of the dossiers, some of the stuff in there went back almost a hundred and fifty years to the foundation of Hong Kong, and, as the explosives man came out carrying what looked like a sheaf of parchment, even before that, maybe as far back as the first European incursions into China itself.

Feiffer said, "I have reason to believe he was murdered because of something he may have been working on or some deal he may have set up for himself for after the takeover that went wrong." He paused, waiting, but there was no response. "I'd like permission to look through his office and his current papers to see if—"

All he did was shake his head, and that was the end of it. Mr. Justice Ang, brushing at his tie for a moment, said, still with no expression either in his voice or on his face, "That will not be possible."

He knew some of the coveralled men in Ang's employ. He

knew at least some of them were Triad people themselves, and he wondered if Ang knew too, and decided he probably did. Feiffer, lowering his voice, watching them as, at the desks and bookcases and cabinets, they watched him, said, "I have reason to believe that—"

"No." He too glanced at the Triad people, his eyes picking them out one by one, and he did know.

Mr. Justice Ang said to make it clear, "In the Law, when it is applied as it should be applied, there are no exceptions. If there was anything to be known about Chief Superintendent Porter, we would have known about it in ICAC, and if it was prosecutable, if it entailed anything that would lead to murder— -"

"It did entail something that led to murder! It entailed something that led to two murders!"

"Then it—"

To hell with it all! To hell with the people watching him, and to hell with— Feiffer, holding the man's eyes, asked directly, "Did you or did you not have an ongoing investigation at ICAC involving Porter or anyone involved with him? Yes, or no?"

It was not his place to use that tone. It was all part of the breakup of the entire society that had been Hong Kong, part of the loosening of discipline, part of the reason everything here had to be destroyed unread.

Mr. Justice Ang, suddenly sounding like Thomas More facing down Henry the Eighth though it might cost him his life, said, "I don't intend to answer that question. I will not answer it to you, or to the Communists, or to anyone else who might ask. What I might know or suspect or speculate about is, like all these files and dossiers and documents here, no longer pertinent."

It was a giant steel door shutting in his face.

Mr. Justice Ang, glancing off in the direction of the incinerators as a signal the conversation was over, said with a nod, "I regret, of course, particularly since the man was a personal friend of yours, that Detective Chief Superintendent Porter is dead, but there is nothing I can do to assist you."

"All I want to do is—" Feiffer said desperately, "Can you at least tell me what he may have been working on before he—"

"No. I cannot."

"Did you have anything on him at ICAC? Anything he was involved with, however peripherally?"

Outside, in the park, all the kites, flying up to the face of heaven were crying, *"See me! Help me! Protect me!"* but there was no help, neither on earth nor in heaven.

Feiffer asked desperately, with nowhere else to go, "Sir, did you have any information on him at all? Anything?"

And then, in Ang's face, he saw it: he saw the flash of anger and the sudden tightening of the jaw, and Ang the Untouchable, the Impartial, the Fair, had done his own deal with the Communists—and his deal was that since he had been forever and always impartial and fair in the past, he could be trusted to be forever fair and impartial in the future. Ang said with a snarl, "Far more pertinent to ask in the light of your own undecided and uncertain future, Mr. Feiffer, is if we had anything and may still have something on *you!*"

And he had him and all he had to do was raise his voice a little and every one of the people listening and half listening to the conversation in the room would have had what they wanted.

He raised it only a fraction. Feiffer said tightly, "You don't have anything on me. You've never had anything on me. My family, like yours, goes back generation after generation in Hong Kong and in China, and my family, like yours, made their fortune at least a hundred years ago in shipping!"

Mr. Justice Ang said, "Oh." He closed his eyes for an instant and had forgotten that amid all the total and utter destruction of all the files and the dossiers in the room and in rooms just like it all over Hong Kong there were other files and dossiers and memories that could not be destroyed or erased, and they were the files and dossiers and memories in men's minds.

Mr. Justice Ang, glancing towards the desks to offer what he hoped all the listeners there might think was the appropriate reaction to that comment, said, "Ah, yes." Mr. Justice Ang said pleasantly, as if he took no real notice of it at all, "Yes, I had forgotten that."

"Yes." It was just a little chat between two acquaintances of similar background. Feiffer, switching from English to Cantonese to make sure the man had no doubt about his intention, said pleasantly, "Yes. My grandfather and his two brothers had a beaten-up tramp steamer they used to ferry cargos direct from India to Canton and the southern China ports almost right up until the beginning of the First World War, just like a lot of other old now well-taken-care-of families here—just, if I may say so, sir, just like yours." He smiled at the man. "Cargos, I'm sorry to say in light of the terrible harm it did to the nation of China and the millions of Chinese lives it destroyed, that consisted almost entirely of *opium*."

Let Justice be done, though the heavens fall. Feiffer said pleasantly, "But I could be wrong in your case." His voice was still too low for the people at the desk to hear clearly. Feiffer asked, "Am I? Am I wrong? Am I mistaken about that?"

He had to give him face; he had to give him a way out. Feiffer said a little louder, as if he pleaded with the man, "Sir, two men are dead! One of them was just an ordinary man who did no harm to anyone! A janitor named Cheng." *Let Justice be done, though the heavens fall. See me! Help me! Protect me!* Feiffer said desperately, "Sir, Your Honor, to let that go as if it were nothing—

surely to God—would put the lie to everything both of us have believed and lived by all our lives! Wouldn't it?"

It was his call, his decision, his dictum from the bench.

But even then he paused to consider it.

Mr. Justice Ang, exactly in his heart what he wanted to be seen to be—a good and fair and incorruptible man administering the Law who, for the sake of that Law, wanted to go on administering it—said firmly, perhaps as a warning to anyone listening, "Yes. Even in the face of chaos, the Law continues and Justice must be served, and there can be no exceptions to that rule."

He saw the men at the desks lose interest and look away, and sighed.

He was a good man: probably one of the best the Colony, or anywhere else, had ever had.

Mr. Justice Ang, putting his hand to his face for a moment, said softly, "Forgive me. I am rather tired." He nodded to the far end of the room where the corridor was: "The late Detective Chief Superintendent Porter's office is this way. Provided you remove nothing from it, you are welcome to look through it in the furtherance of your investigation."

There were no video cameras in there, and he wanted none taken in. There was no need. He was who he was.

His Honor Mr. Justice Ang said to everyone there in that room doing what they were doing, as if it were more than enough to satisfy anyone, "I myself will accompany you."

In the Detectives' Room Claude said, as if there had been no break in the conversation at all, "I think an honest man is one who is always honest in all his dealings with himself, and, therefore, because of either long practice or natural inclination, cannot be other than honest in all his dealings with others."

So obvious. Equally obviously, somewhere out in the middle of nowhere, Auden was involved in at least the entire destruction of the known world, but, since no one knew where that was from his garbled directions, there was nothing anyone could do about it, so why bother discussing it?

Claude said quickly, "But then, truth is relative, isn't it? And a dishonest man might deal with himself in an honest way—accepting his dishonesty as part of his nature—and continue to be dishonest because he believes honestly there is nothing he can do about it but accept it." He leaned forward: "And how would we judge such a man? Like a leopard? A leopard cannot change its spots. We cannot judge a leopard."

"Ah-hah—"

"How do you judge yourself as a man—"

"Ah-hah-ha. Well—"

"How would one honestly judge a good man working all his life to enforce the laws in a place built upon the notion of unlawfulness? How would one judge someone with a badge and a gun and therefore, presumably, the power of life and death, dedicating his life to the preservation of an imperialist colony stolen from its rightful owners as the result of a victory in a war fought only to continue the import of narcotics—*opium?*"

"That was a long time ago—"

"—and so enslave an entire nation to its addiction for nothing more than dishonest *profit?*"

"I don't deal with nations! I deal with people!"

"Are not nations the *essence* of people?"

"No! People are the essence of *nations!*"

"Ah, an honest man being honest with himself? Or a dishonest man being dishonest with himself, honestly?"

God only knew. O'Yee said evenly, "I just do the best I can."

"And when life is too much—when the honesty or dishonesty overwhelms—go to the movies to forget about it all?"

Did he? Maybe he did. Things were simpler in the movies. Especially John Wayne movies and Humphrey Bogart movies. O'Yee said, "Well, I—"

"Or sports. Some people like sports. Sports, some people feel, are the one pure thing left in an otherwise corrupt and venal and confusing world—"

Obviously, he had never followed American pro baseball.

"Except, perhaps, for American pro baseball, which, in my time in America, I briefly followed." He barely drew a breath— "Or football. Now, that is a clear and simple game between men—something easily and rationally followed without too much mental anguish about right and wrong and responsibility and guilt . . ." Claude asked, "Do you like football?"

"Um— Yes. When I was in college in—"

"No, not American football: real football. Soccer. Do you like that? You know, the game with long goalposts and—"

O'Yee said in horror, "No!"

"Ah." Claude said sadly, "Oh, a pity. I enjoy it very much, but lately, at each of the soccer games I've attended back home in Canton, for one reason or another, I just never seem to be able to stay past the pregame events all the way to the end of the match . . ."

He was too late. Porter's office had already been stripped; it was like standing in an empty tomb, and there was nothing to remove. Ang's men had even taken up the carpet to check for hidden floor safes, and all that was left in the gray, cement-floored room was a low, government-issue steel table presumably dragged in from outside with the few things that were clearly Porter's personal property laid out on it for disposition to his family.

In the very center of the line of objects—pens and letter

openers and packs of cigarettes and a lighter and a small, ragged hill of coins and paper clips and ticket stubs and a packet of writing paper with Porter's name embossed on each sheet, there was a single, grainy black-and-white photograph mounted in a heavy Chinese carved lacquer wood frame: a photograph of four people standing on the stern of a boat grinning for the camera: the same photograph Porter had had in his apartment—a photograph of him and Feiffer and Annie and Nicola.

In the photograph, all the friends, standing there on the deck with all the skyline of Hong Kong behind them, looked as if they had all the time in the world to do whatever they wanted. They all looked as if—

Maybe Ang had brought him in there to make a plea in mitigation. Or maybe not. Maybe he had brought him in there to give him a history lesson and make a few things clear. Maybe not. Maybe he was so secure there was no one who could do anything to him anyway whatever they might or might not know about him and his family.

Mr. Justice Ang, with a shrug and a single dismissive wave of his hand that took in not only Porter's office but everything else taking place on the entire floor, said, "None of it really matters anyway. Not now. The Triads are a spent force. They're irrelevant, and everything that was in this place is equally irrelevant."

The Triads—the Secret Societies—had a history in China and among the Chinese that stretched all the way back to the time of the pre-Christian era with the formation of the Ch'ih Mei Huis—the Red Eyebrow Society—carried on in an unbroken line of murder and extortion and kidnapping and terror into modern times in the form of the twin banes of Hong Kong life, the 14–K Society and the Shanghai Bund Society.

Mr. Justice Ang, shaking his head, said, "Now, with the Communists coming in, the Triads don't count. Now, with officials of the People's Republic about to take charge, the Triads know that they have no place in the new society and, with the support of the ordinary people gone, have nowhere to go." Mr. Justice Ang, sweeping his hand for the second time, said to finish it, "So all this is nothing more than window dressing."

He made them sound like brainless thugs who spent all their time beating helpless shopkeepers for the cash in their tills and demanding protection money so they wouldn't come and beat them for the money in their tills a second time.

They weren't. The Triads, formed originally as secret antigovernment political parties, were still secret antigovernment political parties. They were political parties at the ward level, able to wield and deliver massive power and influence at block, at neighborhood, at street level, and, over the years, as they insinuated themselves into the government one member at a time, able to deliver all that power and influence to their own people.

Ang, giving a little history lesson, said as if he were saying it from the bench as a final judgment, as a sentence, "The Triads know what happened to their forebears in China after the Revolution. They know that, unlike British-based justice which requires infinite pains to prove a case beyond a reasonable doubt, the Communist government will simply round them all up and then, without further ado, take them out to some public place and shoot them."

The photograph on the desk was an exact copy of the one Porter had in his apartment, and, looking at it there in that awful, empty dead place, Feiffer tried to remember what else had happened that day when it had been taken, but could not.

Mr. Justice Ang, suddenly talking with all the authority of whatever it was the Communists were going to appoint him to be in the New Order, said fiercely, "The Triads survived so long in Hong Kong because, as an oppressed and disenfranchised people trapped in a foreign system of laws and society they never fully understood, the ordinary Chinese saw them alone as the heirs to all the tradition and history that was China! Now, with the true heirs to all that history and tradition about to take back what is rightfully theirs, all that is finished, and the Triads, with no flag or symbol—no *authenticity*—are finished!"

He paused, waiting for a nod of agreement.

And got none.

"Don't you agree, Mr. Feiffer?"

"You'd agree, Harry?"

And, looking at all the faces in the photograph, all the looks on their faces that day, all the hope, it broke his heart, and he had to look away, back to Ang.

"What was Superintendent Porter working on at the time of his death? Do you know?"

All right. It was quid pro quo; this for that. He knew how to play that game. Ang said formally, "He was working gathering evidence against the 14–K, as he had been for some years, and building up a complete picture of their organization. He was very successful at it. It is my personal belief that, over the years, he had managed to put a number of undercover officers and informers within its ranks and also within the ranks of the Shanghai Bund Triad, and he was using both sources against each other to produce a full picture of the upper-echelon 14–K organization and make arrests."

"And—?"

"And?"

"To benefit who?"

"What do you mean?"

"To benefit the law, or the Shanghai Bund, or himself. What I mean is, did you have anything on him?"

"At ICAC?"

"Yes! At ICAC!"

"As to whether or not, what? That he was corrupt?"

"Yes."

He had made him wait for it, and that made him feel better, reminded him of who he was.

Mr. Justice Ang said, "No."

Mr. Justice Ang, flicking his finger at the photograph, said as a gift of grace and favor, "You may have that photograph you keep looking at, if you want it."

"Thank you." As he picked it up, with the thick, carved lacquer wood frame, it was heavy, heavier than he thought it would be. "According to his widow, Porter made some sort of recent arrangement or deal with someone that meant he would be in a position to stay here permanently after the takeover. Do you know what it was? Have you any information about that?"

"None." It was stupid. There was no such deal. Mr. Justice Ang, shaking his head, said to dismiss it out of hand, "No, that is not true. He was a policeman here for over twenty years, a man, like you, thoroughly identified with the colonial oppression era, and therefore tainted by it, and therefore of no use to anyone." He paused for a moment. "And, I venture to say—" It was a little bit of vitriol payback—"With the same chance of being allowed to stay on after the takeover as a lame Christian's chance of staying on permanently in the Roman Coliseum with the lions!"

"His wife seemed very convinced of it."

"Then his wife is mistaken, or he lied to her about it."

"Apparently, it was a sudden decision."

"No."

"Or a decision he made sometime ago that only suddenly came to fruition."

Still holding the photograph, he felt something jammed in hard under the backing. Feiffer asked, "Then why is he dead?

Why, suddenly, out of nowhere is he—" He saw the question was of no interest to the man. "Is there anything he could have taken from here that would have ensured his future after the takeover? Is there anything he could have had, or found, or known about that might have—" Suddenly, it was so obvious: "That someone could have arranged to get from him in return for protection and then killed him for?"

"No." He just didn't understand the situation at all. Mr. Justice Ang, shaking his head, said positively, "No. All this is over. None of this matters anymore! In the new Hong Kong none of this will have any relevance. All this is nonsense! All these files and artifacts and— There is nothing here of any possible future value to anyone! Nothing that would give anyone any real power! Nothing! Nothing for anyone to be afraid of!"

"Then why are your people blowing open all the locks on the individual cabinets and safes out there and not just hauling the whole lot out to sea and sinking it?"

"What?" Mr. Justice Ang said, a little confused, "What?—because some of the cabinets have been locked so long, all the keys have been lost and—" Mr. Justice Ang said suddenly, "Because there are no keys to some of them and no one knows what's inside!"

The picture in the frame was not a photograph taken a long time ago—it was a color photostat, and the frame, as Feiffer turned it over in his hand, still had the price sticker on it, and that HK $85.00, was not a price from ten or fifteen years ago, it was a price from today.

Feiffer, pulling at the corner of the backing and shaking the thing inside loose, said, offering it to Ang, "One of the keys is here." It was a big, old-style cylinder key, at least fifty years old. Feiffer said, "The top and shaft of it's rusty, but the jaw isn't. The jaw has bright metal scratches and score marks on it as if it's been used to open something recently, as if someone used it in one of the older cupboards here and had to move the key back and forth in the lock to get it to work before he could get it open."

There was silence.

In the bare, stripped-out room, Mr. Justice Ang's face was impassive.

"What do you think that could have been? The thing Porter took?"

"I don't know."

"What do you think it might have been?"

"I don't know." He thought about it for a moment, and in that moment, checked all the logic and planning and beliefs of his life. Mr. Justice Ang said to convince himself, "Nothing! There is nothing here now of value that anyone could want!"

"Whatever it was—"

"There is nothing here that could possibly save any man like Porter—*like you*—from the rightful and just displeasure of the Chinese People's Republic and all its power and authority—*nothing!* There is nothing that—" Justice Ang, himself saved, demanded, "What could it be? All it could be would be a chimera! Nothing! All it could be would be a *shadow,* a—"

In a nation that had survived five thousand years, a nation that had survived emperors and invasion, and war and occupation and rulers and presidents and protectors and chairmen, maybe even the Communists were nothing more than a brief passing shadow themselves, maybe, in the long run, nothing more than . . .

And in that moment, Mr. Justice Ang, seized by a sudden fear he could not put a name to, was Mr. Justice Ang no longer, but only a solitary, ordinary man crying to heaven for help as the men in the park cried out for help with their kites: *"See me! Help me! Protect me!"*

Brushing at his suit as if suddenly both he and it were covered in something—in lint, in ashes, in *doubt*, the man standing facing him in that bare cold room said fearfully, desperately, "I don't know! You knew him! *You tell me what it could have been!*"

He didn't know him. He didn't know him at all.

On the way out through the squad room towards the elevator, there was a phone call for him from the Government Medical Officer, the number passed on to the man by the Commander.

Like a schoolboy afraid the teacher might hear what he said, in a whisper, Doctor Macarthur said, "Harry? Tony."

He almost never used first names. Macarthur said quickly, trying to get it out all at once, "I was wrong. The entire place here is full of Communist liaison people and everything's come to a halt and all my own people have taken off like scared rabbits, and there's just no chance of—" In his office, something must have happened; someone must have moved away for a moment; "And there's no chance of me doing a full autopsy on Porter or the other one at all, and all I got to do before everything went crazy here was take a quick general overall look at both the bodies and make a—" And then, as someone must have passed by, there was a silence.

Feiffer said, "Tony? Are you still there?"

He was. He was just waiting for whoever it was to go by.

Macarthur said quickly, "Harry, around the rectum and anal cavity area—"

He had no time left, he had to say it quickly and be done with it.

Macarthur said, not knowing whether it was important or not, "Harry, your friend, Detective Chief Superintendent Porter . . . You did know he was *gay,* didn't you?"

". . . You'd agree, Harry?"

See me! Help me! Protect me!

". . . Oh, Jesus!"

And then, the moment he put down the phone, there was another call, the number this time no doubt passed on by one of the coveralled men in the other room who had strained to hear every word that had been said.

This time, speaking in Cantonese, the voice was not a whisper, but an order.

It was an order, couched in the terms of a polite request.

The request was made on behalf of someone named Mr. Lee Shih Shu. The caller wondered, did the good sir, Mr. Feiffer, happen to know who he might be?

The good Mr. Feiffer did. He was the head of the Shanghai Bund Society, a man who had held absolute power in the organization in Hong Kong for over forty years.

The voice said, still politely, "Oh. Good."

The voice, repeating on pain of death exactly what he had been ordered to repeat, adding nothing of his own, wondered in that case whether, sometime within the next thirty minutes or so, and no later, the good Mr. Feiffer might care to meet with Mr. Lee at his office for a little chat?

He would?

Oh, good.

The voice, adding nothing, said as an order a moment before he hung up and the phone went dead, "Come, *unarmed!*"

7.

The first sizzling sound of O'Yee's phone had been the sound of the cell phone in Auden's hand disintegrating from the cannon volley of pulverized rock salt.

The second, the even louder sizzling sound, had been the sound of Auden disintegrating around it.

Still, it wasn't the end of the world.

Yes, it was. In Tiger-Dragon Square, looking down at the salt-shot phone as it finally fired off its last spark and melted into the ground, Auden roared, "Are you *crazy?* Are you *insane?* What the hell do you mean it was just their way of telling us that maybe we were using the wrong *compass* to chart our course by?"

He had been salt-shot by cannons, then mashed by the first army of lunatics as they charged him from the east, then mashed again by the army from the west, then, as both armies collided, mashed a third time, and then mashed yet again. And then, for good measure, as all the cannons in all the windows of the Geomancers' Castle blasted out salt all at once—a mashed relic lying on the ground—salted.

Oozing salt, dripping salt, spitting salt, seeing salt floating everywhere in the still-swirling smoke and lying everywhere on the still salt- and smoke-swirling ground, Auden roared saltily, "*What the hell do you mean, 'Oh, well, that's how real knowledge is gained: by experience in the field'?* They shot us! Then they got an army of people with sticks and clubs and swords to rush by to whack us and club us and hack us and mash us just in case the salt missed, and then, after we were all good and whacked and clubbed and mashed and salted, they salted us again, and they—"

The man was crazy. He was crazier than crazy. He was completely and utterly crazy.

Auden shrieked, "Are you *mad?* What the hell do you mean, *'No, no, no, the Chinese geomancer mind doesn't restrict itself to just one philosophical or religious discipline—if indeed it restricts itself to any—it ranges wide over all the disciplines, including the discipline of Zen'?*" Auden yelled, "What the hell do you mean, *'The cannons were just their little Zen way of telling us that maybe the trigrams in the street didn't represent the standard* lo pan feng shui *compass, but instead the* lo shu *one and our thinking was heading in the wrong direction'?*" Auden shrieked, "Are you nuts? Are you completely off your fucking *rocker?* They tried to kill us! They don't like us! They want us to *go!*"

Oh, ho, ho, ho, that was a funny one. Spencer, patting his old friend on the shoulder and wincing as his friend patted him back and almost knocked him over, said with the same happy smile Auden had seen on the faces of lunatics all over the world and on the faces of a line of cows once as they queued up for the big, interesting event just inside the door of the abattoir, "No, see, I was right! Something is happening here, but I was wrong about the way we were supposed to deal with it and interpret it! What it was, was that I mistakenly thought that the trigrams laid out on the ground here represented the standard, old, boring, run-of-the-mill, common or garden variety *lo pan* compass and I was going to set out with that as my basis for nutting it all out, when, in fact—"

He was raving. He was a basket case. He didn't deserve to live.

"When, in fact, obviously, it's not the common or garden-variety *lo pan* compass at all, but the *lo shu* magic square!" Silly him. Such a simple mistake to make. Spencer, glancing up at the now tightly shuttered and silent Geomancers' Union Building through the smoke, said to all of them up there with an acknowledging nod, "Quite right! Quite right! I was wrong, and you were quite right to tell me so."

He could tell he was interested. Spencer, starting to hop up and down with the excitement of it all, said happily, "You see, the old *lo shu* magic square isn't just any old *feng shui* compass used by any old geomancer anywhere in the world, it's *the* ultimate *feng shui* compass used only by the top geomancers only at—" He paused to really give it some effect: "—only at the very center of the Universe! Which is here!"

He could tell old Phil was interested: he just stood there staring at him and looking him up and down and wondering how he knew so many interesting things.

He leaned forward a little closer. (Auden also leaned in a little closer.)

Spencer, chatting away happily, said just to throw in a little background, "You see, in the great Classical Age of China, the *lo shu* magic square was always the most powerful of all the squares. Tradition has it that it was first revealed to the legendary Emperor Yu in a conversation he had with a turtle by a river. Tradition has it that the square is so powerful that the emperor decided to build his capital right where he spoke to the turtle; the entire river changed its course and flowed like a canal and filled his capital with fountains and weirs and places for sweet drinking water—even though, previously, it had always been untamable and tainted. Tradition has it that—"

He was crazy! He was out of his fucking mind! *"Me Lud, it were only when 'ee started ravin' about turtles that I realized 'ee were a danger to me and to people everywhere. And even though I be just a 'umble balloon seller, but a friend to little children everywhere, I knew it were my duty to . . ."*

Auden, getting a strange, unearthly, psychopathic look in his eyes, said in an undertone, "Herr! . . . Herr! . . . *Herr!* . . ."

"Amazing, isn't it?" Well, maybe he was going to do pretty well teaching at Oxford—particularly if he had people with this much basic interest to begin with: people who were prepared to be amazed, people who were— Spencer, starting to point in all directions at once, said brightly, "See, I thought the trigrams were arranged in terms of the basic elements, of Earth and Sky, and the end of the world would come from one of those directions—but, of course, it won't, because the compass incised on the cobbles—isn't to do with concepts like Earth and Sky at all, it's to do with *numbers*—well, they are, but that's only part of it—but they're also arranged in numbers, and the numbers are—"

His was up. That was it. God bless Colonel Colt. Smiling happily, Auden reached inside his coat for his Python.

Spencer, suddenly muttering away to himself as he counted off the squares, yelled in triumph, "I'm right! I know I'm right! I'm right, and all we have to do is settle our minds on the philosophic notion that we have to save the world based on a *mathematical* concept and not a *seasonal and diurnal one,* and all will be revealed to us!" He looked up at the windows of the castle. "And you'll help us do it, won't you? *Right?*"

Wrong.

From all the windows, as, suddenly from both ends of the street, the two armies of black-robed killers appeared for the second time, there was another little sizzle—the sizzle of the fuses of a lot of cannons being lit all at once—and then—just the geomancers' little way of telling them that maybe they weren't dropping a little Zen hint to think again, but instead a large, clear one to just *fuck off*—they were both mowed down in a blast of rock salt that made the entire street and all the temples and pagodas in it and all the multistoried tenement buildings on all four sides around it shake and tremble on the very foundation and sent pigeons falling down dead from the sky.

Enough.

In the Detectives' Room, O'Yee demanded, "What is it? What is it you want from me?"

He smiled. He paused for a moment and gazed at him the way Fiends always did.

Claude, beetling his unbeetled brow, said with a shrug, "Nothing. I want nothing from you at all."

Claude said softly, "Or, maybe, everything. Maybe, even, your very soul." He kept on smiling, and shrugged again. "Or, maybe . . . nothing."

In the Detectives' Room, staring at him, O'Yee thought he had never met anyone like him before in his entire life.

Colonel Kong of the Canton People's Police said, still smiling, "But Mr. O'Yee—Christopher—as an honest man, you already know the answer to all your own questions, don't you?"

And then his face changed and all the brightness went out of his eyes and all they were were utterly opaque jet-black opals staring at him across the desk with no expression in them at all.

Claude said tersely with a new hardness, a tightness in his voice, *"Or do you?"*

In the smoke and what looked like a snowstorm of falling, wadded-up paper mixed in with a rain of still-falling salt, someone screamed at him, "You moron! You lunatic!" and craning his head from side to side from where he lay sprawled across the trigram for *Earth*—no, no, no, that was in the old *feng shui* compass; in the *lo pan* compass it was *eight*—Spencer tried to see where it was coming from.

Next to him on the ground, there were two very large eyes staring at him from inside what looked like a solid mound of salt. It was coming from there.

It came from there like the Voice From Hell.

The Voice From Hell roared, "You imbecile! You cretin! You insane, crazed, academic, *Wind in the Willows*–reading half-wit!"

The salt must have gotten into Auden's lungs. As he roared, he seemed to be making short gasping noises and twitching: "You fucking . . . *menace!!*" But then, as he got his hand somewhere inside the salt case where it hurt a lot—just under his left armpit—and did something, he seemed a little better and made a quick sighing sound of relief. Auden shrieked, "YOU FUCKING *LUNATIC!!*"

Was it *eight?* He twisted his head and read the trigram upon which he sprawled. Yes. *K'un:* Earth. Three broken yin lines set out parallel to each other at the north or winter face of the compass—in the *lo pan* compass, *eight.*

Or was it?

Maybe he had it wrong. Maybe, what he had done . . .

Spencer, getting to his feet and gazing down at it through the swirling smoke, said musingly, thinking it through, "Phil, in the *lo pan* compass, is the standard *k'un* trigram *eight,* or is it—"

He had a stupid mad thought. Spencer said, embarrassed at his own near-gaffe, "Oh, my gosh, I almost asked if it could be *four,* but, of course, it can't be, because in Cantonese, the word for 'four' sounds just like the word for 'die,' and nobody would ever, ever consider that lucky—would they?"

Some . . . people . . . might.

Inside the mound, straining and pushing to get out, Auden, still clutching at his armpit, yelled, "Aaargghhh!!!"

Then there was an explosion of salt, and in one mighty bound he was free! And covered in salt, cured in salt, salted in salt, swathed in salt from head to foot like a Mummy, Auden shrieked, "Now, you're dead! Now, you're fucking dead! Now, for all the innocent little children in parks all over the world, now, you're a fucking—*dead man!*"

All he had to do to kill him was get up. He couldn't get up. He was salted to the ground.

Auden, wrenching and twitching, kicking and pushing and cartwheeling, roared, "AARGGGH—!!"

A blackened, folded-up wad of paper came floating down through the smoke, and Spencer, still looking for inspiration, caught it and opened it to read what it said.

Hmmm. It was just part of a page of a Chinese newspaper—the racing section. No help there.

Rubbing at his chin, Spencer said, still musingly, still trying to think it through, "Look at it from the beginning: go back to the source—"

Yes! Good! Logical thinking!

"—Now, the Duke calls me and says—"

"There is no Duke! The Duke isn't coming! The fucking Duke is off talking to the fucking turtles!" He was getting up. Slowly, one salted joint at a time, he was getting to his feet. Auden screamed, "The Duke is the invention of a twisted mind!"

"I don't think anyone would accuse anyone at the Geomancers' Union of having a twisted mind." That was just silly. "Traditionally, from time immemorial, the role of the geomancer in Chinese society has always been one of doing nothing but good—"

"The fucking geomancers just fired two cannon volleys at us and tried to kill us!"

"They used rock salt. And very small granulations of it at that. That wasn't meant to kill." Spencer, shaking his head and trying to peer through the smoke, said, still nutting it out, "No, why the two volleys were fired at us was to—" His voice trailed off. Spencer said suddenly, "Oh, my Gosh! Not logical thinking, *lateral* thinking—!" Spencer said maybe on the brink of something astounding, "*—if they were even shooting at us at all!*"

Oh, he was dead. Oh, there wasn't a jury in the world . . . Oh, he was . . .

"Maybe, what the volleys were aimed at wasn't us at all! Maybe what they were shooting at was—"

Oh, he was just a memory. He was dust. He was a footnote. He was . . .

He heard a humming noise.

(Oh, confirmations of the efficacy of intelligence!)

Spencer yelled in triumph, "Maybe what the geomancers were aiming their cannons at wasn't us at all, but *them!*"

"What?" He was almost on his feet. Who? Which? Why? *"What?"* Auden, getting to his feet and wondering why he couldn't seem to blink, said, "What? Who? *Who them? What them?"*

"Them! *Them!"* He was so happy. Through the smoke, for an instant, he saw at all the open windows of the castle the cannons' snouts coming out. He saw at the end of the street a crowd, a host of golden—

(No. Wrong country. Wrong quote. Wrong efficacious intelligence.)

He saw, appearing like two evil black clouds this time, not hundreds of black-clad people, but hundreds and hundreds of them, all armed with sticks and clubs and wooden swords. He heard them humming. He looked up at the cannons in the geomancers' windows and saw where they were pointing. Spencer yelled in triumph, "See! See! I was right! It's not us at all! We're not the targets at all! It's *them!* All we are are just two totally innocent bystanders caught in the middle!"

Oh, good. Always reassuring to know that one's death was utterly and completely pointless.

Finally getting to his feet, reaching in for his gun, Auden said, "*—Grrr! . . .*"

"What they're shooting at, here in the street and invisible, are the—"

From both ends of the street, shrieking in Cantonese, both the crowds said it one more time to make it clear, "*—DEMONS!!*"

And then, from the geomancers' building windows, there was a fizz as all the geomancers lit all the fuses of all their cannons all at once, and then—

And then, nothing.

And then, dead set on the demons, all the hundreds of black-clad people at both ends of the square, all humming at once, readied themselves to charge.

In the Detectives' Room, Claude said with a nod, "Your phone's ringing."

In the Detectives' Room, with his eyes again all bright and friendly, Claude said pleasantly, "Please. *Je vous en prie.* Just pretend as if I'm not even here . . ."

It was less than thirty days before the final takeover, and already, everywhere, the Communists were already there, moving into all the instruments of power, talking, probing, being polite, preparing the way for when, after a hundred and forty-six years of national humiliation and anger, they took back what was rightfully theirs and did then only God and they alone knew what it was they intended to do then.

8.

Like hell he was going unarmed.

As Feiffer turned into Empress of India Street, there was a huge crowd of students and demonstrators erecting a hastily built wooden Pillar Of Shame in the middle of the roadway commemorating the Communist massacre in Tiananmen Square in Peking, and at the same time, on his car radio, news that the first contingent of the Chinese People's Liberation Army had arrived to begin the takeover of the British Army's Prince of Wales' Barracks not a mile away, and everywhere, everyone was running out of time.

It was all coming apart at the seams, and as he turned left into Kaifong Street and parked directly outside the traditionally built black-lacquered one-story wooden Chinese villa-style building that was the headquarters of the Hong Bay Kaifongs—the neighborhood associations—where Lee waited for him, even the usual Triad contingent of a dozen bodyguards were not where they should have been, standing guard in front of the main entrance to the place, but, instead, skulking around in little knots twenty yards away talking amongst themselves and looking nervous.

There was no substance left—it was all, now, only shadows and fear and terror.

It was all empty symbols; there was no power, no authority, no future left, and as he went in through the main door unchallenged, it did not surprise him that Lee had opted to meet him there—in the last traditional Chinese building left in a street of modern glass and plastic buildings and that he sat in the farthest corner of the room in a carved red-lacquered chair like an emperor with a single silkscreen painting behind him, and that, as if he were an emperor, the whole thing was set up to look like a nineteenth-century scene of the European barbarian come humbly and at last after many tribulations, to an audience.

Sitting bolt upright in his chair as Feiffer came and sat opposite him in a purposely lower chair, the emperor, Lee Shih Shu—aka Sammy Lee—steepled his fingers under his chin and, for a long moment, was silent.

He was a sleek, oily, round-faced northern Chinese in his late fifties with perfectly coiffed gray hair, wearing a dark-gray business suit that had probably cost more than Feiffer made in three months and wearing on his left hand a jade dragon ring worth more than he would probably ever make in a lifetime.

On the low, carved and lacquered table in front of him, there was a single perfect blue-and-white glazed bowl from the Ming dynasty—half full of water dyed lightly blue, representing the sky, and, resting on the bottom, a fine layer of dark sand, representing the earth. As he thought, Lee gazed into it.

The rest of the room was dark. There, in that corner, they were the only two people on earth, deciding the fate of nations.

Set out on the table next to the bowl, there was a jade-handled calligrapher's brush—the instrument of the scholar—

and, leaning forward a little as if Feiffer were not even there, Lee took it up and, holding it lightly between perfectly manicured fingers, tapped it once on the side of the bowl and made the sky and earth ripple and move.

He thought, because he had lived in Hong Kong all his life, that as well as Cantonese, Feiffer probably spoke Mandarin. Speaking in Shanghainese, which was almost close enough to Mandarin for the man to follow if he strained very carefully at each word, Lee Shih Shu, suddenly looking up, said as an introduction, "Mr. Feiffer, you may know of me as a successful and long-established businessman with many commercial interests here in Hong Kong, but you may not also know me in my other role: that of the unofficial president and advisor to the Grand Council of all the neighborhood progress associations of the Colony—the *kaifongs*—the unofficial and unfunded organizations that for a thousand years have been the sole defenders and protectors of the rights and welfare of the ordinary man against faceless and often bitter and unfeeling authority." He paused again. He asked, still in Shanghainese, "Yes?" and wondered if Feiffer had understood.

He had understood. He had been born in Shanghai, and, for the first ten years of his life, had spoken Shanghainese and almost nothing else.

Feiffer said evenly, in better and more grammatical Shanghainese than Lee's, "No. As a matter of fact, I know you almost entirely as the present head of the so-called Shanghai Bund Triad, an organization of thieves and murderers and thugs that for at least a thousand years, maybe more, has done nothing for the ordinary man except terrorize him and steal from him and torture him."

He paused for a moment and looked the man fully in the face. "I know you as a dirty little guttersnipe who got his start running whores and debt-collecting here in Hong Bay. I know you as someone who has never been to Shanghai in his life because, if you had, the Communists, who have a lot more experience of the Triads than I have, and who have a form of justice sometimes to be wished for here, would have put you up against the nearest wall the moment you got off the train and *shot you dead!*"

He waited for the man to change to Mandarin. Maybe, if he thought it might have done him any good, he'd have taken his gun out and shot him dead himself.

In his seat, Lee was sweating. He was sweating around the collar of his expensive white-silk dress shirt. His power was all gone, and he was sweating. He didn't want to sweat in front of the man, but he was sweating, and he knew Feiffer saw it. He didn't look up. He didn't look Feiffer in the face. Lee Shih Shu, turning the jade calligrapher's brush over in his hand, said without looking up, not even in Mandarin, but in Cantonese, "Even the emperors decreed that one-tenth of all the profits of the farmers in their dominions should be collected in return for protection and security! In the—" He paused. He didn't know which dynasty it was. "In—in ancient times even the greatest Chinese sage who ever lived—even Confucius himself—was a tithe collector! Even Master Kung, working for the emperor, collected one-tenth of all the produce of the peasants in return for—" Sammy Lee said suddenly in English, "The fucking Communists, when they get here, are going to take *everything!*"

"What do you want?"

He looked up. He had eyes like black holes. Sammy Lee asked in street Cantonese, "What do *you* want?"

"I want to know who killed Detective Chief Superintendent Porter and a man named Cheng, and I want to know why."

He ignored it. It was as if Feiffer hadn't even said it. Suddenly looking away and down into the bowl as if somehow he could discern something in there, something deeper, Lee asked again, this time in the careful, slow accent of a scholar, "What do you *want?*"

"I've told you what I want!"

He looked up. "Do you want to stay on?"

"I've told you what I want." He was a slug, a destroyer of lives. He was the evil thing the kite flyers flew their pleas to heaven against—the darkness of their lives—and, as Feiffer looked to one side and glanced out the open door, there were no bodyguards in sight and with everything collapsing, the judiciary, the police, everything, all he had to do was reach in for his gun and—

He must have said something as a preface to it, but Feiffer had not heard it. "Like me, you have nowhere else to go."

"Fuck you."

"And fuck you!" Lee, suddenly balling his fists and snapping the pen in half, said in a hiss, "Like me, there *is* nowhere else for you to go! If you leave here you're nothing! I know all about you! I know who you really are! And *what* you really are, and even though you know all the things you know and even though you may even be the man you think you are, *you are still the wrong color and your eyes are the wrong shape,* and unless you have a protector, a symbol, an emblem—something that makes you *safe*—in less than one month—and do not doubt it for a moment—the Communists, the *Chinese,* of whom you are not one!—will have you thrown out of here like a dog being thrown out into the street!" He looked up and held Feiffer's eyes for a moment. "Unless you have protection from it."

"Whose protection? Yours?"

"Possibly. Possibly that could be arranged."

"Bullshit!"

"It is not bullshit!" Sammy Lee said, to hold out the carrot, still sweating hard, "The Shanghai Bund Triad did not kill your friend Charlie Porter." He shook his head for silence: "And neither did the 14–K." It didn't matter now. "Because, two hours after I learned that Mr. Porter was dead, I had my people take three of the

14–K's top lieutenants out past the harbor limits in a boat and, one by one, the strongest-willed and most loyal first down to the weakest and most wavering, tortured until they told the truth!"

God, he should kill him! It was all over and he had nothing left, and maybe, maybe—maybe, God in heaven! he should just kill him now and have done with it.

He could barely control his voice from breaking with rage. He could barely keep his mind on the fact that he had a wife and son waiting for him in Manila. Feiffer, also starting to sweat, said for the last time, "What do you want?"

He smiled. He changed back to Shanghainese and knew, this time, he would be answered, as was proper, in a lesser language like English. Sammy Lee said sweetly, "I want—I would like, as a man with nothing but the interests of the ordinary, common people of Hong Kong at heart—of whom, Mr. Feiffer, I feel you are one—for you to be able to stay on after the takeover. I would like to help. And be your saviour."

He needed to get out. He needed to get out now. In the bowl, the water of the sky was rippling, making all the sediment of the earth at the bottom of the bowl shift and change color.

Feiffer said in English in a harsh whisper, "It's not within your gift." He turned to go. "And even if it was, the price I'd have to pay—"

"There is no price! The price is only one you have already agreed to pay yourself!"

"What the hell are you talking about? What price? What is it you want? What the hell are you talking about?"

"I am talking about Charlie Porter!"

"What about him?" Sitting there like some sort of well-dressed slug, he was winning. He was winning a game Feiffer did not even know the name of. He was—

All right. Man to man. Plain speaking. Lee said in clear, perfect English, "As the head of the Shanghai Bund Triad, a criminal organization a thousand years old that can trace its origins in China back further than most Western countries can even trace their establishment as nations, I want you to find out who killed Detective Chief Superintendent Charles Robert Porter of the Anti-Triad Unit and I want you to tell me his name!"

Lee said as an oath, that, strangely enough, according to his own principles, he would be bound to follow, "And, in return, within no more than a hour of your doing it, I will guarantee you will be able to stay on after the takeover and no one—Communist or Triad, or anyone else, even I myself—will dare deny any of your wishes!"

He was sweating hard. Lee said as an order, as something non-negotiable, "But it has to be done today. It has to be done today, before dark, because, after that—" His voice trailed off.

Then came back. Lee said with all the terror on his face showing, "Because after that . . . After that, it will all be too late. After that, it will all be too late for *any* of us!"

There had always been a small group of people—the mentally deranged of this world—who, when faced with the cannons of the Russians at one end of the great plain at Balaclava, and the lances and sabers and pig-stickers of the Light Brigade at the other, had but one single urge in life—and that urge was to stand dead in the spot where cannon shot and cavalry charge were going to meet head-on, and shout, *". . . Stop!"*

Needless to say, Spencer was one of them.

Standing in the center of the square facing the crowd at the north end of the square with his hands outstretched in an open, calming gesture of friendship and understanding, Spencer said reasonably in Cantonese in the midst of the humming maelstrom, "No, you must not do this. You must not resort to violence in order to achieve your goals. Violence is not the answer. The answer is intelligence. You must stop, consider all the many, many ramifications of whatever it is that is exercising your minds, ponder all the various means of achieving a solution, and then peacefully, and in a mature and intellectually fair and satisfying way, lay down your arms and all your thoughts of brutish force and negotiate for what it is you want."

Facing the crowd at the south end of the square, Auden also had his hands outstretched in a gesture. It was called the Colt Python Is Aimed Directly At Your Head gesture. Auden screamed, "Or *die!*" He had had all the salt he was going to take—"Or I'll blow the first man who takes a single step forward into the next fucking world!"

He was joking, of course. He wasn't serious.

Spencer, waving the whole thought away, yelled, "He's joking! He's not serious!"

Yes, he was. Salt Man, dripping salt, cocking the hammer, yelled, "Yes, I am!"

"He knows he can't fire that gun here in this holy place!" Spencer said as if it were all nothing but a demonstration of yin and yang—the unity of opposites—and any moment, in a flash of enlightenment, the mobs would see by its demonstration, not what it was, but what they themselves had become, "He knows that an act of violence in this place would throw off the balance of the world and set the universe spinning out of balance—"

He wasn't thinking about the universe; he was thinking about being blown up and being mashed and run over and then blasted to bits by salt, and then— Auden, turning and swinging the gun through three hundred and sixty degrees and taking in Spencer's head as it swung (and at that point in the swing, making little involuntary whinnying noises of pure delight at the thought of it), roared, "I don't care! The next man who tries to mash me or stomp me or shoot me or salt me is fucking *dead!*" Auden, turning back to Spencer to make sure he didn't think he was the one exception to the coming total slaughter, roared, "I've had it, see! I've had it with *lo pans* and *k'ans* and *k'uns* and bloody Dukes and emperor's turtles and bloody invisible demons or whatever the hell they are, and I've had it with being reasonable and I've had it with you, and I've had it with—" Auden screamed at both ends of the street at once, *"And the next person who tries to break one of my balloons, after I've gone to all the trouble of blowing it up and putting a ribbon on it, is dead!"*

At that point, his mind, hearing what his mouth said, should have gone, "Oops! . . ." but it didn't. It was still spitting out salt. Auden shrieked, "Okay? All right? Has everyone got that? *Now get the fuck out of here before I make all your fucking wives widows!"*

What a man of many subtleties old Phil really was! For a moment there . . . But no, it was just his little way of— Spencer, catching on quick, yelled, "See? See what violence maketh of a man? See how this otherwise kind and amiable soul is reduced to empty threats of murder and mayhem by the violence perpetrated against him?" (He had always liked the big, thoughtful, deeply moral poets like Milton and Dryden, and novelists like Galsworthy and— Was it Galsworthy? Yes, it was Galsworthy.)

Spencer, getting into the swing of things, yelled, quoting from . . . from . . . from *Galsworthy:* "'What do it profiteth a man if he gain the whole world but lose his immortal soul?'" Saying it there in that place was a dream come true. Spencer yelled, "No! Let us not try to combat violence by even more violence! Let us *now* rather—" He shook his head and, in the humming, lost his train of thought completely.

The crowd at his end of the square was huge: a solid wall of black-clad and masked figures armed to the teeth getting ready to surge forward like a tidal wave. Well, what the hell? He had nowhere else to go, nothing more to look forward to in life.

Auden, taking his left hand off the butt of the gun and reaching into his pocket to show them what he had in there, yelled, "See? Look! I've got lots of ammo and—" He didn't read nineteenth-century novels as the moral guide to good and evil, he read *Guns and Ammo* magazine as the moral guide to mass murder—"And I'd be more than happy to accommodate you in assisting you on board the train in your little last ride to the next world if that's what you want!" Demons, schemons. The first person to move an inch towards him was going to die.

Up there in all the geomancers' windows, all the muzzles of the cannons watched them.

Spencer, turning and gazing up at the unseen cannoneers, said sadly, "And you, you men of learning and the custodians of all that is ancient and traditional and unchanging and good—"

God! He'd almost forgotten about them! Auden roared, "And you bastards are dead too! I'm not sure that I'll get all of you—"

All he was sure of was that he didn't want to sell balloons.

Auden, swinging the big gun up in their direction and actually seeing one of the cannon muzzles shake as the cannoneers behind it must have ducked, screamed in Cantonese, "But by God, I'll huff and I'll puff and I'll *blow* your house down!"

Okay. Enough of the yin and the yang—now for the unity. Spencer, dropping his voice a little, said sweetly, "We want to be reasonable, you see, and help you, as indeed, in their hearts, all men want to be reasonable—" Time for the Light Brigade to stop in the middle of the plain and give their poor horses a drink of water. "So let us help you and be reasonable. Let us first identify the problem—what it is you're afraid of—and then, having done that—"

They moved. At both ends of the street, both the crowds, as one, seemed to move a single step backwards.

"—and then, having done that—"

It twitched. Up there in one of the windows, another one of the cannon muzzles twitched. Below it, at the top of the stone steps, the big wooden teak main-entrance door opened a crack.

"—and then, having done that—" Spencer, taking another step forward to the north end of the street, asked sweetly, helping them along, giving his class a little hint, "And then what? What do you think we should all do then? . . ."

Spencer asked in the utter, absolute silence, "Hmmm? Well, come on now . . . what do you think should happen next? . . . Hmm?"

It was a hard one.

You could see them thinking about it.

"Well? What do you think? What is the problem?" He hated to make it easy for people—to stifle original, creative thought and personal research—but sometimes, well, you just had to start people off a little and . . .

He started them off.

Spencer said pleasantly, starting them off, "Well? The problem . . . What is it exactly?" Spencer asked politely, academically, "Hmm? Well?"

"DEMONS!!" At both ends of the square, the two crowds of black-clad men, as one, shrieked as one, *"DEMONS!! . . . DEMONS!!"* and then, as all the cannons from all the windows blasted out all at once, charged.

In the Detectives' Room, O'Yee yelled into the phone, "What? What? *What?"*

Goalposts, halftime, everything, nothing, souls, Chinese puzzles mixed in with French and American enigmas and—

But on the phone there was nothing, no sound at all on the line.

There was only, ever, the presence of Claude in the room watching and listening.

Claude said helpfully, "Perhaps merely a wrong number? . . ."

On the phone, all there was was silence.

O'Yee said formally, "Colonel Kong—"

On the phone, there was a single sound. That sound, as if someone had just heard all the jaws of hell snap open directly in front of him, was *"Aaaiiiyaa!"*

O'Yee said tightly, "Colonel Kong, in the light of all the recent history of the past twenty or thirty years of the People's Republic of China—of the Cultural Revolution and the Hundred Flowers and the deification of Mao and all the denunciations and all the twists and turns of official favor, and then the rise of Deng and then the death of Deng and then—" O'Yee asked as the phone suddenly went dead, "Just how the hell have you managed to keep yourself from getting *killed?"*

"Ah. A good question."

And it fazed him not at all.

Colonel Kong said with his index finger raised and waggling in the air to underscore his point, "Ah. But an even better one, and certainly one much more intriguing to me—in the light of all the recent history of Hong Kong, all the venality and corruption and oppression and plain, simple, government-sanctioned *evil*—might be, Just how the hell have *you?"*

Sitting there in his chair like some sort of disgusting, evil slug, Lee had it all worked out.

Well, so did he. Standing above the man with his finger stabbing in the direction of the man's heart, Feiffer said as an accusation, "He *had* something, didn't he—Porter? He had something the Triads wanted! He had something he took from one of the cupboards in the Anti-Triad Unit room and he took it back home that night and—"

It hit him like a physical blow—"Because you offered him the same deal you just offered me. That's why he suddenly told his wife they'd be able to stay on! Because you offered him the same deal for it you just offered me! But before he could get whatever it was to you, someone killed him for it and took it, and just to make sure you knew about it—just to make sure you knew you were going to have to deal with someone else now to get it—killed some poor innocent doorman on the way out and left him lying in full view of the street for everyone to see!"

Everything about Charlie Porter's life had been a lie. Feiffer said with a pain so deep he had to shake his head hard not to be overwhelmed by the immensity of it, "He *worked* for you, didn't he? Porter? He was your man, bought and paid for!" It was the only thing that made sense. "That's why he had so much success against your rival, the 14–K—you fed him what he needed to know, and why he got promoted so quickly: you made his success *for* him. And in return—" He was a slug. He was worse than a slug. He was a slug that had been eating away at the heart of everything for decades. Feiffer demanded, "What did he have? What was it he promised you in return for everything you'd done for him over the years? What did he have that he'd promised you in return for being allowed to stay on? What was it that he had that would give you the power to *allow* him to stay on?"

"Nothing." He had it all worked out. Lee, smiling and shaking his head, said easily, "He had nothing that belonged to either us or the 14–K. All Mr. Porter ever had from us was—was nothing."

"What did he have?"

"He had *nothing!* He had—" Lee said suddenly, "The Triads are the heirs to the history and tradition of China, not the Communists! The Triads can trace their line back into antiquity as the authentic voice of the people, not the Communists! The Triads are China, not the Communists! The Communists are nothing more than a fly spot on the pages of history! Porter, like you, was not even Chinese! He was a barbarian, a ghost person, an invisible entity, and even if he had had something we wanted he would not have known its worth or understood its import anyway! He would not have understood its import to the Chinese—to the real Chinese: to the mass of ordinary Chinese—to the *people!* And, even if he had, even if he had in his barbarian's mind, some small inkling—" Lee said, "Even if there was such a thing, he would have thrown it away for something pointless and useless like money!"

God only knew what it was.

Lee said, "And he did not work for me. I never even once met the man or spoke to him."

"Then where did he get his network of informers?"

"All I ask of you in return for that which you want most is the name of the person who killed him. Nothing more."

"No."

"Then you will have nothing when the Communists come!"

"And neither will you!"

"Then both of us will lose!" Lee, suddenly leaning forward, said tightly, "Listen to me. All this—the taking back of Hong Kong—is nothing; in the long view, it is all nothing. It is nothing more than a dress rehearsal for the taking back of Taiwan; and how the people react to it here, how they accommodate themselves to it here, who and what organizations here they give their loyalty to, will be a touchstone for all the people on Taiwan, and then, through them, to all the ordinary masses until finally—"

"Until finally, what? The Triads get to rule all of *China?*"

"The Triads have always ruled China! The Triads have always been the invisible empire of the people! The Triads, like the emperors of the old Confucian days, have never taken more than their rightful one-tenth share of their labor from the people, while the Communists have taken everything! The Triads are the people! They are the power controlling the people, controlling their labor, controlling their every waking hour! The Triads have the power to make the people rise and—" He had said too much. Lee said suddenly, "You are being offered an arrangement that no other round-eyes has ever been offered! I am offering it to you! I am offering you—"

"Perhaps the 14–K could offer me something better."

"The 14–K, within the next three weeks, will cease to exist! Within the next three weeks there will be no 14–K!" He was a Mandarin. He was going to merge all the Triads into one single awesomely powerful group. Lee, leaning back in his chair and tapping himself on the chest, said as an order, "Look at me! Do not see who you think I am or who perhaps once I was, but see who I might become in the future! Consider that! Consider that before you decide to deny me what I want!"

What the hell had Porter had? Whatever it was, it wasn't some B-movie little jade statuette or some magic powder or all the other things beloved of filmmakers whose closest acquaintance with the Orient had been learning how to use chopsticks in some New York restaurant—whatever it was was something awesome, something sacred, something holy. Feiffer, following the man's theme, demanded, "Did he know what it was that he had?"

And got him. Lee said with his contempt for everything Western showing, "No! He did not! He was too stupid!"

"Who did?"

"Someone."

"Someone Chinese?"

"Yes! Of course!"

"Did Charlie Porter work for you or not?"

"No, he did not!"

"Then who did?"

"Someone."

"Someone Chi—?" Feiffer said in a whisper, "Oh my God! . . ."

In all the years he had known her, he had never even kissed her on the cheek—he had never known anything about her. Even though she was originally from Shanghai and had been born there as he himself had, in all those years he had never once spoken to her in anything other than English, and in all those years—

Feiffer demanded, "Was it Annie? Was it his wife? Did *she* tell him what he had?"

"Yes!"

"And was she the one who worked for you? Not her husband, but *her?*"

"Yes!"

"And was she the one who promised you the—"

Sammy Lee said, "Yes! All these years, since she married him ten years ago, one week exactly after he told her as a joke what he had, she has been guarding it for us—making sure it stayed where it was, waiting until the exact moment we would need it—which is now."

She had not been the one who had killed Porter. If it had been her, Lee would have known about it. "And what was the rest of the deal?" Feiffer said with his voice rising, *"To kill her husband after he had handed it over to you and—"* Feiffer said suddenly, "You weren't going to let him stay on, were you? *Annie* was going to be allowed to stay on! Wasn't she?" Barely holding himself back from reaching down and throttling the man where he sat, Feiffer roared, "And is this the same deal you're offering me? To do you a small favor and then, in return, find myself shot dead in a ditch in a few days *at your fucking convenience?"*

"Perhaps."

"Are you completely *insane?"*

"Are you? Let us assume for a moment there is such a thing—that marks the possessor as the true, the real, the authentic voice of the ordinary people and you find it. Who *will* you give it to? The *Communists?* The slaughterers of the people in Tiananmen Square? The heirs to Mao's Great Leap Forward that killed five million people? To the Marxists? To the murderers? To *them?* To the takers of everything? Or to us? To the Triads—the takers of only one-tenth of the labors of the farmers, one-tenth of—" He believed it all. Lee roared, "Who would you give it to? Whose rule would you have the ordinary people of China—the one billion men, women and children—live under? Theirs, or *ours?*"

He rose. The audience was over. He had it all, all worked out.

Lee, a player playing now in the biggest game there was to play, said to silence any further discussion, "All you have to do is give me the name of the person who killed Charlie Porter, nothing more. And as for his widow, as for the woman you call 'Annie,' there is no point in asking her—"

Standing above the table between them, he glanced down into the wonderful Ming bowl, and then with his hand, flicked it away onto the ground and smashed it as if it were nothing.

Lee Shih Shu said a moment before he turned to go out of the room through the open door into the street, "Because she is dead. She was killed in the underground car park in her apartment building less than a hour ago. And not by us." And God only knew who had died to give him that information. "And not by the 14–K either, but someone else."

Between the chair where he had sat and the open door all there was was darkness.

In that darkness, Lee said from the door as an order from the man he might become, in the language he had begun in, in Shanghainese, "Find out who, and then come back here—this time, as you were told to, *unarmed*—and tell me his *name!*"

9.

He exploded.

In the Detectives' Room, leaping up from behind his desk, O'Yee yelled at the bland, the unbeetled face looking at him, "I managed not to get killed all these years because I never did anything to anyone that would have *gotten* me killed!"

He was a man who knew all the questions, but none of the answers. Snarling at him, O'Yee yelled, "I never did anything to anyone that would have made them *want* to kill me! I never did anything to anyone that wasn't legal or justified or just plain brought on by what they did themselves first; and I never did—"

"Ah. The truly good and honest man in action."

"That's right!" To hell with it—he didn't need this. O'Yee, still snarling, yelled, "That's right. You're right! I am a good man! I don't have to wonder about what a good man is, or answer questions about what a good man might be, because I am one! I am a good man! I have people who love me—family, and friends—and anything I might regret having done wasn't because I set out to do it that way, it was just—"

Claude said helpfully, "Bad luck?"

"Yes! Just plain bad luck!"

He understood. Claude said, nodding, "Forced upon you by the times and circumstances. Promises unfulfilled and aspirations denied." He seemed to cast about for an illustration—"Like Mr. Sun Yaoting, for example." He saw O'Yee did not know who he meant. "The last eunuch of Imperial China, who, I read in the papers, is at the moment either dying or dead—here in Hong Kong." He was trying to be helpful. "Now, there is a man who was a victim of his own times and circumstances, a man who, when he was eight, in 1911, had his genitals cut off so he could be introduced to the Imperial Court as a eunuch, one of the group of inner officials, a person who, as you may know, wielded enormous power and influence within the court. And a man who, less than a year later—at age nine—was the victim of the 1911 Nationalist Revolution that swept away the entire imperial system and everything that went with it." Poor bastard. "And then, during the wartime Occupation of China, a man hunted mercilessly by the Japanese as a dangerous anti-Occupation rallying influence and forced to work as a mere peasant in the fields to hide his identity—and then, after the Communist Revolution, a man seen as representing an evil and feudal past, and expelled during the Cultural Revolution as an enemy of the people. And now, at ninety-five years old, and either on his deathbed or already dead; as the People's Republic stands on the point of reclaiming Hong Kong—" Claude said with a shrug, "Well, a man who just had bad luck all his life. Like you."

"I haven't had bad luck all my life."

"No?"

"No." He wasn't going to tell him anything—nothing. O'Yee, shaking his head, said firmly, "I've had good luck all my life. I have a good family and friends and I have the respect of people and I—" O'Yee said in a sudden, uncontrollable storm of anger, "And I've done a good job here! I've done a very good job here, and I've—"

"We all want to do that. We all want to do a good job. It is the nature of Man to want to be moral, to feel pride in his own behavior. But can it be done here? Can even a good man working in an evil system ever do good? Or, must he, perforce—" He smiled. "—or must he, perforce, be capable of doing only evil in that evil system?"

There was nothing to say.

"Or are all such feelings of having done good in that system mere delusions?"

Nothing.

"Chimeras? Phantoms? Lies told to oneself to justify one's own doubts, one's own—"

Nothing.

He leaned a little forward in his chair. Claude said softly, intimately, "I refer to the doubts that come in the nights, in the silences, in the moments when we are most alone with ourselves, the moments when we are no longer surrounded and safe with our friends and our family. I refer to the coldest, loneliest moments just before dawn when we cannot sleep, when the body is at its weakest ebb and the soul at its most vulnerable, the moments when, like tentacles, all our doubts and fears come out of the night to claim us, the moments when—" Claude asked, "Do you have such moments, Christopher?"

"No."

"Never?"

"No! Never!" Suddenly, moving back and forth behind his desk, he could not get his breath. Suddenly, there, in that tiny strip of space at the back of the room, there was no air.

O'Yee, gasping for breath, said, "No, I don't! I don't have any doubts in the middle of the night or any other time. I know what I've done and I know why it happened and—*and I know why I did it, and I don't have any doubts about any of it! Ever!!*" He couldn't breathe. He almost couldn't get the words out. "And if there are some things I wish hadn't happened, they just happened, and they weren't of my doing!" (God! He was starting to talk like him!) "And at least—"

O'Yee roared, "At least I never took busloads of prisoners out to the nearest football ground and tied them to the goalposts and *shot* them!" (To hell with it! If he was going to go down, he was going to go down firing!) *"The way you did!"*

"What?" He seemed surprised.

Yeah, he hadn't thought he'd known that!

He shook his head as if to make sure he'd heard right, then blinked and shook his head again.

Claude said as if he still could not quite believe he had heard it right, "I've never shot anyone in my entire life."

"What?"

He pulled back the flap of his coat a little: "I don't even carry a gun. I never have. I wouldn't even know how guns work."

"What? But you—"

"No." Shaking his head, Claude said, to dismiss the idea completely, "No, I've never shot anyone. No one. Not in my entire life." He paused for a moment.

Claude said pleasantly, matter-of-factly, "But you have, haven't you?" He glanced down for a moment at the open dossier on his knees. "You have. You've shot people. In the course of the last fifteen years, you've shot and killed a total of seven human beings, one of them a member of your own family." He paused again.

Claude asked, "How do you feel, in your stated complete and utter lack of self-doubts and conscience, about that?"

He had to sit down.

Claude asked, to make sure he had it right, "It was your wife's cousin, wasn't it? The member of your own family you shot to death? A man named—"

O'Yee said softly, "Yes."

"Yes." He did not look down at the dossier.

He blinked, and suddenly, everything in the room was gone and all there was in front of his eyes was darkness. O'Yee said into that darkness, "I didn't know who he was at the time."

"No. He was just a man who called the police and told them that he was in a hotel room with hostages and that the only person he'd negotiate with was you, and then, when he shouted out from behind the door of that room that if you came in alone, he'd give up the hostages—"

O'Yee said, "It was dark. There were no lights on. All he was in there was a shadow—"

"He made a sudden move with something in his hand and—" O'Yee said, reliving the moment, "I thought it was a *gun!* I thought he had *hostages!*"

"Did he? Did he have hostages?"

"No."

"Did he have a gun?"

"No, he didn't have a gun!"

"I see."

"No, you don't see!"

"He was a man who often visited your family, wasn't he? A man your children, when they were young, called—"

"Yes!"

"A man who—"

O'Yee said desperately, "He committed suicide! He couldn't do it for himself so he used me to do it for him!"

"Ah." He nodded. He was a man who had never been in the same situation himself, but maybe could understand it. Claude said softly, "I'm sorry." He was a good man: he gave something to O'Yee as a gift.

Claude said sadly, sympathetically, "Maybe, is it possible—I don't know about such things—is it perhaps likely that, meeting death, he wanted the help, the assistance, the company of his friend, of a good person, someone he loved? You perhaps?"

"No." He could not look up. He shook his head.

O'Yee said so softly Claude had to crane forward in his chair to hear what he said, "No, it isn't. It isn't likely at all. What is likely, what is not only likely but true and indisputable, is that if I had really been the person he thought I was, I would have seen all the signs of it all coming long before it happened—all his pain and sadness and despair and hopelessness and loss—and never even allowed it all to come to that in the first place!"

In Tiger-Dragon Square, being beaten, bonked, buffeted, smoke-blown, salt-peppered and being bashed to bits by a thousand bashers, Auden yelled in a panic, "Get to the door of the castle! Find the door! Get to the door and then kick the door open and then get in behind the door and then close the door and we'll be safe behind the—"

They were already at the door. Auden yelled, "Aha! The door!"

It was a good door, a big door, a castle door, the door to the Geomancers' Union Castle.

Shoving at it, pushing on it, being clobbered and clubbed by a cast of thousands, Auden yelled as someone clobbered and clubbed him yet again, "Push the fucking door!" And then someone else clubbed him and he crashed against the door and felt someone grab him and hold him up and thought it was Spencer and was glad he had decided to— But it wasn't him: it wasn't Spencer—it was someone else. It was a man wearing black pajamas and a mask carrying a wooden sword, bent on slashing him into ribbons, and Auden, reeling backwards, as said black-pajamaed man let fly a blow that missed his head by an inch and bounced off the door, roared—

"Get to the door!"

It was Spencer.

Spencer, suddenly coming out of nowhere and barging his way through a knot of other black-pajamaed people slashing at the door with clubs and sticks and—one of them at least—swinging a huge wooden sledgehammer, yelled as if he hadn't heard a single word Auden had said, "Phil! Find the door! Get to the door and then kick the door open and get in behind the door and then close the door and then we'll be—"

And they'd be safe behind the door!

Good idea!

Well done!

About time he used his brain for something.

Auden, shoving and pushing, getting to the door and pushing on it, yelled back, "Good idea!" and in a blast of cannon fire that seemed to pour directly down on him, got to it and with a mighty kick got it open, got Spencer in, and with a slam, got the door closed.

Good door, great door. Funny how it didn't seem to have an inside lock. Funny how it just seemed to lock itself automatically, but still, good door, nice door—just the door they needed.

Auden, resting his shoulder on the door and giving it a little affectionate pat as outside what sounded like a thousand rioters smashed at it with hammers and sticks and clubs and swords, said in relief, safe at last, "Phew!"

Well, at least he was out of fucking Tiger-Snake Square or the center of the known world, or whatever the hell it was—at least he was—

Letting go a long sigh of relief, he wondered exactly where it was he was, and turned to have a little look.

And then another, a longer look.

And then another, a very long look.

And knew in that moment, exactly, precisely, where he was.

Standing behind the locked and sealed door with no way out, gazing down a long, stone-walled and ceilinged corridor lit by nothing more than flickering candles, he had not even the faintest shadow of a doubt exactly, precisely, where he was.

Already starting to break out all over in scabs and warts and buttons, Auden shrieked in horror, "Oh, no! Oh, no! Oh, no! *Oh, no!* It's the secret one-way passageway leading straight into the tomb of the Mummy's Curse old Whatever-His-Name-Was found!"

In the Detectives' Room, Claude asked, "Your family, and his . . . And your wife . . ."

For a moment, he didn't seem to quite know how to put it. Claude asked, "Did they forgive you for what happened?"

"Yes."

"And your children?"

"Yes."

"And is that the worst part of it?"

"Yes."

All there was in those silences before dawn when he could not sleep and his body and soul were at their lowest ebb, was the pain.

In the Detectives' Room, O'Yee said softly, "Yes, that's the worst part of it."

And could not help it, and, in front of the man, put his hands to his face and wept.

"Extraordinary . . . I was wrong . . ."

Inside the Geomancers' Union Castle, unlike Auden, Spencer wasn't staring down the Passageway To Hell with his eyes like saucers: he was standing with his back to the Passageway To Hell looking at the door to the street, looking past it, through it. Spencer, standing there, staring at it with the same fascinated expression Mr. Spock wore on his face as he computed how many microseconds the *Enterprise* and its crew had left before they were all sucked into the Fifth Dimension, said in a curious little mutter, "Hmmm . . . extraordinary . . . I was *wrong* . . ."

Well, yes, it was. Yes, it certainly was. What was extraordinary was that, on the other side of that door, there were two heavily armed hordes of totally black-clad maniacs bashing and hammering to get in, while, on this side of the door, at the far end of the passageway where there was only darkness, there was—

He had a little question. He asked it. Auden asked in what he thought was a calm voice, "How do we get out of here, Bill?"

"Amazing . . ."

Yes, it was. Well, well, well. Who would have thought it?

Auden asked again in what he thought was a calm voice, just in case the man had not heard for the sound of the bashing and hammering, "Um, how do we get out of here, Bill?"

"Astonishing . . ."

He shook his head. Spencer, turning and glancing down the corridor—the one that ended in blackness and warts and scabs and buttons and slow, lingering unspeakable Death—said yet again, "Amazing. Extraordinary . . ."

"How do we get out of here, Bill?"

"Amazing. Extraordinary. I was wrong!" He looked over at Auden in case he had a question.

He did. Starting to hop up and down like a toad—like a living, breathing *wart*—Auden screamed at the man in horror as suddenly, with an unseen breeze, all the candles down the entire length of the place all went out at once, "Bill! Bill! *How the hell do we get out of here?"*

In the darkness, trying to help the man along, Auden shrieked in a panic, *"Right?* Or *left?* Or *straight ahead?* Or—?"

Auden shrieked, "OH, MY GOD!!!"

And in the same instant, as all the candles came back on all at once, something under his feet suddenly opened up with a bang, and, with Spencer just a moment behind him, kicking him in the head as he went, his direction was settled, and, like a hanged man falling instantly through the trapdoors of a gallows to Eternity, where he went, flailing and punching and kicking and yelling in terror, was straight . . .

Down.

In the Detectives' Room, as O'Yee sat silently with his head in his hands, gazing down at his desk, all there was was silence.

Standing alone above the empty chair where Lee had been, gazing down at the smashed bowl on the floor with all the blue water of heaven and the brown sand of earth spilled out from it, all Feiffer could think of were the kites and how they flew uselessly, pointlessly, powerlessly up in a deaf and uncaring heaven.

In the darkened, ancient room, as he put his hand to his face, all he could think of were the kites.

10.

His voice carried down the entire length of the Morgue corridor.

In Doctor Macarthur's little glassed-in office off the post-mortem room, Inspector Burtenshaw, no longer sounding or even looking like the same man, roared in answer to something Macarthur had said, "They're everywhere! They're not just in here—they're everywhere: the goddamned Communists! They're everywhere!"

He saw Feiffer come in through the door and look at him for an explanation. He gave him one. His shirt was ripped where he had torn off his badge and thrown it away. Rank didn't matter anymore. Burtenshaw, furious, said with all the pent-up anger and frustration of a civil-service accountant wantonly denied the opportunity to tot up the very last column of figures in a ledger book he had been working on all his professional life, "No sooner than one of my constables radios in to Headquarters to get either you or one of your detectives down to the scene to where the body of the infernal, damned woman is than I'm ordered to call in on a land line and informed that, because the body is Chinese, no action is to be taken by any part of the present administration about it! I'm simply to call up an ambulance and have it transported directly here to the Morgue and placed in a secure area! And then . . . and then—"

He was breathing hard. He stopped to catch his breath, but couldn't. "—and then, after that, I'm to go straight home, pack my uniform, and either stay on a few days as a civilian tourist if I like, but, preferably, *book myself on the next available plane back home to Australia!*"

His badge was gone, but not his gun. The way things were, he was going to keep that to the very end, maybe even longer.

Burtenshaw, putting his hand on the butt as if he thought any moment he might have to draw it to defend himself, shouted, "And by the time I get back from the land line—less than two minutes because I timed it!—both my constables have taken off and left the body lying there in its own blood and—and— And *deserted* me!"

He still had his hand on the gun. With his eyes flickering back and forth in the office as if there were enemies hidden everywhere, he was out of control, and in that moment, extremely dangerous.

He kept his distance from him. Feiffer, standing, as Macarthur did, at least five feet away from the man, asked with no threat in his voice at all, "Are you sure it was Annie Porter?" He tried to think of the man's first name, but could not.

Everything was a threat. Burtenshaw, spinning on his heel and thrusting his hand even harder on the butt of his gun, yelled, probably answering the question from Macarthur that had set him off in the first place, "No, I'm not sure it was Annie Porter! I'm not sure it was Annie Porter because I didn't get a chance to examine her or any identification or papers she might have been carrying! And, yes, I'm sure it was Annie Porter because—"

It was Annie Porter. He had seen her face. Burtenshaw, suddenly turning back to Feiffer to give him the information he should have been able to give him at the scene, shouted as if everyone, everyone, were part of the conspiracy, "Yes, it was her! Unlike her husband, whoever killed her didn't use a shotgun—they used a small-caliber pistol! And, unlike her husband who had his whole fucking head blown away, all she had was a neat little hole in the back of her head behind the left ear and—" Burtenshaw said before Feiffer could ask, "The car-park attendant found her when he did his rounds and ran out into the street where I was on street duty—but, of course, by the time I got back with my fucking marching orders, like my *cops* he was gone too, and everybody, everybody seems to know more about what the fuck's happening than I do, and all I am anymore is just a fucking, a fucking little—a fucking little errand boy and I don't give a fuck about any of it anymore, and I was just a fool to try to behave in a responsible, adult, honest way towards anyone I ever came into contact with in this whole goddamned place when all the time, *because everyone I ever came into contact with here in my entire career was nothing but a thief and a liar and a cheat!"*

He was going home. He was going home, not as a man with wonderful, exotic stories of his last few weeks as a real street cop to tell, but as a failure. He was going home—never to speak about the subject again to anyone—as a fool.

He looked away, and then down to the floor, and for a moment it seemed as if he might suddenly sink down to the floor and sob.

Feiffer said, "Tony?" but Macarthur said nothing either, and shook his head.

Maybe Macarthur's life had gone too. Maybe something had changed and everything he thought or hoped for had also changed. Or maybe not. Or, maybe worse, he didn't know what had happened.

Macarthur, still shaking his head, said, doing the best he

could, "I don't know, Harry. All I know is that it was made known to me by—by people I have to listen to—that—"

He hardly knew how to characterize it himself.

"All I know is that I wasn't to touch her or have anything to do with her—and that any examination or autopsy of the body would be done later by someone else, someone Chinese, and that—" He shrugged. "I didn't even see the body. After it came in, it was—"

Burtenshaw said suddenly, "The ambulance got as far as the receiving door in the back and then two men in white coats came out with a stretcher and took it in by hand, and then another man in a suit—"

Macarthur said, "The Chinese People's liaison officer, Doctor Hsang—"

"—said very politely, 'Thank you very much,' and then went in with it, closed the doors, and then left both me and the two ambulancemen standing there in the roadway looking stupid and wondering who the hell was going to fill out the forms that we all had in our hands that were supposed to be filled out and—"

Macarthur said as if he could not quite believe it himself, "They—Doctor Hsang and his people—they said, in future, Chinese bodies were not to be touched by barbarians, and then they took over the whole place, turned out the only European body we had, and dumped it in the undertakers' pickup room out of sight."

"Charlie Porter?"

"Yes." He glanced for a moment up at the ceiling, and then nodded. Macarthur, quoting exactly what Doctor Hsang had said, said softly, "Yes. 'For almost a hundred and fifty years, the Europeans have treated the Chinese people like dogs; now, rightfully, it is their turn to be treated by the Chinese people as dogs!'" Macarthur, still trying to understand it, still gazing at the ceiling, said in a whisper, "Jesus Christ, Harry—!"

"And you!" He hadn't finished. Burtenshaw, turning back to

Feiffer, with his hand still on his gun, shouted, "And you! Mr. Big Fucking Shot! Mr. I'm-Your-Superior-Officer, I'll-Tell-You-How-Things-Are-Done—Bigshot— This is for—*you!* This is *yours!*" For the first time, he took his hand off his gun and, reaching past his holster, rammed it into his pocket and brought something out. "It was stuck on the front window of the car next to where the body was when I came back from calling in and everyone, including the car-park attendant, had taken off like fucking frightened rabbits!" He held it up. "It's for *you!* It's *yours!*"

It was a scrap of folded-up paper. Thrusting it in Feiffer's direction, Burtenshaw yelled, "Take it! It's yours! It's even got your name written clearly across it in big letters so even a dumbo like me can read it! It's a note, a letter! An order from your fucking *masters!*"

He could not take any of it anymore, and, suddenly yanking his hand back before Feiffer could reach it, looked down for an instant at the paper and balled it up in his fist and threw it down to the floor.

In his anger, in his frustration, in his pain, all he wanted to do was take out his gun and kill someone, maybe, in that moment, with his eyes running with tears, most of all, himself. Burtenshaw shrieked, "You bastard! You cheat! You liar! You—"

Burtenshaw roared before Feiffer could even move to get it, "Don't bother reading it! I can tell you what it says! It says, 'To Detective Chief Inspector Feiffer, Yellowthread Street Police Station, Hong Bay—' It says, one line, in English, 'Keep in mind and consider for your future that any arrangement you may have previously come to with Mr. Lee of the Shaghai Bund Society can be more than bettered with one phone call to Mr. Heng at 14–K.' " Burtenshaw said so softly it was almost inaudible, "The fucking Triads . . ."

The hand on the butt of his gun wasn't for himself or anyone else. It was for Feiffer.

Standing there in that awful place, the most alone he had ever felt in his life, Burtenshaw screamed in his fury, "You *bastard!* You cheat! You thief! You *liar!* You're one of them! You're like everyone else in this whole, stinking, corrupt, rotten place! You're a goddamned, stinking, lousy *thief!* And a *cheat!* And a *liar!*"

In the Detectives' Room, after what seemed like a long time, Colonel Kong, glancing up from his open dossier, asked as a matter of record, "He was a Communist, wasn't he? Your wife's cousin?"

O'Yee had a cigarette burning between his fingers. He put it to his mouth, but it tasted like salt and he stubbed it out in his ashtray.

"Wasn't he? A member of the Party here in Hong Kong since the mid-seventies, a man named—"

"I know what his name was!"

"Wasn't he? He was a Communist, wasn't he? A sworn enemy of everything that you and the colonial regime you represented as a policeman stood for—wasn't he?"

"No."

"Wasn't he?" He looked down into the dossier. "I have it here that he was a—"

And saw him. And saw him in that awful moment when the first shot lit up his face in the darkness, and, before he could stop, because he was so frightened there in that little room, the other five shots from his revolver came so fast that— O'Yee said, "No! He was my wife's cousin! He was a—"

"He was a Communist. A—"

He saw his face. He saw, as all the bullets tore at him and ripped him apart and killed him, he saw his face see him, and in that moment, he saw his eyes, so sad and lost—

O'Yee said desperately, "I don't know what he was! He was

my wife's cousin! He was my friend! He was my children's friend! He was a man who brought gifts to my children and never forgot any of their birthdays, and—" O'Yee said suddenly violently, "He was a man who ate at my table! He was— He was— *He was a human being!"*

"Who you killed!"

"Yes! Who I killed! Yes, who I killed! Yes, who I shot six times because I was so fucking frightened because it was dark and I thought he had a gun and who—" O'Yee said on the edge of losing it, *"He was a human being who was the friend of my children and who I liked very much!"*

"And a Communist, and, therefore, by definition, a bitter ideological enemy of everything you believed in, and, no doubt, in your discussions together over your table, a deep and frustrating thorn in your side and an influence within your family for nothing but evil—"

"Go to hell!"

"Was he not?"

"No, he was not! He was a—" O'Yee, withdrawing inside himself, giving no more, having no more to give, said as an order, *"You go to hell!"*

In the ashtray, the stub of the cigarette was still burning, and he reached for it and took it, and then, holding it between his fingers, suddenly could not remember what he had wanted to do with it and stubbed it out hard again.

O'Yee, with the muscles of his neck and jaw clamped so tight he had to close his eyes for a moment to bear the pain, said with an effort, "He was a— He was— He worked in a library—"

O'Yee said with no tone at all, as a recitation, "His name was Robert Wing and he was forty-two years old and unmarried and he worked for the Hong Kong Public Library and he brought little gifts of books and pictures and prints of China the library was throwing out for my children and he sat with them after we'd all eaten and read to them or pointed things out to them, or told them about the history of things, and he was a very good and kind and gentle person. And then he was told by his doctors that he had—"

He could barely say the words—"He had cancer of the bowels and he was in pain all the time and then his eyes went and he couldn't read anymore, and he was embarrassed to be around people because he couldn't control his bowels anymore and he—"

O'Yee said with the pain in his neck and jaws becoming unbearable, "And then—and then— *And then I killed him!* I went up to the room he'd rented thinking he was some sort of criminal with a hostage and I shot him six times in the chest and I killed him! He never told anyone about his disease or his pain and I—"

"Then how could you have possibly known about his fear of embarrassing himself in front of—"

"He left a letter!"

It was almost more than he could bear.

"Addressed to me!"

"To the man he knew would kill him?"

"Yes!"

"A man who, because he was a police officer and therefore used to guns and violence, would kill him quickly and cleanly?"

"Yes! I don't know! Maybe!"

"Or because he knew you would be so frightened you would shoot without hesitation?"

"I don't know that either! Maybe!" Maybe that was true too.

"And did you?"

At his desk, he needed something desperately. He needed a cigarette, but somehow—somehow, he could not think where to find one, and— "Did I what?"

"Did you kill him quickly and cleanly?"

"I don't remember!"

"Really?" It was a simple question. Colonel Kong, looking a little surprised, asked as if perhaps the man had not quite understood how simple the question was, "Did you take no interest in the matter after he was dead? Did you just slaughter him as if he were some sort of wounded dog in the street and then walk away to let—"

"Yes, I killed him cleanly! I shot him six times in the heart at close range!"

"With a revolver?" He glanced over and craned his neck towards the top drawer of O'Yee's desk as if he could somehow see through the wood and see what sort of gun he had in there. "Or a pistol of some sort? Or with something bigger? Like a shotgun, or a—"

His neck was rock hard, and he was paralyzed by it, and at his desk he could not move, and, sitting here at his desk, staring at the man with his hands clenched into fists, he was like stone and could not even blink his eyes.

Kong said conversationally, as if he did not notice O'Yee's pain at all, "What I am getting at is this: I wonder, if, when this poor gentle man, this friend of your children, this sad, hurting creature—I wonder if, when he was finally buried, he went to his grave intact. Or if—" He leant back in his chair to impart a little information—just a little snippet of interest in a casual chat between two friends over tea: "There are those, you know—and it is a deep-rooted belief in Chinese culture—who would say that a person's body and soul are inextricably linked together, and that a person who is sent to heaven with only part of his body intact is sent there with only part of his *soul* intact, and can therefore never find peace—and is forever condemned to the limbo of the half world between heaven and earth to roam as a ghost, as a spirit, and to—"

"It was a revolver."

"The one you still have there in your desk?"

"Yes."

"So he did not—"

"No. He didn't."

"Ah." He looked down and made a little note in his dossier with his pencil. "Then I am relieved as a Communist that the killing was not done for political purposes, and I am relieved as a Chinese that, if he believed such things or your children believe such things, he went to heaven intact, and I am relieved for you as a friend that because of all that, you are not haunted by his spirit, or see his face staring at you in your dreams with a strange look upon it that you can never, never, quite comprehend."

He looked up from his dossier and smiled.

Colonel Kong, still smiling, still nodding, said to simply put an end to his unimportant little query, "Good. I am pleased that is out of the way."

He leaned forward and touched at the teapot.

It was still hot.

Colonel Kong, still being Mother, asked pleasantly, *"Tea?"*

He had nowhere else to go, and, after what Burtenshaw had said, not even Macarthur would go with him, and he had to go there alone.

Taking one of the little-used utility corridors that ran down the side of the Morgue to avoid running into any of Doctor Hsang's people, or, for that matter, any of Macarthur's, Feiffer went to the far rear end of the place to the undertakers' pickup room to where Porter was.

There was nothing else: nothing else to be done, and then, even when he got there, all there was was a cold, stone room with a body ready to be taken away outlined under a sheet on a chipped and peeling metal Morgue gurney whose wheels were jammed and black with dried-out grease and dirt, and there was nothing.

All there was in the empty, windowless room was the body of

a dead man, bereft of all symbols, stripped of all he had ever once been, ready to be taken away by the undertaker and disposed of like a dog.

There was no sound in the bare, cement-walled and -roofed room—not even the hum of the refrigerators that permeated the entire Morgue—and no sound of traffic on the other side of the unpainted heavy steel door that led out onto the street, and with half the head blown away and the outline of the body under the sheet somehow wrong and incomplete, the room was not a room at all, the body of the dead man not the body of the dead man at all, and all it was was nothing, was silence, was *Death.*

And it was as far as there was to go: there was nowhere else. And no one else to ask. He had had something and whatever it was, it had gotten both him and Annie killed, and, standing there under the single flickering dirty sixty-watt bulb on the ceiling that lit the place, Feiffer, talking not to him, but to himself, said softly, with, now, no answer to be had, "What did you have, Charlie? What was it? What was it you took? What was it? What did you have?"

But all it was under the sheet was rotting, dead meat.

Whatever it was, it was not money, not something worth anything, not something precious. It was something important, something vital—something the Triads, with everything they already had, wanted: something they *needed.*

And whatever it was, it had gotten both Charlie and Annie killed.

He was never going to know the answer. Like Charlie and Annie, in less than a month, everything would be changed and none of it would matter, and, like Charlie and Annie, everything he had ever done all his life and everything he had ever been would be gone, disposed of, and forgotten.

In the awful, dead silence, Feiffer said with all the anger suddenly come to the surface, "You lied to me, Charlie! You lied about everything! You lied about the Triads and you lied about being gay and you lied about— You lied about everything! *Your whole life was a lie!* And now—"

And now, there was nothing left, and outside that door, in the street, everything was changing—changing so massively and utterly and quickly that there was nothing anyone who was not part of it could do except be overwhelmed by it.

It was all pointless. What he should do now was go home, pack the last of his things into a suitcase and, pleasing everyone, take the first available plane to Manila to his wife and family and be gone from it all.

And, with his life over, disappear, like Charlie, into oblivion.

If Annie had been telling the truth—if she hadn't lied too—if Lee hadn't lied—if everyone hadn't lied right up until the last two days, Charlie had been planning to take a plane a month after the takeover and go.

And then suddenly, he had not. Suddenly, suddenly—if Annie hadn't lied about that too—was going to stay on permanently.

In the cold, stone room, Feiffer, starting to pace up and down, demanded, *"How?* How were you going to stay on permanently? And with *whose* help? The Triads? The Shanghai Bund people? The 14–K? Or, if it wasn't any of them, with maybe the help of your *lover* or—"

It was crazy. No one had the power to do that. All the power was gone. "Who was going to make you *untouchable?* Who was going to—" It made no sense at all. "And why so suddenly? Why, so suddenly, over the course of a day or two, after all the years you had to arrange something *and couldn't,* why did it all happen so suddenly? *And why the hell did you leave the key in the back of that picture for me to find?* When was I supposed to find it? What was that for? What was that supposed to tell me? Why the hell would you have wanted to tell me *anything?* And once you stayed on here, Charlie, you and Annie—you an ex-cop and your wife embroiled in the Triads—*what the hell did you think the Communists were going to let you do?* And if whatever it was you had wasn't worth *money,* how the hell did you expect you were going to live here? On what? On good will? On the gratitude of the Triads? On the— Or was it all just a smoke screen for something else?"

Instead of disappearing anonymously down the rear stairs, whoever had killed Charlie in the middle of the night in his own apartment had then gone down in the elevator in plain sight to the front lobby and killed the night janitor who he knew would be there.

In the pickup room, talking no longer to the thing on the gurney, but into blackness, Feiffer demanded, "Why? Why did he do that? Why did he make sure of that? What was he trying to say or cover up?"

If all it had been was that he didn't want the janitor to remember him going up to the apartment through the front entrance, why the hell hadn't he simply gone up to it by the rear? Why, maybe *couldn't* he have gone up to the apartment from the rear? And why the hell hadn't he killed Annie then, when he had the chance? Why wait? Why—? *Why go to all the trouble of stalking her and finally get her alone by her car in the car park and then killing her?* She had had nothing, knew nothing—if she had known anything, she would not have been killed—she would have been taken and tortured—*why wait?*

The thing under the sheet, his friend, was a liar. Everything in his entire life had been a lie.

And it hurt.

Standing there with his mouth dry and arid like dust, it made everything, everything the two families—his and Charlie's—had ever done together a joke.

It made all the smiles and grins and days on a boat out in the harbor mugging for the camera a *lie.*

Under the sheet, dead and extinct and silent, there wasn't the outline of a man he had known for over fifteen years and who had been his friend—under the sheet, dead and extinct and silent, there was a man he had never known at all. And outside in the streets, everything was changing, and after four generations of his family in China, there was nowhere for him to go, no way to save himself, no kites flying up to heaven that would do him any good at all, and suddenly, standing there, shaking, it was all Charlie's fault, and Feiffer, with everything welling up in him all at once, screamed down at him, "You fucking bastard! Who were you? What the hell did you have planned? If you had some way to stay on, why the hell didn't you at least tell me how you were going to do it *so maybe I could have stayed on too?"*

But he couldn't, and what he should do now was simply go home and pack his bag and—

All their lives, in all the lives of all their generations, all that had kept the kite flyers down in the park from despair and suicide was the struggle, was the hope, however vain, that somehow, up there in heaven, someone or something heard . . .

That someone at least gave a damn.

He gave a damn. He gave a damn about a man called Cheng lying cut in half in an apartment lobby staring forever at the reflection of his own face in the big glass doors to the street.

He gave a damn about Annie, about—

But all there was in the cold, concrete pickup room was the dead and mutilated body of a man he had never known.

In the silence, facing that man, Feiffer asked, "Who were you, Charlie? Who were you? Who were you *really?*

—With everything going, with everything being overwhelmed, with everything coming to an end, standing there under the dim, flickering light, Feiffer tried to think of maybe one place, one place that maybe no one had gotten to yet and taken over and changed irrevocably where he might be able to find out.

11.

In the worst place on the face of the Earth—actually, not on Earth at all, but at least ten feet below it—like some sort of mad, loquacious, hair-rollered housewife settling in at the back fence, he wanted to continue with the little chat he had started upstairs at the door.

In hell, in the flickering candlelit Black Hole of Calcutta, in the awful, dank, candlelit oubliette under the passageway, lying against the corner of an awful, dank wall dripping with ooze, Spencer said, to get the little chat going again, "I was wrong!"

Who said that? Lying in a terrible confusion of pain and salt and dank and ooze and arms and legs, Salt Man, growing warts and scabs and buttons by the moment, said, "Huh?"

He thought he heard a voice. He turned his head to see where the voice had come from and couldn't turn his head.

Auden, reaching up with one of his limbs—it felt like an arm—to turn his head in the right direction, said, "What?"

It wasn't an arm. It was a thing covered in ooze.

Auden, staring at it in horror, said, *"Oh, my God!"*

He was in some sort of room below the ground in a pyramid—not the room where the old Mummy had sat around laying curses on people, but in the room before that room where the old priests had sat around with the old Mummy embalming the old Mummy and pulling the old Mummy's brains and viscera out through its nose and tossing them on the ground. He was lying in them. They smelled bad. They smelled like ooze. The ooze was all over him. Auden, not a man to waste words, shrieked, *"Oh, my God!"*

Spencer, nattering away to himself, said with a sniff, "I was wrong about everything! I was wrong about heaven and earth and I was wrong about the *lo pan* compass, and I was wrong about the geomancers, and I was wrong about—"

Well, he was dead. The old Mummy had got him and he was gone. In the ooze, with some sort of droning sound in his ears, Auden lay down in the ooze to go.

"I was wrong about *everything!"* Like all happy *hausfrauen*, yapping nonstop, he was pleased his neighbor didn't try to get a word in edgewise. Spencer, raising his eyes up to where the sky should have been but wasn't, said to the closed trapdoor above his head, "I was *wrong!* All those people out there—the hordes of people—the ones with the sticks and the clubs and the swords and the— They weren't trying to get into the Geomancers' Castle at all—everything I thought about them was wrong! And the geomancers with their cannons and— They weren't trying to keep the hordes out at all! What everyone was trying to do was to get both of us *in!"*

Balloon? Nice balloon? Balloons for sale? Buy my nice balloons . . .

Spencer, leaning back and hitting the back of his head over and over against the wall, shrieked, "See? It's all so clear! It was all so simple! Or, at least, it would have been so simple to anyone else except *me*—"

He hit his head again: "I didn't kick the door hard enough to get it open, and you didn't kick the door hard enough to get it open! We couldn't have! It was too big! The door was already half open, and—"

Hit! "And all those people out there weren't trying to stop us getting *in*, they were out here making sure we didn't get out!"

He gave himself another good hard bash.

Spencer yelled, "What a *fool!* What a *fool!* Anyone else would have simply walked up to the door and asked the geomancers what the trouble was, but not me! No, me, I have to think everything's so complicated and arcane and I have to—"

He hit the back of his head so hard he almost knocked his brains out.

Spencer screamed in self-loathing, "Moron! Idiot! Imbecile!"

Balloons? Sinking down, Wart Man said in a bubble of air on the top of a deep, scummy pond, "Bloop! . . ."

"They even told me what it was! They shouted out 'Demons!' and, of course, being me, I had to assume they meant—but no, they weren't saying there were demons in the square, or that we were demons, what they were saying was that there were demons in the *Geomancers' Castle* and they wanted us to—"

Spencer yelled, hating himself, "God Almighty, all the Duke asked for on the phone was for me just to hold the fabric of the world together for a while until he could get there—*he didn't ask me to try and work out every stitch of the fabric the world was made of!*"

He was disgusted. He was disgusted with himself.

Spencer, disgusted beyond measure, shrieked, "See that? Hear that? Listen to me! 'Every stitch the fabric of the world is made of'! What's wrong with me? I can't even talk in a simple way! I talk in metaphors, in similes, in *tropes!*"

He went down. He went down into the ooze. Auden said, going down, oozing, ". . . Blurp!"

Spencer yelled as an order to himself, "Just for once in your life, talk simple! Stop all this and talk simple!"

He couldn't.

Giving his head a good bash, Spencer yelled, "But I can't! I'm an intellectual *poseur,* an empty shell, a vessel full of the half-digested and little-understood snippets and anecdotes of other men's thoughts! I'm full of crap! I'm a moron, an idiot! I'm a—" Spencer said suddenly just to check Auden hadn't fallen asleep on the floor there out of boredom, "Phil—"

Spencer said as a confession, "Phil, the truth is that the job at Oxford is only mine subject to a personal interview!" Spencer, laughing hollowly, said, "Ha, ha, ha! That's a funny one! One earful of the sort of crap I talk and anyone with half a brain—*let alone a panel of Oxford dons!*—would go away shitting their pants with laughter and suggest that maybe I might be better off selling fucking balloons in the park!"

There was a heavy sucking noise like an enormous wart sinking down into a sea of ooze.

Spencer said sadly, "You were right! *You* were right! You said that this place was the place where the Ghostbusters kept all their caged-up ghosts—something not from some esoteric tome, some impenetrable ideography, some sacred, secret, senseless screed that *I* would have read, but from some stupid Hollywood *movie*—and you were right! —And I was wrong!" Oh, the pricks and arrows of outrageous fortune—a tale, full of sound and fury, signifying nothing! Spencer yelled, "The simple man was *right!* The ordinary, good and simple and uncomplicated nature, the noble savage still in touch with Nature, was, as always—as always he should be and has been since time immemorial—right!"

The simple man was a single eye staring out of the ooze and wondering why his flippers didn't work anymore.

Spencer said sadly, "And I'm sorry. I'm so sorry." He tried to bash his head one last time, but suddenly he no longer had the strength. "I am so, very, very sorry . . ." Spencer said, dropping his head to his chest, "It's finally come to pass. Right at the end, the thing I most feared has come to pass, has been revealed to me—the thing I was most afraid of— It's happened. Finally, at last, it's been revealed to me that I'm a fool, that I'm not clever at all, that all I am, is just a fool! . . ." Spencer yelled suddenly, "Demons! Demons! *Demons!*"

Oh, God! What else? What next? Auden, getting his mouth up above slime level, yelled, "Oh, no!" It was the Mummy. It was the Curse of the Mummy! It was the Curse of the Mummy laid on Old-Whatever-His-Name-Was that—

Auden yelled, "Where? Where? What demons? Whose demons? Where?"

"Mine! My demons! Everything I feared most in the world! Everything I feared all my life was true! *My* demons!"

He was in tears, sobbing.

Sinking back against the wall, a destroyed man, Spencer said with his face running with tears and all his dreams as dust, "Oh, God! Phil, what do we do now? Have you any idea? Have you any idea at all? Phil! Phil! Phil, how the hell do we get out of here? Phil, I'm useless, *stupid!* Phil, what the hell—? *What the hell do we do now?"*

Or maybe he already knew.

He did.

In a whisper, Spencer said as his final, his last words at the fence, and on earth, "Oh, God—!" and reaching in under his coat with a moan like a hurt, wounded animal, took out his gun, and, cocking the hammer back with his thumb, raised the barrel up to his head and began to squeeze the trigger.

No, he didn't want fucking *tea!*

In the Detectives' Room, what he wanted was to be rid of it, to stop being frightened and to remember who he was, and to take control of his life again, and to—

He didn't give a damn anymore. Reaching over and speed-dialing Ong's number, O'Yee, hardly waiting for the man at the other end of the line to say who he was or who he wasn't—or whatever the hell he was going to say—roared into the phone in Cantonese, "Ong! This is O'Yee! And, yes, Colonel Kong of the Chinese People's Police is in the room with me, and, yes, he can hear what I'm saying, and what I'm saying is this: I have money for you that you earned as a police informer putting criminals into jail where they belong, and I owe it to—the people of Hong Kong owe it to you—and whether you like it or not, I'm going to pay it to you!"

He looked over at Kong and didn't give a damn.

O'Yee said determinedly, "And Ung, and Eng, and anyone else on the list—tell 'em all that everyone is being paid exactly what they're owed, and if they're worried about Kong getting to them, tell them not to worry, because I'm going to wait until Kong goes and then I'm going to come around to each and every one of you in person and deliver the money, and then I'm going to come back here and destroy every record there is, and then I'm—"

All he could feel in his stomach and behind his eyes was pain—"And fuck 'em! And fuck 'em! And I'll die before I tell them anything!"

There was a long silence.

In that silence, thinking only of a man wasted with cancer

who died in the flash of the gunfire with the saddest, softest look on his face, O'Yee could not stop his lip from trembling.

It was Ong. On the other end of the line, Ong said softly, "Okay."

"You know me! You know I'll do what I say."

"Yes."

"Good." That was settled. He hung up.

And then, after that—

After that, he had to go.

There was no choice.

After that, there was no choice and—from Hong Kong, from everything he had known all his life, from the place he wanted to be most—he would have to go and never return.

It was the end. It was all over. And in that awful moment, in the Detectives' Room, as Claude looked at him with no expression on his face at all, there was silence.

Auden.

Auden the sinking in the slime, Auden the soon to be swallowed up in the swill.

At heart, he did not have the heart of a balloon seller.

At heart, he had the heart of a German shepherd dog. Give him a role, even if it was only to bite somebody, and he was happy.

Call him up. Let him hear a whistle, and if ever once you had been nice to him—just once in his entire lifetime—he was yours and would protect and defend you to the death.

He heard a whistle.

He heard a whistle from someone who, more than once, had been nice to him.

Slime, *Schlmime!* Curse, *Schlmurse!*

Rearing up from the ooze like Neptune come up from the

sea, Auden, making the distance between them in a single step and ripping the gun from Spencer's hand, roared, "Are you *crazy? Are you *insane?* If it hadn't been for you, we wouldn't have even got this far!" (His one remaining brain cell said, "Huh?" but it wasn't the one connected to his mouth and his mouth went on moving anyway.) "If it hadn't been for you, by now, God only knows what would have happened out there in the square! God only knows what would have happened to the Universe!"

All the light was going from Spencer's eyes. Auden, reaching down and hauling the man up to his feet and holding him up straight against the wall, yelled, "If it hadn't been for your fine mind—*which impresses everyone you meet*—why do you think the Duke would have called you in the first place?" He shook him. Auden, covering the man in salt and ooze and slime and good intentions, roared with his face an inch away from the fading eyes, "Aye? Well? Well, come on! You're the intelligent one, not me—tell me that!!"

He was a beaten man, and he knew when he was beaten.

Spencer, looking distraught, said sadly as the last intellectual conclusion he would ever make, "Because it wasn't the Duke. You were right. It wasn't the Duke, it was someone else. It was just someone playing a game . . ."

"What game? The Duke Game? There is no fucking Duke Game! Of course, it was the Duke! It was the Duke of—" He couldn't remember the damned man's name, "The Duke of—"

Spencer said sadly, "The Duke Of Extended Sagehood, the Yen Sheng Kung, the—"

"Exactly! The spirit of China! The authentic descendant of the greatest man in the history of China: Confucius himself! Him!"

Spencer said in wistful echo, "The one person who no emperor or feudal lord dare command or rebuke, for he is—"

Yeah. Him. Auden, nodding hard and getting the man to nod hard back with him, said, "Right! Right! And—"

Slowly but surely, the light was coming back into Spencer's eyes. Spencer said as if in a trance, "The person for whom the good of the All is the one true moral path to be taken, the person who—" He was still wandering a little—"Who personifies all that is good and true and noble and moral and constant and . . ."

"Right! And who did he pick as his number one guy, as his henchman? He picked you! Old Bill Spencer! Bill the Brain! Bill the—"

He looked down at his feet. No good. Spencer said, "And I failed him!" Propped up there against the wall with all the flickering and fluxing candles making deep hollows and shadows on his face, he was inconsolable. "And I failed him! I failed him the way I failed myself! I failed him because I'm a *poseur,* a sham, a pseud! I'm someone too stupid to realize how stupid he is, someone so stupid he thinks that what he knows is all there is *to* know—in other words, a *fool!*"

"What was it he wanted you to do?"

"He wanted me to—" Spencer said, "What I thought he wanted me to do was somehow decipher all the runic signs and omens of the Chinese spiritual world and discover through logic what had upset the balance of the world and, once I'd done that, find the hole in the fabric of the universe and, going where no man had gone before, go there and—"

His life was full of ideas and aspirations, but all of them the ideas and aspirations of other men.

Spencer, shaking his head in a vain effort to make it fall off his body and roll away into the dirt where it belonged, shouted, "Listen to me! Who the hell do I think I am—the last great explorer on the final frontier of the mind?" Spencer, shaking even harder, yelled, "I thought it all had to do with *lo pan* compasses and runes and signs and symbols and the perfection of the spirit and all the great questions of life and death and I had the power and knowledge to take us both on a great spiritual journey to the center of it all, but it didn't! It had to do with demons in the Geomancers' Castle, and look where I ended up taking us! I ended up taking us *here!*"

"Which is where?"

"Which is—" He looked up. "Which is—" Spencer said curiously, "Which is in the central demon-halting passageway in the Geomancers' Castle . . ." He stopped shaking his head: "Which is—" Spencer said suddenly, "Gosh!"

His dog, proud of him, said with a nod, "Well done."

"Which, obviously, is—which, obviously, is here to protect something important from the demons who have upset all the balance of the cosmos and thrown out of kilt the answers to all the great questions of life and death, and . . ."

Auden said softly, "I'm proud of you. You've done it again."

"Which is—" He looked into Auden's face. "Really? Are you sure?"

"Yes." He turned for a moment and glanced down the long, candlelit corridor. Warts. Scabs. Even buttons. Sometimes they didn't matter a shit.

Auden, putting his hand on Spencer's shoulder and, not knowing it, echoing word for word exactly what Old-Whatever-His-Name-Was—Howard Carter—had said at the entrance to the final mound of debris blocking his way before he uncovered the greatest treasure in the history of archeology: the tomb of the boy-king Tutankhamen, said with an encouraging squeeze on the man's shoulder, "Well, we're here now. Let's go on and see what's down there. Shall we?"

12.

In all of Hong Kong, it was the one—the only place—the Communists had not gotten into and changed irrevocably. It was the one place they wanted to go on working, untouched, doing its job, to the very end, and then move intact ten thousand miles away to London to continue doing that job until the last remainder of the British presence in their nation—the last heir of the spoils of the humiliation of the Opium War—was dead and forgotten.

It was the Hong Kong European Civil Servants and Police Officers Pension and Retirement Benefits Office on the second floor of the old Victorian four-storied stone and iron-lacework-balconied building on the corner of Prince Albert Street and Admiral Nelson Road that, right up until the Japanese Occupation, had been the Government Finance and Accounting Department.

Outside the main entrance in Prince Albert Street, at the bottom of a flight of stone steps, there were two empty stone plinths where the Japanese had removed the two stone lions guarding the portals to the place that had never been replaced.

There was no need. What guarded the place—what had always guarded the place, what had always guarded every part of the world the British had spread to or legally colonized or illegally taken or simply killed for was not lions or men with hearts of lions, it was money, and the bureaucracy, unflinchingly immovable and impenetrable in its complexity, that dealt with that money.

Inside the still, heavy-walled building, as Feiffer waited at the main enquiry counter for someone to come back with Porter's file, in a huge room filled with shirt-sleeved Chinese clerks working away in rows at their desks below turning fans, it was as if nothing had changed in a hundred years.

It hadn't. Ten years ago, in a burst of uncharacteristic liberalism, the British Government had given the Hong Kong Chinese a locally elected Legislative Assembly so they could have a democratic voice in the running of their own affairs, however powerless and ineffectual in the real world it might be.

But they hadn't given it here. No one had ever given it here.

As he swept by with a sheaf of folders and files under his arm, the sole European in the whole place—a short, prematurely bald, pinched-faced man wearing a chief clerk's waistcoat lined with silver pens—said sharply to one of the clerks at his desk who looked up at him as he passed, "Get on with your work!" and then, pausing for a moment to wait as the clerk complied, glanced around the entire roomful of clerks to make sure the warning was taken by all of them as well.

Standing there watching him, Feiffer knew the man would have no first name, and he didn't.

Coming over and depositing the files on the counter and then putting his hand on top of them to make sure they were safe, the man, close up with eyes that had no light in them, said impatiently, "Mr. Coughlan. Yes?" He turned back quickly to make sure no one in the room was doing anything they shouldn't while he had his back to them—"And you are?"

No first names, merely identifying title and cross-references.

Feiffer said formally, "Detective Chief Inspector Feiffer, Yellowthread Street Station, Hong Bay."

Feiffer said before the man could look around to check on his clerks again, "I'm investigating the murder of Detective Chief Superintendent Porter of the Anti-Triad Unit, and one other, and I need to see Porter's file to see if he made any recent changes to the disposition and place of payment of his pension payments after the takeover."

"No." He glanced over his shoulder at the clerk he had disciplined, to check the man was not looking surly and insubordinate. "Not possible. All our files are confidential."

"I don't need to take them away, I just need to—"

He knew Feiffer didn't have it, or he would have had it on the counter ready. Mr. Coughlan said with a sigh, "Death certificate attested to by a Government Medical Officer?"

"I don't have one. The Government Medical Office has been taken over by—"

"And a Hong Kong Police Interdepartmental Request for Information and Assistance Form 37A signed by an officer of Divisional rank certifying the need to—"

"No." The Commander had gone, and there was no one else left.

It didn't matter that the lack of the first form was reason enough to say no; he was going to list—because they were all on the list—all the forms that should have been there before he could even possibly contemplate saying yes—and even then, only after he had filled in his own forms. "—and, additionally, if the information required is of a personal or financial nature, or one that may involve the possibility of court proceedings, an Order in Chambers from a judge of no less than Quarter Sessions level." He was saying it loudly so all his clerks could hear, so they knew exactly what power he had. Here endeth the lesson: "Do you have any of that?"

He had nothing.

All he had, outside there in the streets, was a place running out of time.

All he had was a picture in his mind of people flying their kites uselessly up into the heavens to be heard, and *hoping,* hoping only not that things would get better, only that perhaps they might not get any worse.

"No, I don't."

"Then you are wasting my time!" He turned to go.

Feiffer said sharply, "—'Sir!' "

"What?"

He didn't like him one little bit. Feiffer, raising his own voice so the clerks could hear, said as a reprimand, "Then you are wasting my time, 'Sir!' Unless you've forgotten for some reason, or you were never informed—or you were too stupid to remember—a Detective Chief Inspector of Police outranks you in the civil-service list by at least two grades, and you are requested to address me with respect and not speak to me as if you are some bad-mannered guttersnipe speaking to what you consider to be just one of the local fucking *natives!*" He had nothing to lose. Leaning forward across the desk and putting his finger on top of the pile of papers, Feiffer said with steel in his voice, "And furthermore, if you refuse to assist me in this matter, I will arrest you on the spot on a charge of obstruction of justice and have you taken out of here in handcuffs!"

Behind him, all the clerks in the office looked up. Coughlan did not turn around to see them do it.

And then he did turn around, and, as all the clerks looked away, he remembered who he was and what protected him.

Coughlan, shaking his head, simply stating the regulations, said evenly, "No. You cannot do that. I am not required by law to assist you without the appropriate paperwork, and since you do not have the appropriate paperwork, my position is clear and indisputable and legal and would stand up in any court." He turned back for an instant to the clerks.

He had thought maybe the possibility of the man's losing face with his clerks would have been enough, but it wasn't—the opinion and respect of the clerks—the locals, the *chinks*—was nothing to him, and it needed something more, something deeper, something he understood, something he feared.

Feiffer said with a nod, "You're right."

"Yes, I am."

"And any such charge, heard in a court in England where, considering the continuing breakdown of the system here, it would have to be heard, would undoubtedly exonerate you in full."

Mr. Coughlan, standing like a ramrod, like a stone lion guarding the Empire, said as a matter of fact, "Yes. It would."

"I don't intend to return to England after the takeover."

"What?"

"No." As all the clerks looked up, Feiffer said as an admonishment, "Obviously, you didn't bother to check my file before you spoke to me. I am not English. I intend, if I can, to stay on after the takeover. I have only been to England once in my life. I have no connection to England. All my connections are here. I was born here, in China. *So any court action in England you might have to enter into to have the record of an arrest on criminal charges removed from your file before you get your own pension would have to be conducted through the Chinese People's Republic's legal and bureaucratic system for however long that might take!"* Feiffer said in barely a whisper, "And in that case, I wish you good luck and a very long life—because you will need both of them!"

In the entire place, there was an utter silence.

In that silence, all he would have had to say to the man was, "Come on, now look here, Coughlan, as a fellow European, as a fellow white man . . ." but it would have been something he could not have lived with.

Feiffer demanded, "Well? It's your fucking pension, not mine!" And then, as suddenly as his face seemed to dissolve away in front of him, he saw who the man really was and how frightened he really was. "All I want to know is what changes Porter may have made to his pension plans. Nothing more. All I want to know is whether or not he intended to go back home to Australia after the takeover, or whether he might have suddenly—" Feiffer said, "For God's sake, man, he was murdered! He had his entire face and head blown off with a shotgun! And then his wife was killed! He was a friend of mine! *I just want to find out who killed him before it's all too late!"*

But it was not the humanity of it that made him open the file and look down into it—it was the threat.

Mr. Coughlan said tightly, "Yes, he changed his pension disposition. He changed it three days ago, in this office, with me. He filled out the appropriate form and, even though I advised him that in the long run it would make better financial sense not to do it, he opted for a lump-sum payment in cash in the form of a check made out on a local bank."

Then it was true.

He had found a way to stay on.

Porter had found a way to stay on. Charlie had . . .

He had been lonely all his life because, like the old stone lions, all his life, all he had ever been was not something living and breathing and alive, but merely a copy of it, a representation. Coughlan, suddenly speaking again, said out of nowhere, "He was your friend, was he?"

And Feiffer, not looking at the man, not seeing his face pinch up into a look of utter hatred, said softly, "Yes."

Coughlan said, "Then your friend was a pervert! Your friend was degenerate! Your friend was a shit-stabber! A homosexual! Your friend was a *queer!* The next day when he came in to collect the check, he had me make it out to someone else—someone he brought in here with him! Someone called Robert Arthur Sims—someone he called 'Bobbie'—someone who sat there in my office with him holding his hand, and who, on the way out, when he thought I wasn't watching, leaned over and kissed him on the face!"

He didn't represent all the things the lions had represented, only all the worst things they had represented.

He was talking not to Feiffer but to the clerks. Coughlan, coiled like a spring, full of malice, shouted, "You don't believe me? Then go ask him yourself! Ask your friend's little bum boy! Go ask Robert Arthur Sims! He's still at the Hong Kong Victoria Hotel here just around the corner waiting for the check to clear!" Coughlan said with a little mincing flourish of his shoulder, "Or, maybe, 'Sir,' you already knew that."

Coughlan said suddenly very angrily and loudly for everyone in the room to hear and learn by in the most imperious accent he could muster, "He wasn't British either! He was an Australian, like Porter! He was second class, just like you! He didn't understand how to do things, how things are done properly and discreetly, *either!*"

* * *

In the geomancers' passageway, Auden, stepping back and letting Spencer support himself against the wall on his own, demanded, "Well? Go on? *Go on?*"

In the dank, flickering candlelit hole to nowhere, there was silence.

Still with his back to the wall, Spencer said hesitantly, "Um . . ."

"What?" He put his hand to his ear—"I can't hear you!"

"Um . . ."

"I *still* can't hear you!"

"Um . . ." He wasn't sure. He just wasn't sure.

"Go on?"

"Um—!"

"Go on?"

"Um-um . . . maybe, um—"

Auden said, "Good!" and turning, going down the passageway towards God-only-knew where, to God-only-knew what, with Spencer only a single step behind him, in the terrible, continuing, absolute silence and foreboding of the place, went on.

If people like Coughlan were the thing that had made the Empire great, then it was long overdue for collapse.

It was now only a question of whether what came next might be even worse.

Two blocks from the Hong Kong Victoria Hotel, talking on the public phone at the corner of Queen Victoria Street and Fortune-Tellers Lane, with all the tables full of twittering fortune-telling birds in bamboo birdcages pecking at piles of facedown fortune cards and taking the single one out that was the true and authentic fortune of the customer, Feiffer said directly to Mr. Justice Ang as a simple question-and-answer, "Did you or did you not know that Porter had transferred his pension over to someone else?"

He was in his office at ICAC, the Independent Commission Against Corruption, the place where they knew everything about everyone. After a pause, Mr. Justice Ang, not liking Feiffer's tone in the least, said, "No, any information that comes here from the Pension and Retirement Benefits Office only comes here as the result of a court order. Unlike every other department in the Colony, there's no automatic notification of any officer's sudden change in status or financial situation."

Even he was afraid of them.

Ang said, almost as if he were defending himself or he thought the conversation might be being taped, "The work of the Pension and Retirement Benefits Board is something I take very seriously and I would never countenance using any information from them I had not obtained other than through proper channels and in the proper way."

And he had a pension himself! Probably two—one from his time as a judge and the other as head of ICAC!

And probably, by now, he had put in a few phone calls, and if Porter had had something from one of the cabinets in the Anti-Triad Unit and the Triads were after it, still in the business of covering every base there was, he knew what that was too.

Mr. Ang said, to finish the conversation, "So I can't help you."

All down the street, the birds were picking out the little cards from the tables along the sidewalk, and, behind them, in stalls and shops and in doorways, other fortune-tellers were reading palms, considering the shapes of heads, consulting their numerology books, and everywhere—everywhere—there were people worried and fretful and frightened, milling about and looking anxious.

He had nothing to lose. Feiffer, taking a breath, said as a matter of fact, "The pension was converted to a lump-sum payment, and, at Porter's request, made out to the order of one Robert Arthur Sims—"

Feiffer said quickly before the man could interrupt, "It was done only two days before Porter was killed—" He got it in before the man could react: "—not by the Triads, and, obviously, while the one person Porter should have made it over to—to his wife, Annie—was still alive. Before she was murdered. Before she was executed with a single bullet to the head like a put-down dog!"

There was a silence, as, for a moment, Mr. Justice Ang considered his fortune, or read his card, or considered his numbers.

In that silence Feiffer said, as if he and the man had been friends for years, "Eb Coughlan at the Pension Office said that in his mind there was no question that Porter was gay. Was he?" He had no idea what Coughlan's first name was, only that it was probably something appropriately Dickensian. "Can you confirm that for me?" and prayed that Ang did not know what Coughlan's first name was either.

But, from the other end of the line, there was only a silence.

"Eb said you probably knew, that you—"

"The mere fact that an officer may be—" He went silent again for a moment. "The mere fact, as Mr. Eb Coughlan would be the first to point out, that a serving police officer may have private sexual preferences—*none of which in any way impinge on his office and none of which he actively practises while in the employ of the Service*—in no way amounts in the view of ICAC as a cause for investigation or the withholding of benefits or—" And Mr. Justice Ang had one hell of a pension, and one that he had arranged with the Communists and the British to keep; "And in no way—"

They monitored the Net.

Up there, in ICAC, they had two full-time people whose only task was to surf the Net. They had got Porter through the Internet.

"Well, Eb says you—"

Ang said slowly and clearly, as if each and every word were for the tape, "It came to the attention of ICAC some months ago that Detective Chief Superintendent Porter was in contact with various homosexual sites on the Net, and that he—" He was measuring every word. Goddammit, he knew what Porter had had; he knew the *truth!* "However, the question of privacy and the legal complications concerning any information gained from that source is still dubious in the eyes of the law and—" He was a man for all seasons, a man who would do anything to continue to be that man, a judge of all men except himself—a *fraud.* "So, I regret I can only—"

It was a long shot. "And do you know about the insurance policies too?"

He considered that one—God only knew in reference to whom. "Yes."

"And that they—"

"There was only one."

Everywhere in the street, the desperate were bargaining with the gods. They were bargaining with the gods on the phone too. "How much was it?"

"A million six US."

"Originally made out to Annie. And then changed over in the last few days to—"

"Yes."

Feiffer said, nodding, "To one Robert Arthur Sims of Australia. Right?" Feiffer said suddenly formally as if he also thought the conversation were being taped, "You knew about that straight away, didn't you? That warning flag went up on that one real quick, didn't it? Or did it? Your office didn't miss that, did they? They didn't let that one go?"

"Of course we didn't let that one go! We have an automatic notification agreement with all the banks and financial institutions in Hong Kong in the case where there's a sudden and abrupt change in—"

"Yes. And you were notified."

"Yes."

"And did? What? *Nothing?*"

He sounded a little desperate. "The fact that an officer may have private sexual preferences and may or may not be planning *after his retirement* to engage in those preferences or somehow financially favor his partner in those practices *in the future and in another country . . .*"

"He wasn't going back home to another country! He was staying on here!"

"That is not our current information."

"That is what his wife told me. She told me that, suddenly, just a few days before he was killed, he informed her he had found a way to stay on and he—"

"What someone may have told you in a casual conversation is not the same thing as someone telling it to ICAC in a formal disposition!"

"It seemed pretty formal to me." He wondered if anywhere, in any of the stalls or the shops in the street, any of the fortunes were good and told of a future full of hope and success and prosperity. "She told me while the dead body of her husband was still lying in her front living room covered in blood with his head blown away and all the walls covered in his fucking brains!"

"You will not *swear* at me!"

If Ang had made his calls and found out what Porter had had—if he had had anything—then it was probably all too late anyway, and if Sims had been the one who had killed Porter and taken what he had, Ang already had it, and the matter was as good as closed and finished and done away with, and all there would ever be left would be—

And it had to be today. Everything had to be finished by today. After that, at least according to the Triads, all deals and bets were off, and standing there, gazing at the birds on the tables and the customers—ordinary people, people in working clothes with dirt and calluses on their hands—nothing made sense, nothing was clear, and everything Charlie had ever said was a *lie,* and everything was blocked, sealed off, and all there was was Sims, and if Ang had made his call, all there would be there would be a dead body, and whatever it was Charlie had had—if he had had anything—would be gone.

And so would he. Standing there, gazing at the fortune-tellers, with nothing left, left in limbo—made unnecessary and irrelevant to whatever great game was being played out—so would Feiffer, and everything he had ever done or believed in all his life would have been for nothing.

"I apologize for swearing at you."

"I accept your apology."

"Thank you." And fell silent and waited. Feiffer said politely, "Thank you, sir."

He was a good man, a just man, a lenient man. Mr. Justice Ang said suddenly understandingly, "I appreciate, Mr. Feiffer, that the late Chief Superintendent Porter was a friend of yours, and how long your family has been connected with Hong Kong, and how difficult it must be for you to realize that you have no place left in the new order of things, but you must appreciate that the island of Hong Kong was never legally *ceded* to the British by the Chinese, but was *stolen* as the result of an evil war fought by a militarily superior nation solely to continue to protect its profits from the enslavement of the Chinese people by *opium.*" Whatever his own family had done back in those days was now safely covered up. "It is time for you to consider your own personal future with your family and make a new life for yourself in another place and in—"

"Yes."

Mr. Justice Ang said, as if perhaps Feiffer might have had a doubt about it, "There is no question that you have always behaved here in the most responsible and upright and honest way, and I, for one, and indeed this office, would certainly be more than happy to attest to that fact in writing and offer any very positive reference to you that might in any way assist you in your future— If it would help."

"Thank you."

Mr. Justice Ang said as if to a hesitating child, "Time to go, Harry."

"Yes." He brightened up a little. "Thank you." Feiffer, not this time watching the street, but looking down into blackness, said as his final words, "I want to just say how much we in the Force—the honest members of the Force—appreciated all your work and—"

He cut him off: he had done only what had to be done. "Every organization has its share of bad apples. It does not necessarily reflect on the good members of that organization."

"Yes, I understand that."

"You were always a man the Force could be proud of." It cost nothing now: "You should be proud of yourself and your time here."

"Thank you." He paused for a moment. Feiffer, sounding bitter and let down, said in a harsh, self-recriminating whisper, "He was my friend, you know, Charlie Porter, and I . . ."

He was a very understanding man. Mr. Justice Ang, forgiving

all, said, softly, "Yes. 'I know who my enemies are, but God protect me from my friends' . . ."

"I suppose all it was, was just a sordid little case of blackmail and murder, and that—and that this man Sims, whoever he is, paid someone up here to—?"

"Yes. Undoubtedly." Mr. Ang said brightly, cheering him up, "See? You were always a good detective."

And he didn't *know.* Or did he? Coughlan hadn't told him, and he really didn't *know,* or had he? Or—

And it had to be now. It had to be today. And he had to keep his voice steady, and he had to—

Feiffer said softly, sadly, "This man Sims . . . One day, just for my own personal satisfaction, just to make things right in my mind, one day, I'd like to ask him face to face about—" Feiffer said as if it were the remotest possibility in the entire world, "One day, I'd like to ask him about what Charlie was really like— You know, just for my own personal . . ." He paused a long, awful, stomach-twisting moment. "But I don't even know— I don't even know what nationality he was, and I don't suppose you do either . . ."

"Australian. His nationality is Australian."

"Oh."

Mr. Justice Ang said, "Domiciled in Brisbane in the state of Queensland, address 145 Graham Road, Aspley, website *www dot mantalk dot com,* name of user, 'Bobbie.' "

And he didn't know! He didn't know Sims was there two blocks away from where Feiffer was calling from! He didn't *know!* And Coughlan, true to form, hadn't told him, and he didn't *know!* And there was still one chance left, one last day, and it had to be, and was, *today!*

In his last official words he had to say to the man, maybe the last official words he would ever say to anyone, Feiffer said a moment before he hung up, "Thank you. Thank you very much," and then, going quickly down the street, went into the first numerologist's shop he could find, and, putting a ten-dollar bill on the man's table, asked him, according to the Chinese calendar and all the portents and fortunes and numbers, just what today was.

In 1997, in the Year of the Ox, Harvest Year—the year, the ancient, deep-lined, white-haired man sitting in there and smoking a long, hand-rolled cigarette packed with pungent, vile-smelling cheap Chinese tobacco told him, when we all reap all the fruits and ills of all our past efforts—it was, counting from the moveable date of Chinese New Year, Day 111, the best day of its kind there was, the most propitious day of its kind there could ever be.

It was a lucky number, one-one-one, the luckiest for certain things there was, the one day in the year the gods in heaven had ears for the woes of men, the best day there was for the one event important to the Chinese mind above all others.

Behind him in the little shop, there was a half-drawn curtain to the little room where, like all old Chinese men and women afraid of what might happen to them after they were gone, there reposed, beautifully oiled and tended to, his coffin.

Looking back to it for a moment, a little sad perhaps that today was not the day his turn had come, the numerologist told him that today, day one-one-one in the Year of the Ox, the Year of Change—at least for another two full calendar years—was the best day there would ever be.

For a funeral.

13.

At the end of the flickering candlelit corridor there was another corridor leading off from it to the left at ninety degrees, and then, at the end of that, another leading off to the left at thirty degrees, and then, at the end of that, with the arrow point of its angle throwing flickering shadows like sharpened teeth on the candlelit wall opposite it, another turning back on itself, and then, ten feet down that, another turning back at forty degrees, and then, at the end of that, reached by a step down and then a step up, another that seemed to end against a blank wall in a little stone ornamental pool of still water, but, in the shadows against the wall, turned off again and went back a full one hundred and eighty degrees into an unlit tunnel full of nothing but darkness.

Fifteen feet below the foundations of the Geomancers' Castle in Tiger-Dragon Square, set on the walls between the candles, there were ancient tiny circular bronze mirrors that, in the darkness, reflected nothing. The tunnel, as Auden craned forward to see it in the yellow light, paved with ancient, perfectly circular cobblestones, went downwards.

It went downwards, lit by the candles, with no end in sight to it, into . . . into, in more darkness. Into more tunnels.

And then, instantly, all the candles in the corridor behind him leading to it went out and even the darkness was gone, and in the glow of his lighter all he could see was his own hand holding it.

And then, with no wind, with no breeze, that too went out.

He flicked hard at the wheel but the lighter didn't even spark. On the brink, snapping the lighter closed, Auden said tersely to Spencer a single step behind him, "What is it, Bill? You know. What is it?"

He didn't know, or, if he did, it was probably wrong. He had been wrong about everything else. "I don't know."

"You do know! What is it? What is all this?"

He couldn't be wrong about everything, not *everything!*

Or could he?

He *had* been wrong about everything! He had been wrong about the cannons and the attacking crowds and the Earth and the Sky and the *lo pan* compass and the—

Spencer said—surely to God not wrong about even the simplest thing—"Um, it's a *feng shui* entrance passageway! It's a series of mazes and turns and steps and arrow corners and mirrors designed to make a demon lose his way and decide to go somewhere else or back where he came from, or, or—"

"Or what?"

"Or it's a—" He made a sniffing sound. "Or it's a—"

Spencer said suddenly, "It's a—" Spencer said desperately, "I don't know! I'm not sure! What the hell do I know? I don't know *anything!* It's a maze designed to keep the demons in! And that passageway going down is the passageway straight down into the place where they all live!"

Spencer said, in this case talking not about the corridor but the place in his mind where he lived, with no fear in his voice, but only anger, "It's the place where all the fear and uncertainty and self-doubt and terror of this world reside! It's the exact center, the vortex, the entrance gate to all the nameless fears and terrors of every living man's nights!"

"Like selling balloons in the park, huh?"

"Yes, like selling balloons in the park or whatever else you're afraid of."

"Or like—"

He was going to say something about teaching at Oxford.

Spencer said, "Yes!"

"Or like—"

"Yes! *Yes!*" Suddenly pushing past Auden and in a flurry of movement rushing down the tunnel and then stopping halfway, a broken, humiliated, disappointed man, Spencer said, "Yes! Yes! Like the Duke lying to me and making me feel important when all he wanted was someone useless and expendable to keep the demons busy while he did more important things! Like—"

Now it was all clear to him.

Spencer yelled, "Don't you see? He picked me because I was stupid! He picked me because I didn't count! He picked me because I was nothing but a filthy, useless, no-account *foreigner!* A person of no consequence—someone who wasn't even Chinese! Someone who—"

Maybe he had sunk to his knees: his voice sounded farther away, different.

Spencer yelled in his humiliation, in his disappointment, "Don't you see? *He picked us because we're going anyway!* He picked us because we don't count! Because we're nothings! Because, all we're going to be after all this anyway is still nothing more important than a pathetic, posing little half-read dilettante, and a fucking wart-and-button-covered balloon seller in a park!"

In the darkness, he thought he went down the tunnel and stood above where Spencer knelt.

In that darkness, Auden said softly, "Is that what's at the end of the tunnel, Bill?"

"No! That's what's at the end of my tunnel!"

"What's at the end of this tunnel?"

"At the end of this tunnel is the demon hole! At the end of this tunnel is where all the demons of the world live—all the demons all the spells and devices and prayers of the geomancers are designed to quell and keep from getting out into the world and destroying it! All the—"

He reached out, and Spencer wasn't kneeling at all—he was standing with his back to him, swaying slightly from side to side as if he balanced on something on the floor. Auden said, not looking ahead to where Spencer stood, but suddenly down, "It's my last day on the job, and I still haven't collected my free air ticket back to England . . ." On his answering machine in his apartment, there had been so many reminder calls from the Government Travel Office that the tape was full. Auden said softly, "You know, I keep thinking about it, but I just can't bring myself to do it."

He was still balancing, tottering, rocking back and forth. Spencer, also talking into the darkness, said softly, dreamily, "It's wet and damp, England, even at Oxford, and when I was a kid, I used to come down every year with flu, and everyone I really know and like isn't in England, they're here."

"Yeah." Auden said in a whisper, "Me too. And the Travel Office keeps telling me I should pick up my ticket, and Stores have already called me three times telling me where to drop off my gun, and—" Warts and scabs and buttons and balloons, and—Auden said as a question he had never been able to find an answer to, "But Bill, if I did that—if I picked up my air ticket and handed the gun in, *where the hell am I going to go?*" He was desperate. "Tell me that! You know everything! I don't care what the Duke thinks of you—you know everything! *Tell me that!*"

His voice was a whisper. It was all he knew. It was all he could say. Spencer said, in a whisper so faint Auden had to strain to hear it, "There is a rent in the fabric of the universe and the demons are about to break loose and rise out into the world to destroy it, and all that will satisfy them and keep them from rising up is us—is us being destroyed by everything we fear most and suffering an eternity of torture at their hands as their playthings, and I think you and I, both of us, should go down there and face it!"

Well, how bad could that be?

Auden, again a dog with a role, said happily, "Well, it can't be any worse than balloon selling to children in the park—"

"It will be balloon selling in the park! In your case, *it will be balloon selling in the park!* And in mine— And in mine— *And in mine—*"

Suddenly, standing there in the darkness, it was important to him to say it. Auden said softly, "You know, in all the time I was here I never did anyone a bad turn all the time I was here. Never!" Auden said, as maybe his last words, but in any event as words he needed to say to someone while it still mattered, while someone still cared, "In all the time I was here, whatever the Communists or anyone else is going to say, I never treated anyone unfairly and I never took graft and I never—" Auden said, suddenly happily, "And I had a hell of a good time, the best I ever had in my life."

"You can always turn around and go back."

"No." Auden said softly, "No, no I can't. Not now. There's nowhere to turn back to."

"There's the air ticket."

"Fuck the air ticket!"

"Yes."

Auden, moving up and standing next to the man where the tunnel suddenly seemed to widen, asked, "And you?"

"Yes."

"Fuck Oxford?"

"Yes." Spencer said, suddenly sure, "Yes. Fuck it all!"

And they weren't going. They were staying. They were staying. They were staying there dead, but they were staying—they were staying on.

And in that moment, he was full of joy and peace and—for some reason too deep for him to understand—hope. Auden asked, ready for it, "The demon hole, huh? The demon hole, huh?"

Spencer said, "Yes."

"Lead me on to it. Where is it?" In the darkness, standing next to Spencer all he could see ahead of him was black.

Spencer said softly, "Here. It's here. I'm standing on the edge of it. It's a hole. It's a hole, a pit. It's a bottomless hole just one single step ahead of me straight down into all the terrors of hell!"

Go on? Go on? In that moment, there was nowhere else in the entire world he would rather have been.

Auden asked, "Step off? Step off? *Step off?*"

"Yes!"

Auden said, "Good! The hell with it then! Let's do it!"

And together, after all the years, after all the best the world had had to offer, wanting no more, believing that there was no more, nothing better, nothing else in the future that the world had to offer after all they had already had from it and could have no longer, they stepped off and fell straight down through the darkness into the hole.

In Empire Plaza, at the end of Victoria Road, where once the huge, set-back English gardens of the Hong Kong Victoria

Hotel had been full of quiet walks and pergolas and bronze statues of Queen Victoria and Prince Albert and all the other great architects of the nineteenth-century British Empire, everything had gone, been changed, and all that was there framing the massive five-story stone verandahed and private-balconied edifice of the place and its place and role in its previously settled and unchanging world was a huge red-flagged electronic clock just outside the main entrance, counting off the hours and minutes until the takeover.

It was where the flagpole had been that, for over a hundred years, had flown the Union Jack above two of the British Navy cannons that had opened fire on Canton to begin the Opium Wars and as memorial to all the brave sailors of that Navy who had died at the hands of the evil Chinese who had tried to resist them.

The gardens were full of unarmed soldiers from the Chinese People's Liberation Army—officers and men—all dressed in their olive-green uniforms with no badges of rank on them, the officers standing talking in knots to other men in blue business suits as they made arrangements for their quarters and the enlisted men wandering aimlessly in twos and threes, smoking cigarettes and from time to time glancing back nervously at the officers.

And it was all too late, and standing there in the street gazing at it with a sick feeling in his stomach, suddenly Feiffer was nobody, just an irrelevance, and everything he had—his badge, his authority, his life, everything he had ever been—was nothing, and none of it mattered anymore: not Porter or Annie or a dead night janitor named Cheng; none of it mattered anymore.

It was all gone. Everything, like the flag and all the statues and everything Hong Kong had once been, had gone, had faded, and there was nothing left.

And all he had to do was walk away and go back to his apartment and pack his bag, and in less than four hours he would be gone too, and with his family in Manila.

In the great movement and change of things—in the life of nations—like all individual men, he was a nothing, like the kite flyers and all the people crowded around the fortune-tellers seeking the attention of an uncaring heaven, not important.

He had no authority, no power, and if Porter had had something that mattered to someone, some totem, some object, some sign or symbol that mattered to all the people who would go on after the takeover, it didn't matter to him, because, after the takeover—clearly, set out there in miniature, educational tableau before him—after the takeover there would be no place for him and he would not be there.

He wished in that moment he had someone to talk to, to turn to, but there was no one, and in his own way, even though he was still living, standing there, he was as dead and silent as Porter. And as overtaken by events and discarded and extinct.

Gazing up past the clock to the top floor of the hotel and the wonderful Italian tiled roof that surmounted it, Feiffer said, lost in the maze of it all, "Goddammit, Charlie, you must have known that the Triads would have killed you the moment you gave them what they wanted! You must have known they wouldn't have let you stay on to tell people about it! You must have known if they had something that protected them from the Communists they wouldn't have let you stay on to tell the Communists that you were the one who gave it to them! You *must* have known that! It was your job! It was what you *did.* It was what you did for over twenty years! You must have known what they were like!"

It was all crazy. It made no sense at all, none of it. Still gazing at the roof, gazing through it, gazing into nothingness, he could not understand what the thing Porter had could have been or how he thought he could have used it.

It wasn't anything worth money. Charlie had given all his money away to his lover Sims, and then, just to make sure his lover Sims was well cared for in case something happened to him—that the Triads killed him—*which he undoubtedly knew they would!*—he had made Sims the beneficiary of his insurance.

It was all crazy.

Above the roof of the hotel, the sky was gray and overcast, in the late afternoon, starting to darken towards evening.

Feiffer asked, "And if Sims had killed him, that made no sense either. Why would Sims kill you for whatever it was you had? What use would it be to him? And if you had managed to somehow beat the Triads and stay on, how the hell did you expect to live with no money? How the hell did you expect to even pay the fare to get down to Australia from time to time to see the man you obviously loved so much? How did you expect to do any of it?"

And Annie? Why did she die? All their married life, and probably before, she had been his conduit to the Triads, his private source, the informer who had got him promotion after promotion—maybe even the one person who could keep him alive after he had given the Triads what they wanted—why the hell was she killed? What the hell had she known or seen that someone didn't want her to talk about? And Cheng, the poor bastard, lying in the lobby of the Pearl Gardens Apartment Building, cut in half by the blasts of a shotgun—why him too? He knew nothing. He was a no one. What the hell did he know or had he seen that made him a danger to— To whoever it was who had taken Porter's head off and left him as nothing more than an unrecognizable mass of blood and pulp on the floor of his apartment? What the hell had he—

Then suddenly it hit him like a physical blow. Feiffer, suddenly looking straight ahead, said in a gasp, "Oh, my God!"

It mattered. One man mattered. One individual life mattered.

Taking out a cigarette and lighting it with a shaking hand, and then instantly tossing it away again onto the ground, Feiffer said softly, "It matters. This is my home. This is where I live. And it matters. It matters to *me!*"

Sims. Robert Arthur Sims of 145 Graham Road, Aspley, Brisbane, Australia.

Up there, in the hotel, in one of the rooms, was Sims.

Still shaking, touching at his gun under his coat to make sure it was still there, Feiffer said softly, "Sims. I know why you did it! I know all about you! I know what you look like! I know who you *are!*"

Inside the lobby of the hotel, an army of workmen were taking down all the old oil paintings and pictures of all the great events of the Empire from the walls and replacing them with framed Chinese flags and portraits of Mao and Deng and Jiang, but as he passed quickly through them to the reception desk for the number of Sims's room, no one stopped him or asked what he was doing there, and, as he got out of the elevator on the fifth floor and went quickly towards the door of Room 502, the entire place was deserted and there was no one there to ask him by whose authority he carried the gun he had in his hand, cocked and ready to shoot.

They fell straight down exactly three feet, three and a half inches straight onto a cold, hard, dead-level marble-tiled floor and landed flat on their faces.

Getting to his feet and hauling out his gun, Auden yelled—as somewhere off to his left there was a flash of sparks as Spencer tried to get his lighter to work—"Where are they?

Where are they? Where are the demons?" Auden, turning in circles as the lighter went flick, flick, flick and did not catch, yelled, "Come on! Here I am! This is Auden—not Auden the fucking balloon seller, but Auden the fucking *cop!* Here I am! Come and get me! Here I am! *Here I am!*"

There was a final hard flick and then, suddenly, the wick on the lighter caught and Spencer's face was lit up in a circle of yellow light.

Auden yelled, "And he's over there! The smartest man you'll ever meet in *your* fucking lives! Come on! We don't care! We're not afraid! Come on! *Come and get us if you can!*"

He looked around in the darkness, but there was nothing, no movement or sound at all.

Auden, still turning, still aiming, still ready to fight, asked, "Bill? Where are they? Where are the demons?"

And then the wick went out and there was only darkness.

Auden said, "Bill? Are you there? Are you all right?" He was ready for the demons. The demons didn't know what they were going to be up against. Auden said urgently, trying to locate the man by sound in the blackness, "Bill? Are you still here?"

"Yes."

"Are you okay?"

"Yes."

Maybe he was. Auden, heading in the direction of the voice, said to encourage the man, "Don't be afraid. What the hell can some demon do to us? We're the boys who—"

"I'm not afraid."

"Great!" He was The Auden. Neither was he. Auden said fiercely, "No, neither am I and I—"

In the darkness, all there was, was darkness.

There was nothing.

The place was empty. All it was, was only . . . darkness.

Auden said in amazement, "My God, it's all just a story! There aren't any demons here! It's all just— It's all just a story and there aren't any demons or phantoms or warts or scabs or buttons! It's all just a story, made up, and—"

"Yes."

"And they're gone! There's nothing here anymore at all!"

"Yes."

"Those old demons—" He still didn't quite get it. Auden said in triumph, "By God, we scared the living shit out of them, and they've gone back into their pit and they've pulled the ground back over them and they—" Auden said, "Haven't they?" Auden said in utter admiration, "My God, the old Duke knew what he was doing when he picked you for this job, didn't he?" Auden said in the best imitation of an Oxford accent he could manage—which wasn't much of an Oxford accent—"Well done, that man! Well done, that man!"

"Thanks."

"And we—" Auden said, "And that's it, isn't it? That's all there is, and now . . ."

It was their last great battle and not a single shot had been fired, not a single blow thrown or received.

Auden said, suddenly overcome by an awful sadness, "And, I guess, what we do now is just go back the way we came and . . ." Auden said, "And pack up and go out to the airport and . . . and go home, and . . ."

"Yes." And in the darkness, Spencer's voice was the voice of a small boy told at the end of a long, wonderful afternoon's adventure that all that—all the strange and baffling mysteries he had found in his garden and in the woods—were nothing, were merely chimeras, and all that was real was home and clean hands at the dinner table and then, after dinner, a bath and then bedtime.

Spencer, suddenly lighting up the wick with a single flick and looking down into the glow of the flame with his eyes full of that small boy's disappointed tears, said in a whisper, "Yes, I guess we do."

He had always thought being a man when it really counted meant being hard, like grit.

It didn't. Sometimes, being a man when it really counted meant feeling a strange, almost sad, gentle feeling and a loss, and—

It was the end. Auden said quietly, "It's over, isn't it? There's nothing more, is there? Not for us. Not now."

"We beat the demons."

"Yeah." They had. "That was something." He put his hand to his face and there were no scabs or warts or buttons there, only tears.

Auden said in a whisper through the tears, as now, nothing more than an echo of something that once had been, "Go on? . . . Go on? . . ."

Spencer said softly, "No. Now, there's nowhere else to go."

"Right." He was always right. He was going to be great at Oxford. Auden said, firmly, nodding, being a man about it, *"Right."*

Wrong!

Suddenly, without warning, as if it were the place they had always been meant to arrive at, as if it were the place it had always been their fate to finally discover, like the last, final few inches of debris falling away in front of Howard Carter's eyes and blinding him with all the riches of Tutankhamen's tomb, on every side of them all the walls slid away down into the ground and they stood in the light of a thousand candles burning everywhere in a huge ancient green-marble-walled room full of carved mahogany and amber and coral and everywhere, everywhere, on the walls and the ceiling and on all the carved, gilded doorways, everything glittered with gold and jade and majesty and light.

* * *

In the Detectives' Room, Colonel Kong, glancing at his watch, said suddenly out of nowhere, "Detective Chief Inspector Feiffer is a great friend of yours, isn't he?"

He could barely get the words out. O'Yee, sitting at his desk, staring down at it, said in a whisper, "Yes, he is."

Kong said sympathetically, thinking about it, "A good man. And a man, I imagine, whose friendship you will miss very much when he is gone."

Yes, he would. O'Yee said softly, "Yes. I imagine I will."

"Yes." He looked again at his watch. He smiled his nice smile.

Kong said almost sadly, "Yes, I know Harry quite well myself. I think, when he's gone, as I think he soon may be, I will probably miss him too."

It mattered. It *mattered!*

At the end of the fifth-floor corridor, taking a measured step backwards to brace himself and then smashing open the hundred-year-old polished-brass lock with a single massive kick, Feiffer burst into Sims's room and took him by surprise by the window before he had time to get to the sawed-off double-barrel shotgun and pistol lying on his bed.

Covering the man with his gun, Feiffer said evenly but with his face full of anger and hate, "Good afternoon, Charlie. Well, I must say, you look in remarkably good health—for a fucking *dead man!*"

14.

He looked different. Standing there in the little single room dressed in a light sweater and slacks, Porter looked different, out of context, like someone else who had lived inside his body in secret hidden under all the uniforms and badges of rank and expensive suits and ties—someone somehow younger, thinner and alone, and, with his eyes darting for an instant to the two guns on the bed, someone out to protect no one but himself.

It was his hair: he had dyed the gray out of it and where it had always been thick and full, shaved it back at his temples to make it look as if it receded, and then, brushed it straight back.

It was probably what Sims's hair had looked like, what his photograph looked like on his passport.

He saw him looking. Touching at his temple, Porter said easily, "Oh. He had a full beard. I got him to shave it off. Passport photos are bad enough, and once the poor old Passport Control guy realizes you've shaved your beard off since it was taken, well, the poor bastard would let the Devil himself by even if he told him he was Santa Claus."

"You lied to me, Charlie. You lied about everything."

"Yep." Standing there at the window, he had been smoking a cigarette. The ash at the end was long and there was no ashtray. "Sorry about that, Harry, but, well, that's life, you know." He looked over to the little console table by the bed for the ashtray.

Closing the door behind him with his free hand and glancing in through the open door of the bathroom to check that it was empty, Feiffer said coldly, "If you make any sudden moves towards either of those guns, Charlie, I'll shoot you dead on the spot." Feiffer said, still watching the man like a hawk as he shrugged and put the burning cigarette filter-end-down on the windowsill to let it burn away there, "You lied to me and you lied to Annie and you lied to Sims and you lied—you lied to everybody! And you lied to the Triads about having something they wanted, and you lied— *You lied to everyone!* There never was anything, was there? It was all nothing more than a smoke screen for some pathetic fucking insurance scam! *Wasn't it?*"

"There's nothing pathetic about a million six, Harry—at least, not to normal people. What's pathetic about one million six is not having it. What's pathetic is spending your entire life in a place like this and then ending up at the end of your life chucked out into the street like a dog with nothing. Now, that's pathetic. That's real pathos!"

He didn't give a fuck. Standing there, having a little chat, safe and untouchable, he didn't care. He was even enjoying it.

Porter, raising a finger to give Feiffer a little friendly lesson about life, said earnestly, "What's pathetic, Harry, is believing in certainties. What's pathetic is still believing in middle age what you believed as a young man—believing things will never change. What's pathetic is believing that at the end of a long, useful life, self-satisfaction is enough. What's pathetic is not realizing that at the end of your life, at the point of death, there is no morality, there is no satisfaction, and that in order to stay alive just one more single second the human animal would slaughter millions of his fellow man!" He looked hard at him. "What's pathetic, Harry, is a grown man standing there with a gun defending some sort of unchanging morality about life and death and murder that doesn't even count anymore and in less than a month will never have counted at all, and will all be swept under the carpet of rewritten, politically correct history and totally forgotten! Which is very gratifying for all the poor bastards like you and me living on their fucking pensions and boring people in bars somewhere about the good old days in the Empire and then going back to their fucking little rooms with nothing to look forward to in the world except putting a gun in their mouths and blowing their fucking brains out!"

"All these years, you were on the take from the Triads, weren't you?"

"No, I never was." He turned, and the cigarette had burned down to the filter and gone out. "Like you, I never took a penny." He almost turned to go towards the bedside table for another cigarette, but then, glancing at Feiffer's face, changed his mind. "Not because, like you, I was always a white knight and on principle I wasn't going to take anything ever, but simply because it occurred to me at a very young age that the take was wasted on the young and that the only real take worth having was the big one at the end."

"You took money from the Triads. You took money from the Shanghai Bund through Annie and then, when she was all used up, when the Triads wanted something back in return—"

"No. I never took a penny from them either. All I ever took from them was the information they supplied me about the 14–K so I could earn my promotions and at least end up with the pension of an ex–Detective Chief Superintendent—which is hardly enough to live on for the rest of my life— As opposed to the pension you're going to get as an ex–Detective Chief Inspector, which will be hardly enough for you to have the bus fare to the nearest dole office to pick up your unemployment money!"

He didn't give a damn. He had time, while he waited for the pension check to clear, and he might as well spend it talking to Feiffer as standing at the window smoking a cigarette.

Porter said softly, "Look at you, Harry. After all your years here—after all the things that you thought mattered—what the hell have you got? Nothing. Less than nothing. This is your last day. There isn't any more. It's all over. And all you've got at the end of it is a fucking *gun* that you've got to hand in—you can't even keep that and sell it on a street corner somewhere for food!"

"You killed three people, Charlie! You killed them in cold blood: Sims, and Annie, and the janitor whose name you probably don't even know, Cheng!"

"So what?" It was a ludicrous statement. "So what, Harry?" He couldn't understand why it was so difficult to follow. "So what, Harry? *So what?*" The man was a fool: everything had to be explained to him. "You can't fake your own death for the insurance by killing *yourself*, Harry—you have to find someone else to kill."

"And you found him through the Internet, didn't you? On some sort of gay date website: someone who looked like you enough that Annie would—"

"He didn't look like me at all. That would have been a bit odd even to old dumbo Coughlan at the Pensions Board. But he had the same approximate physical age and build and coloring and that was all I needed."

Porter, glancing again at the bed, said with a smile, "Thank God for gays, Harry, promiscuous bastards that they are: it was like flicking through *Choose a Bod*—they just list everything about themselves in the hope you'll find them attractive." He seemed a little bored by the conversation, by having to explain it all. "And then, once I got him up here, all I had to do was buy him—as a little love-gift—a suit and a watch just like mine, and then, take him over to the apartment and blow his face off."

"How long have you been planning all this?"

"Oh, years. You don't find people like Sims overnight, you know."

"And Annie? She was taken in by it? Or was she part of it? When she saw what was supposed to be your body lying there on the floor—"

"Annie was a piece of crap! The last time Annie saw my body lying anywhere was never! The last time Annie and I even fucked was never. The last time—"

He saw Feiffer's face, saw what he was thinking.

Porter said as if he were talking to a child, "No, Harry, I'm not gay. I'm not even straight. I'm not anything! What I am is a man who wasn't going to end up the way I've seen other people end up: on the fucking beach eating fucking dog food and talking about a life that no one even gives a damn about! What I am is a man, at age fifty-one, who intends, thank you very much, to live at least another twenty or thirty years on my terms, *with money!* As Mr. Robert Sims of Australia. Well, at least until all the insurance money is through to me down there in that name—and then, after that, *as whoever the fuck I please!*"

"And they don't count? Sims? And Annie? And Cheng?"

"No." He paused for a moment. "Unlike you, Harry, I don't believe anyone counts—and certainly not some fucking gay and some fucking dumb Triad bitch, and most definitely not some fucking no-account, nameless fucking chink janitor!"

"He saw you and Sims go up to the apartment, didn't he? The janitor?"

"Sure. Hardly good form, don'cha know, to take your lover up to your apartment by the back stairs—especially not if you don't want him to suspect you're going to kill him when you get there. Also, cements the idea in the minds of the Triads that the thing I had they wanted was gone, that that was the motive for my murder. Which, thank you, no doubt by now you've established very firmly as the reason for my poor unfortunate death."

"And Annie?"

"Loose end." He smiled again. "Thanks for all your hard work. I knew you'd find the key at the back of the photo. I always said you were a good detective."

"It isn't too difficult to be a good detective when the major clue you're looking for has been salted there in front of your face for you to find!"

"Yeah. Sorry that the photo was only a Xeroxed copy. I intended to get a proper copy to make it look a little better, but things kind of moved a little faster than I anticipated and I just had to make do."

There was something wrong about it all. There was something so wrong about it all, but whatever it was, for a moment, Feiffer could not put his finger on it.

Then he could, and what was wrong was that the man didn't care. What was wrong was that he was going to get away with it. What was wrong was that . . .

What was wrong was that he knew there was nothing Feiffer could do about it!

What was wrong was that—

Feiffer said suddenly, "I can't tell the Triads and just let them kill you, Charlie—can I?"

"No." He smiled. Porter said softly, "Aha! At last, you've got it!"

"And I can't tell the insurance people either, can I?"

"Nope."

"And I—"

Porter said sadly, wistfully, almost sorry for the man, "Ah, Harry, you've no idea how many times over the years I've really felt sorry for you—you and your white-knight complex, you and your belief in good and morality and justice. You and your pathetic desire to be part of something you can never be part of. You with your understanding of all things Chinese and your love of the common fucking masses and your need to be part of it all—*and your fucking white skin and your round eyes that mean you never can be!* No. No, you can't tell anyone. You have to let me go. You have to be part of it—because I have got something the Triads want. It was stolen in my 'murder,' and I've still got it. I've got something a lot of people want!"

He didn't give a damn. He was safe, untouchable, bulletproof.

Porter, reaching into his pocket with no fear of the gun in Feiffer's hand, said with a grin of triumph, "It wasn't all a smoke screen—the so-called smoke screen for my 'murder'—there really is something a lot of people want and I've got it. And all you have to do—and you haven't got any choice in the matter because of who you are and what you believe—is let me go and say nothing—*and you can have it!*"

He paused.

He was, as he had always planned to be, a winner. He had beaten everyone.

He didn't look at the guns on the bed. He didn't need them anymore. All he needed was what he had in his pocket.

Pulling it out, Porter said like a schoolmaster talking to a callow, stupid adolescent child, "The only question is—and I know you don't even have the faintest idea on earth—is this thing that's so important, this object, this sign, this symbol that's so vital and urgent and necessary to everybody . . . What is it? . . . *Do you know?*"

With his eyes wide in all the glory and candlelight, Auden said in a gasp, "What is it? What is this place?" Everywhere in the huge marble-floored room there were incense burners set into the walls filling the air with a heavy smell of camphor and sandalwood, and in the fumes and smoke from the candles, he had to keep blinking his eyes and wiping them with his hand to stop them running. Brushing the smoke away and backing into a wall to get out his handkerchief, Auden said in astonishment, "Oh, my God, Bill, the floor and the walls— They're not marble, they're jade!" He looked up and saw the ceiling through the smoke. "Oh, my God! Look at the ceiling! It's the color of the sky! It's jade too, full of diamonds—like stars!"

Everywhere, along all the walls, there was more jade—pots and bowls—and everywhere, between them, bronze urns and bowls—and, standing between each of them, a line of full life-sized jade and soapstone and bronze statues of men and gods in long robes, all marching like a procession towards a huge painted screen at the end of the room.

Touching gingerly at the first statue, Spencer said in a whisper, "God, it's a contemporary statue of Fu Hsi, the inventor of writing, from at least three thousand years B.C.!" He touched another—"And this one—the next one—"

He could hardly believe it: "It's Shen Nung, the inventor of agriculture—and this one . . ." It was the most magnificent thing he had ever seen in his life, rich with the patina of antiquity. "It's the Emperor Yu, the Tamer of Floods! From the Legendary Period!"

He hardly dared look at the next. Spencer, like Carter at the tomb of Tutankhamen, said in a gasp, "I don't believe it! It's all from the most ancient period of Chinese history there is—a period so old that no one is even sure it ever existed! It's a contemporary statue of an unknown god from the Legendary Period five thousand years ago when men and gods walked the same earth!"

On his side of the room, all the statues led towards the great screen too. Touching at the first of them, recognizing it from a thousand cheap copies, Auden said, "It's Confucius!" It was a wonderful stone sculpture set a little back into a niche in the wall with a stone Dog of Fo on either side of it guarding it.

It was a statue of Confucius dressed in the robes of a traveller holding a tablet in his hand. There were only two characters on the tablet, simple ones, but all, perhaps, any man needed to know.

Auden, reading them aloud, said, "'*Jen*'—love, benevolence, loyalty. '*Cheh*'—wisdom." He looked up from the tablet to the next statue marching towards the screen. Auden said, "And Lao-tze—there's another one of Lao-tze, the founder of Taoism and—" And then the next. Auden said, "And Mencius, and—and all the Sages of China, all together in the one place!"

Confucius and Lao-tze and Mencius were only from the period of the Chou dynasty states, only from about two and a half thousand years ago. Where Spencer was, there was something so old it had no date. Spencer, leaning down and touching it, said, "Oh, my God, it's from the—" It was something of twisted black rock full of iron and oxidation and fused minerals with a single, wonderfully carved pictogram carved into it. Spencer said with an effort to get his voice, "I think it's a— I think it's a meteor of some kind, a magic stone, from even before the dawn of China! I think it's a—" He hardly dared say it—"I think it's—I think it's a rock from the Creation of the Universe—part of the great bolt of lightning and matter the Chinese believe the gods sent down from heaven that first created their world!"

It was all in an underground room in Tiger-Dragon Square, Hong Bay.

Auden said, "What the hell's it all doing here? What *is* this place? What's it all for?"

Spencer said, "It's a procession! It's a procession of homage, a continuity, leading to—" He looked up. "Leading to the screen! Leading to the—" In an instant, he went the length of the place to the screen. "To the—"

And, with his heart in his mouth, looked behind it and saw there, set on a golden bier, a carved teak coffin with its lid open containing, dressed in saffron robes with all the badges and devices and honors of his rank . . .

Spencer said in awe, in reverence, in wonder, "It's a procession! It's a final procession! It's a final, great procession of all the things that China ever was to the last, the final link to it. It's a procession of all the emperors and sages and gods to the last of their own, the last of the line! It's a procession to the coffin of the last eunuch of Imperial China, Sun Yaoting! It's *China!* It's the last, the final moment of everything China ever was, a procession of homage and honor to the last, final link left on earth with all the gods and legends that created it!"

Still standing at the window, Porter said, to explain a few facts of life and living that maybe Feiffer had missed along the way, "You see, the one thing you have to understand about the chink, Harry—about all Orientals—especially when you're trying to run his affairs for him in a nice, paternal way—is that he's an ungrateful little bastard who, rather than accepting the fact that you're better than him, still always remains totally and utterly convinced that, whatever happens, he's always still better than you."

Whatever he had in his pocket was not a gun. As he held his

hand around it in there, it was not big enough, not the right shape.

"And I don't just mean better than people like you or me—the big-foot barbarians from across the sea and all that, who tried to run his affairs—I mean, *anyone* who tries to run his affairs, including presidents and premiers and commissars and Communists—anyone at all. Old Hundred Names—the eternal Chinese—may nod and bow and scrape and pay lip service to it all, but unless it has the backing of heaven, unless the authority stretches all the way back to the fucking first bit of dust on the Chinese soil—the first bit of clay the first Chinese was made from—he just doesn't believe in a fucking word of it, and never will."

He had never thought he could feel such hatred for anyone. Still holding the gun on the man, Feiffer said with his voice shaking, "What are you talking about, Charlie? Do you know?"

"I'm talking about the Communists and the Triads and the—And anyone else who wants to have power here in Hong Kong when we poor old colonials have gone!" He shrugged. "Not that we really ever had any power anyway . . . I'm talking about legitimacy, authentication, certification—I'm talking about who the ordinary Chinese are really going to look to for direction and who they're going to pay their fucking protection money to, and who they're really going to give their loyalty to when we've gone!"

He drew a breath: "I'm talking about their Cloth of Gold, the thing that makes them what they are. Their links with heaven and who controls those links. I'm talking about who, through a great deed that gives him the right to it, possesses the symbol of an unchanging link with heaven all the way back into the darkness before creation! I'm talking about who—Communist, Triad, whoever—now that the last eunuch of Imperial China is dead, is going to be seen as his authentic *heir,* his trusted friend—his authentic and undisputed *successor!*"

He grinned and shook his head at the stupidity of it all. "Children, Harry. Just like children, living in their own private, secret little world of gods and ghosts and trees and flowers and animals that talk and fortunes and prayers and kite flying, and—"

"What have you got, Charlie? What is it you stole this time?"

"I stole nothing! It was already stolen!" He stopped and shook his head. "No. Actually, not stolen so much as given away, and then, not so much given away as taken."

As well as a lecture on life, he had another little lesson to give on the subject of history. "During the Japanese Occupation, it was something so dangerous to keep that they gave it to the Japanese Secret Police just to get rid of it, just to prove they had nothing to do with it, just to show that they wanted nothing to do with something that the Japanese, being Orientals themselves, saw as yet another symbol of the real, secret loyalties of the Chinese—something they saw as an idea that had to be destroyed as quickly as possible if they were to rule China undisturbed. And so it was handed in to the Kempeitai, the Japanese Secret Police, and the Kempeitai took it and stored it, and then, after Liberation, when all the Kempeitai's files and papers and records and archives in Hong Kong fell into our hands . . ."

Feiffer said coldly, "You promised it to the Shanghai Bund Society, didn't you? You did a deal with them years ago that if they'd help you in your career, you'd pass it over to them after the takeover, didn't you? So they'd be untouchable. So the Communists wouldn't dare go after them. So they could continue on robbing and murdering and thieving from— So, whoever was in power, Communists or colonial, as the holders of the mandate of heaven—the Annointed Ones—no one dared touch them at the risk of rebellion because—"

"I always said you were a good detective, Harry."

"And, having control of it kept you safe all these years, didn't it? Even from the 14–K. And probably even from Ang and the ICAC."

"Sure."

It was so obvious.

"Because you'd promised it to the 14–K too, hadn't you? Even when you were rounding up their people on the information you got from the Shanghai Bund, they didn't dare do anything to you *because you'd promised it to them too—hadn't you?*"

"Oh, yes." He couldn't help smiling. Porter said with a grin, "Oh, I promised it to everyone. I promised it to anyone who might help me along in my career."

"And then you— You knew once you'd handed it over you were dead—so you set up the insurance thing and—"

"No, other way around, Harry. It was always the insurance thing first, and if old Sun Yaoting, the last eunuch, hadn't died a little prematurely, I would have been well away in Australia the last few days before the takeover and everybody'd be still hunting for whoever killed me and took it, and you—"

"And, as your friend, I'd have worked it as my last case before I left and provided the motive for your killing and certified it so the insurance money was paid out."

"Yes."

"And if the last eunuch hadn't died on time?" He knew the answer. Feiffer said in disgust, "You'd have had him killed too! Wouldn't you?"

"Sure."

"What have you got, Charlie?"

He couldn't help sniggering. Porter said with heavy irony, "Poor old eunuch, not what you'd call a lucky man, really. Here he was at age ten in 1910 with all his manhood sliced off ready to serve the old Manchu emperor there in Peking, and what happens? A year later, everything changes, the Manchus who have ruled China for three centuries are swept away and the Republican government of Sun Yat-sen is in power. And then, just when the Nationalists are about to be swept away thirty years later and maybe the Imperial Throne might return, what happens? The Japanese occupy China, and then, once they've been gotten rid of by the Nationalists and the Communists, the Communists come to power, and then—"

He thought it was hilarious.

Porter said with all the sympathy of a stone, "And then, when the old eunuch comes here to Hong Kong to die—to at least fulfill his own, single role of interceding with the gods in heaven for all those who are loyal to all the things that once was China . . . well, guess what, Harry? He can't really do even that because he's lacking something. He's lacking something the Kempeitai took and that I have! He's lacking the one thing he needs to even get himself into heaven in the first place! He's lacking his *balls!* His *genitals!* And there is no way known to man or God that he can enter heaven and be powerful without them!"

He took a single step forward. Porter, still grinning, still sniggering, said, pleased with himself beyond measure, "And the man or the group or the Triad or even the Communist Government who returns them so he can go to his grave with them and enter heaven on behalf of all men—on behalf of *China*—is the man or the group or the Triad or the Communist Government who has all the loyalty and the gratitude and the unswerving devotion of all the ordinary, little people who believe all this stuff, and he's the man or the Triad or the government that can rule them whichever way he likes, complete with the mandate and anointment of heaven, *forever!*"

With a sudden jerk, he pulled his hand out of his pocket and held out what looked like a little oblong cedarwood box wrapped in torn and tattered brown paper with the seal of the Japanese Kempeitai on it.

Tossing it over, Porter said, "Here! Take it! It's yours! You can have it with my best wishes!"

He thought it was the best joke he had ever heard.

Unable to control himself any longer, laughing uproariously, Porter said, leaning forward a little so Feiffer could catch every word, "Only one problem, Harry—only one little catch to, you know, your going down to the jolly old funeral and handing the box over with a flourish and becoming untouchable yourself by your good and noble action, and it's this: *there's nothing there!* The box is empty! The bloody thing must have rotted away into nothingness years ago, and, inside that box in your hand, *there's nothing there anymore!*"

Then, in the great jade and gold and silver and incense-filled hall, without warning, in the wall behind the great bier, a long, sliding door opened, and there, standing in a line, dressed in white and with their heads shaved, were the geomancers, the demon-scarers, the cannon shooters.

In the center, taller than the others, and with his hands outstretched towards them, was the Chief Geomancer: the great magician, the keeper of order in a universe full of chaos and evil and hell, and when he spoke to Auden and Spencer as one man, he spoke to them not as men at all in the common language of Cantonese, but in the high, classical language of Imperial Mandarin.

He spoke to them not as mere mortals, but as slayers of demons.

The Chief Geomancer, his face twisted in pain and fear, begging them, stretching out his hands to plead with them in humble, respectful supplication, said desperately, "Help! Help us! Please! Please—! *Help us!!*"

15.

Even with Feiffer's gun pointing at him, standing there still grinning at the thought of the empty box, Porter was still in control.

He had been in control all his life. All his life, people had been cowed by him, people like Annie, and—because he had thought through every move before he made it—even people like the Triads and maybe even people like Justice Ang at ICAC.

It was what he did best. He enjoyed it.

He enjoyed it now.

Standing by the window, still grinning, Porter asked pleasantly as Feiffer looked down at the package in his hand, "Well, Harry, will we call it quits and just part as friends and say no more about it?"

He could see Feiffer had no idea what the hell to do next. "Or, of course, now that you've got the magic box, you could walk out of here and give it to the Triads—either of them: the Shanghai Bund or the 14–K, it doesn't matter which—and ask them for the same deal they were going to give me: their official protection and blessing so I could stay on, and all the riches and business connections they promised me to make staying on luxurious." He couldn't help laughing. "Which, of course, is bullshit, because the moment they get it they're going to blow your fucking head off to stop you talking about it, but you could try it anyway if you liked."

It was all a great joke, all of it, all the symbols and flags and devices, all the things lesser, stupider men held important. "Not that you'd give it to the Triads anyway, would you?"

"No. I wouldn't."

"No." Suddenly he had a bitter twist to his mouth. "No, because the Triads are naughty, bad people, and let's hear it for the white knight! So who would you give it to? The Communists?"

"No, I wouldn't."

"No, you'd give it to the common people. Old Hundred Names. The poor old downtrodden chink in the street who needs all the help he can get from heaven—your buddies, your friends in the fucking tenements and sweatshops, the people you give a damn about, the people you've spent your entire life protecting and caring about— Right?"

"Yes! If you like! Yes!"

"Oh, great. That's just so clever! That's just so fucking bright! Their most sacred little relic, their connection with the ear of heaven, everything that's China and the Chinese, and you're the one, towering above them with your round eyes and your white face, you're the one who gives it to them! And just what the hell do you expect them to say to you when you stand there and patronizingly hand it to them *at the very moment when everything you represent is going?* 'Oh, thankee, Master, John Chinaman he veree, veree humbly grateful to nice white man'?" Porter said in a rage, "You fucking moron, they'd cut your throat from ear to ear and leave you lying dead in a gutter with the fucking dogs!"

Maybe he hadn't thought of everything. Maybe he didn't know quite everything he thought he knew.

Feiffer, feeling a cold hatred towards the man he had never felt for anyone before in his entire life, said as a matter of information, as something he knew that Porter did not, "The box doesn't have to have anything in it. For the very reason you pointed out—because it is something so sacred and important and connected with the blessing of heaven—no one is going to open it to check. And it doesn't matter who I give it to. I don't have to give it to anyone! All I have to do is make a phone call to whoever's entrusted with the burial of the body—*whoever the common, ordinary people trust*—and tell them where to come to pick it up—*and then just leave it somewhere safe for them to find!*"

There was a momentary silence, then, very slowly he clapped his hands three times.

Porter, full of mock admiration, said, still grinning, "Well done! Terribly, terribly . . . straight! As they say in that old Chinese proverb, 'In the presence of the truly noble and moral man, the evil coward slinks away in shame.' " He was in control, enjoying himself. Porter said with a nod, "Wonderful idea. Great plan."

And then his eyes changed. "Except for one thing. Except for the fact that the moment you try to do that I'll put in a call to the Triads and the Communists and anyone else I can think of and tell them the box is empty because you took what was inside it, and then everybody—*everybody!*—will have just one thing uppermost in their nasty, vicious, murderous little minds—*and that'll be to cut you into a million pieces in revenge to show the common people just how much they care about the common people and how much they deserve their loyalty, and you'll be right back where you started!*"

Porter said as if it were the simplest thing, nothing at all, "All I want is the pension money and the insurance, Harry. All I want is to leave here as Mr. Sims. The check for the pension will be cleared and on its way by electronic transfer to Mr. Sims in Australia by the end of the day. All you have to do is just let me walk away. And then, if you've got any sense at all, call it quits, call it an object lesson in life, and go home, pack your bags and spend the rest of your life with your wife and son in Manila or—or wherever the hell you want to spend it, doing—whatever the hell it is you want to do."

"No."

"You're not a cop anymore!"

"I can still fuck up your insurance money!"

"Can you?"

"Yes, I can!"

"How? By telling everyone what happened? Telling them what I did? Telling everyone the box is empty? Telling poor, put-upon, oppressed Mister Chink In Rags that you had the key to heaven but that, for some moral reason of your own, you had to fuck it all up by bringing me in to some sort of idea of justice known only to you as well as telling everyone the box was empty anyway?"

Every way he turned, it seemed there was nothing. Suddenly, standing there, he was nothing but an irrelevance.

"Put the gun away, Harry. You look ridiculous standing there with it in your hand."

He turned slightly and glanced behind him out the window and nodded in its direction. "Just walk away, Harry. Just go. Just walk away with nothing in your hands and call it a day." He couldn't resist it. Porter said with a casual shrug, "Maybe we'll meet up again somewhere on the planet and I might even be in a position to offer you a job, or at least maybe a handout."

The window faced the street. When Feiffer had taken the door down, Porter had been standing there with the cigarette in his hand almost smoked down to the tip as if he had been doing something else and forgotten to smoke it. He looked down at the badly wrapped package in his hand. It was not badly wrapped, but badly rewrapped.

Feiffer said in a storm of hatred, "You bastard! You dirty, fucking bastard, Charlie! There was something in the box, wasn't there? It didn't rot away years ago! It was intact! It was intact, *and when you saw me out there on the street, you destroyed it, didn't you?* You destroyed it to protect your final, fucking base, didn't you? To protect yourself from your final, fucking obstacle! To protect yourself from *me!*"

He was glad he had seen it. It was nice to have one's genius fully appreciated.

Porter said with a wink, "Well, at least, to protect myself from your white knight's view of morality and the welfare of the lesser races of this world." Porter said before he could ask, "I flushed it down the toilet in the bathroom in there. It was tiny—well, of course it would be, since they chopped the old eunuch's nuts off when he was about nine—and it—"

He saw Feiffer's face.

Porter said fiercely, "You can't win, Harry. I've thought of everything. You can't win. You can't beat me, Harry. Harry, trust me, believe me, whatever you do or whichever way you turn, you simply cannot *win!*"

He had the gentlest voice. In the great hall, speaking in a whisper, the Chief Geomancer, with his ancient, lined face all twisted in anguish, said in desperation, "Please, he is not *intact.*"

He glanced down to the face of the old, old man in the coffin, a face full of years and lines of sadness and suffering. "Sun Yaoting: the last great link with everything that is China—the symbol of everything the gods bestowed upon our race—he is not *intact!*"

He was speaking in classical Mandarin: "People have lied. Things that were to be returned—things that were promised to be returned—have not been returned, and if he goes to his grave mutilated and unwhole and not as the man he was born as, he cannot come back in the next life as a man again to walk among us and protect us with his power. He can only come back as something else—as something low and evil and vile—as an insect, as the lowest life that crawls on the ground! As a slug!" It was a thought he could not bear, and he had to look away to say it: "Or worse—!"

On top of the huge, carved coffin, just below the open viewing port where the sad, dead face lay with its eyes closed, there was an ancient jade box encrusted with what looked like rubies and emeralds, with nothing inside.

The Chief Geomancer, changing to Cantonese so there could be no mistake about what he said or how desperate he had become to say it to two barbarians from the West, said as a plea, as an entreaty, as a prayer, "You. You two. You two souls who have dispersed all the demons from the Demon Hole with the power of the goodness of your characters, please, please, assist us one more time!"

He glanced at a flight of steps that rose from the floor up to the wall facing the street that seemed to go nowhere. The Chief Geomancer said desperately, running out of time, "Soon, today, within moments, because it is the only day it can be done, we must take the coffin out into the street for the people to carry to the cemetery for burial. They are all waiting. They have done all they can with their swords and sticks and clubs to clear the street from evil, and, with our cannons, we have done all we can . . ."

He could barely get it out: "—Please, once we go out there with the body, please, *please,* you must help us from being torn to pieces by them once they realize we are not bringing out the complete body of Sun Yaoting to be transported to the panoply of the gods as a Benevolence, but instead, only a mutilated, unintact creature, to be turned by the gods in their anger and fury and displeasure, into the worst and most evil demon who ever infested all the fears and terrors and nightmares of men!"

Out there in the streets, the kite flyers were flying their kites up to the heavens for nothing.

In Fortune-Tellers Lane, what all the fortunes foretold of the future was nothing, was evil, was suffering.

In the little hotel room, gazing at the man standing there, at a stranger, Feiffer said in amazement, "I can't believe I didn't see it coming, Charlie. All those years I thought we were friends—I just can't believe I didn't see it coming . . ."

"Thank you." Porter said with sudden vehemence, "Because you weren't supposed to! You weren't *supposed* to see it coming. What you were supposed to see was your buddy, your friend, your *pal,* and then, after I got my head removed by a shotgun in my own apartment with my wife asleep in the next room, what you were supposed to see was an indignant rage at the unfairness of it all, and, even as everything was falling to pieces around you in the last few days before the takeover, you were supposed to obligingly go out as the good white knight and make sure the insurance company knew officially it was a fucking murder in the line of duty, and didn't try to get off the hook by saying it was an unexplained death, or a suicide, or whatever those vultures might have tried to say."

He nodded his gratitude. "For which, I thank you. And now,

if you don't mind, I've got a few things to do, like disposing of guns and—"

"You murdering bastard! You killed three people! Cheng, and Sims, and even your own wife—even Annie! You slaughtered three human beings as if they were nothing!"

"Yes. And I betrayed all my friends."

"Yes! Yes, you did!"

"And?"

"What do you mean, 'And'?"

"I mean, 'And so what?' I mean, everyone dies, Harry. And everyone kills. And so . . . And so the only real question when it all boils down is whether or not—" He was starting to lose his facade of calm. "The only real question is whether or not all the dying and killing is of any use or importance or worth in monetary terms! *Because none of it is of any use or importance or worth in terms of glory or morality or dignity or respect or gratitude or anything else along those lines!*"

He glanced for a moment at the two guns on the bed. Taking a step towards Feiffer with his hand at his side kneading itself over and over into a fist, Porter said with his eyes blazing, "Because I know all about that, Harry! I know about killing and dying for morality and glory and all the rest of it! I saw it up close all my life! I saw exactly what *that* was worth! I saw it every day of my life when I was a kid when there was no money because my fucking father had gone off in the name of glory and morality and decency and all the rest of that *crap* to fight in the war and gotten himself fucking killed the first fucking day he got off the boat in Korea when I was six years old! I saw exactly what it was worth to my mother and me! It was worth, exactly, a medal, a certificate of commendation, and a pension that was barely enough to pay the rent: exactly the same things that both you and I are due to get for our years of service and morality and—"

He was breathing hard. He had to stop to catch his breath. "I saw what morality cost! I saw it when all I wanted to be all my life was a fucking doctor, and all I could ever afford to be was a fucking *cop!* I saw it when—"

Porter, shaking his head, suddenly huge and dangerous in the little room, said with his hand still kneading and his eyes glancing to the guns on the bed, "No, I don't share your view of right and wrong, Harry. The only view of right and wrong I have is that it's wrong to die the way my mother did—worn down and broken from work—and it's wrong for anyone to live the way I did as a kid: always second-rate, never as good as any of the rest of the kids with fathers and with money—and the only thing that's right is to take whatever the hell you can get and make sure the same thing doesn't happen to you!"

Suddenly, as he thought about it, his face changed. "Do you know what I'm going to do with the money, Harry? Nothing! I'm going to do absolutely nothing with it! Now, to your mind, isn't that the worst, the most morally disgusting thing you've ever heard in your entire life? *What I'm going to do with the money is nothing!* What I'm going to do with the money is just know I've got it—and, by God, thank you very much, that'll do me nicely!"

He looked Feiffer directly in the eyes. "And as for all your people—all your swarming, poor, desperate people with only their fucking gods and their superstitions and their fucking eunuchs and all the rest of it, I can sum that up very simply as far as I'm concerned in three simple words. As far as I'm concerned, I-don't-care! As far as I'm concerned, I don't *care!*"

He was bulletproof. There was no way of getting to him. Every way was closed, was a dead end, was a road that led nowhere.

Porter said softly, "You can't win, Harry. You can't beat me. The only way you can possibly beat me is to *be* me—and to kill me in absolute stone-cold blood and with as little feeling as the way I killed Cheng and Sims and Annie—and that, because I factored you in years ago for exactly what you are and what you believe in, is something you won't do! That is something, in your fixed and firm and human world of morality and decency and honesty, in all the panoply of things you might be prepared to do for all your little chink friends, for everything you believe in—that is something you would never do!"

Standing there smiling, Porter looked again at the two guns on the bed.

Porter said with a shake of his head, "They're not loaded, Harry, so any sort of half-baked, bloody TV–cop-show notion of shooting the bad guy as he goes for his gun isn't going to happen. The bad guy is definitely not going to make any halfhearted try for his gun in this scenario so the good guy feels better about murdering him. No, the bad guy is just going to stand here until you finally get tired and go away, and then, the bad guy—" It was like talking to an idiot, to a moron. He wondered why the man simply couldn't see it, why he still stood there. "And then the bad guy is going to wait for his check to clear, toddle off to the airport with his new identity, and sit around in Australia waiting for his next check—the big one, the insurance—to clear. And then— Well, who knows?"

Porter said slowly and clearly, "The problem is, Harry, the only way you win here over the bad guy is to become the bad guy yourself and shoot me down in cold blood—and you can't do that, Harry, not you."

Porter said to make it all clear, "No, Harry, you can't do that because, all your life—and I took careful note of it all these years—you never once did *anything* you couldn't live with! And that's your problem, your one weakness, the thing I factored in about you years and years ago when I planned all this: nothing and no one, not even your poor little chinks out in the streets, justifies the white knight doing something he couldn't live with!"

And then, the way it had at all the dinners in that apartment over all those years as they swapped stories and drank and were friends, his voice boomed out to silence any further discussion.

Laughing uproariously, in that instant making all the years of friendship and trust nothing more than they ever really had been, nothing more than a mere *joke,* putting his hand to his face to wipe away his tears of hilarity, of victory, of success, Porter demanded, *"You'd agree, Harry?* It's not because you're such a good, fine fellow or any of the other things you might think—it's all just because you're fucking *weak!"*

In the silence of the great hall as all the geomancers waited, Spencer said in total and absolute bewilderment, "But *how?* How can we help?" He turned to Auden next to him, old Salt Man still covered in salt: "All we are, are just a couple of cops—a couple of— All we are, are a couple of soon-to-be ex-cops with nothing to look forward to in the future except a life of—" Spencer said at last, "Being a failed teacher, and—"

Auden said quietly, "And a balloon seller in a park."

He looked down at the still, parchmentlike ancient face of the eunuch, of a man born to be in the company of kings, dead now in the company of failures, and very gently reached out and touched him on the cheek to comfort him.

Auden, glancing around the great room, said with a shake of his head, "That's all we are now. We don't have any part in any of this anymore. Maybe we never did."

"Your spirits must have had some part in it or they would not have vanquished the demons in the demon holes! And you would not have been the ones that the heavens would have chosen to come if you had not—"

No, it was all wrong. Trying to put it right, Spencer said, "No, we didn't just come—we were summoned to come. We were—I was called on the phone by—"

"By who?"

"By—"

It was what they were waiting for, what they had prayed for, what, in that moment, they all willed he might say.

Spencer, suddenly standing straighter, said with his voice full of confidence, "By Yen Sheng Kung himself. By the Duke of Extended Sagehood. By the direct descendant of Confucius himself." Go on? Go on? By God, why not? Spencer said with a nod in Auden's direction, "In order to hold the tearing fabric of the universe together until he can get here! Until—"

They didn't have his *balls!* The open, empty jade box was for the final thing that meant he could ascend to heaven as a man, and they didn't have them! Gazing at the box, Auden said in a whisper, "Oh, my God!" Auden demanded, "Until what? Until he can get here with—" He had to be careful what he said: *"Until he can get here with whatever goes in this box?"*

"Yes!" He was trembling. The Chief Geomancer, suddenly changing to English, said intensely, "If we go out there without it it is the end of all the *feng shui* magic in China: the end of everything men have trusted in and believed in for generations! It is the end of hope! If the Duke is not out there waiting for us with the box that goes into this box in his hand, it is the end of sagehood, of history, of trust, and of the common hopes and trust and dreams of ordinary men and women with nothing else in their lives to sustain them! It is the end of everything!"

The Chief Geomancer, suddenly going back to Cantonese and making all the other white-clad, shaven-headed men around him nod in agreement, said desperately, "You know, you know because your souls are the ones he chose to perform the task of clearing the way for him to be here. When we open that wall up there and carry the body of this man—this last, great symbol of everything that China ever was, out into the street before the waiting people—will he be there or not? We haven't heard from him since he spoke to us on the telephone out of nowhere in the middle of the night and we don't know! *Will the Duke be waiting there with the object that goes into that box to see this poor, good, dead man clear on his way to heaven and rebirth and continuing spiritual strength for the poor, ordinary, toiling masses of this world or not?*"

Hope. It was all about hope and needing and fear of the future. It was all about the human spirit: what drove it. It was not about Oxford or teaching or balloon selling or what might matter or what one might fail in tomorrow: it was about now. It was about what was important now.

In a whisper only he and the ears of the ancient, lined, dead creature lying there in his coffin heard, Auden said softly, "You know, I really loved every moment I spent in this place. It was the best thing I ever did in my entire life . . ."

In a murmur only he heard, Spencer said quietly to himself and to all the things that drove him that mattered, "Saint Crispian's Day . . .

> And gentlemen in England now a-bed
> Shall think themselves accurs'd they were not here,
> And hold their manhoods cheap whiles any speaks
> That fought with us upon Saint Crispian's Day . . .

If the Duke was not out there when they got outside into the street, they were all going to die.

Hope.

In life, that was all there was.

"Yes." It was Auden. He looked at Spencer for confirmation, and confirming it, Spencer nodded back.

Spencer, speaking for them both, said as a statement of fact, "Yes, he's out there. Yes!"

"The Chief Geomancer said softly, "You are blessed men."

Yes. Yes, they were.

Auden said, "Yes!" Glancing down for a moment at the face of the eunuch and then up the flight of stairs to the wall, Auden said, "Okay. Fine. That's settled. Get him ready, and then let's get on with it and put everything that's wrong with this whole, stinking, fucking world back the way it all should have been from the start!"

Standing there gazing at Porter at the window of the little hotel room, it was like hearing the sound of a death sentence being passed.

It was a death sentence being passed.

There was no point in threatening the man with his gun anymore, no point at all, and letting it drop loosely to his side, Feiffer said with his voice suddenly full of sadness and disappointment and pity for the man, "I'm sorry for you, Charlie. I'm sorry you see things the way you do. I'm sorry you see me the way you do, but you're seeing it all through your own prism and what you're seeing is wrong. And you're the one who can't win, not me."

"Sure, Harry, and if it makes you feel better about it all, I'm sure God, who's undoubtedly up there in his heaven, will see I catch some sort of awful, lingering and painful disease the moment I get off the plane and all the money I've stolen from the three people I've killed won't do me a scrap of good and I'll die a terrible, repentant death and then go straight to hell—okay?"

He was getting impatient. "But now— Well, I hate to be a bad host, but—" He was still watching the gun. He watched as Feiffer put it back in its holster under his coat. "But now, you know, time is money and all that, and I've got a lot to do, so if you don't mind . . ." He indicated the door. "If you don't mind, I'd like you to go now and—"

"I'm sorry that this is what life did to you, Charlie. I'm sorry you think it's so worthless." He sounded so disappointed for the man.

"Sure." He had lost interest. As Feiffer walked apparently aimlessly in the direction of the bed and looked down at the guns, he turned away and glanced out the window.

"I'm sorry for you that you got everything so wrong—that you got me so wrong . . ." Gazing down at the guns and shaking his head, Feiffer said softly, "It was never them and me, Charlie, the way it was with you. It was never me wanting to be one of them—I *am* one of them. This is my home. This is where I've lived all my life. I've never known anything else. This is what I am. There's no duplicity or pretending or self-delusion about it—all this is what I am!" It was like having an enormous hole opening wider and wider in his heart that was never going to close. "And I'm sorry! I'm so sorry that you think that this is what life is all about. I'm so sorry that you thought I only ever did things I could live with, that I was weak; and I'm so sorry, sorrier than I can tell you, for you, and what the world you must have lived in all these years must have been like—"

"The world I lived in all these years has been pretty good, thanks, and, once you finally finish saying your little piece and get the hell out of here, it's going to get a fucking sight better!"

Feiffer said tightly, "And I'm sorry, most of all, that you did all this on an assessment of me seen not through my eyes, but through yours. I'm sorry, Charlie, that all the years we knew each other, that we were friends, you were always so busy talking that you never once listened, or, if you did, you never once heard what you were listening to." Feiffer, starting to shake all over, said to try to make him understand, "Charlie, I never did anything solely because I could live with it—that wasn't my weakness! It still isn't! My weakness is that I did things because they were *right!*"

"Sure, Harry, whatever you say . . . Whatever makes you feel better."

He was bored by it all, irritated. He turned and gazed out the window. Porter said philosophically, offhandedly, just wanting the man to stop talking and go, "Well, Harry, there you are." He meant everything—everything that was inside that room and outside of it. "As the poet says, 'This is the way the world ends. Not with a bang, but a whimper.' "

No, it didn't.

It ended with a bang.

The shotgun on the bed—as Feiffer knew it would be—was loaded, and taking it up and crossing quickly with it over to the window, without another word he put it straight against the side of Porter's head, and then, pulling both triggers at once, blew the man's head and face off in a blast that took all the glass out of the window in a massive roar and an instant explosion of blood and bone and viscera.

. . . And in that moment, felt the hole in his heart open up and devour everything inside him, and had to reach out and hold onto the wall by the window to stop himself from falling.

Then, tossing the gun back on the bed, and putting the little wrapped box safe in his inside coat pocket, he went quickly out of the room and down in the elevator to the hotel lobby and out on to the front steps to get to his car.

And saw instantly, everywhere in the plaza, all the people who must have followed him there or been told he was there: the Shanghai Bund people, the 14–K, the local Communists—all of them—all getting out of their cars with guns and coming towards the sound of the shot, and as he ducked quickly back into the hotel to get out of sight, he knew, if he was not very careful in the next few minutes, exactly whose funeral it was going to be a good day for.

If he wasn't very careful it was going to be a good day for his, and as he went quickly back across the lobby and down the first side corridor he found, he looked urgently for somewhere, anywhere, there might be a phone so he could put in a call to the one person left on earth he trusted who might be able to help.

16.

In the Detectives' Room, Claude looked down at the last page in O'Yee's dossier and made a note.

In the Detectives' Room, Colonel Kong said with no expression on his face or in his voice at all, "Finally, on the subject of honest men . . ."

No, it was all over, finished. There was nothing more to be said. It was over.

At his desk, shaking his head, O'Yee said, sadly, beaten, "No, you win. I'll go. You win."

He closed the dossier and looked up. Claude said softly, "No, Christopher, you do," but before O'Yee could ask him what he meant, the phone rang, and, before O'Yee could even ask who it was, Feiffer's voice at the other end said urgently through the speaker, "Christopher, is that you?"

From his chair, Claude said, "Harry?"

"Claude?"

"Yes."

Feiffer's voice said urgently, "I need an address. I need the address of a funeral service to be held today for—"

Claude said quickly, "Tiger-Dragon Square!" He looked at O'Yee to explain, "I heard it on the phone from your man Auden. Auden and Spencer are already there." Claude asked, "Harry, where are you? Are you in trouble?"

"I'm at the Hong Kong Victoria Hotel and I'm in a hell of a lot of trouble!"

"Stay there!" He was in charge. He was going to be in charge sooner or later anyway. "Stay where you are!"

Colonel Kong of the Chinese People's Police said, with no doubt in his mind about his power to do it, "I'll have a truckload of the People's Liberation Army soldiers around there to pick you up in two minutes! Be in the front lobby. As soon as you see them, go straight out and get into the back of the truck with them! After that, it's only about three or four minutes to the square, and Christopher and I will meet you there!"

He was already on his feet, already gathering up his papers and bag. Reaching over the man to push the button on the phone to hang up, he glanced down at O'Yee still sitting at his desk and saw the look of utter perplexity and confusion on his face.

Kong said fiercely, "Oh, yes, you're very important in all this too."

Kong said quickly as he tapped out a number on the phone to call God-only-knew who, "You might say, in this entire, extremely important little affair, you may well now be the most important person there is in the entire place—"

Standing next to Spencer up on the funeral ramp with all the geomancers behind him in two lines on either side of the coffin ready to pick it up and carry it, Auden said as an order, "Okay!"

The Duke was out there. He had to be.

Auden said, "Open the wall!" and as the entire wall slowly slid back expected to see maybe a hundred or so people out there waiting with him.

What he did not expect to see, and what was out there waiting for them all, were *thousands.*

17.

Stepping out through the open wall into the square at the head of the procession, Auden said in horror, "Oh, my God—!"

They were everywhere, thousands and thousands of them, filling the square, pushed up shoulder to shoulder in long lines and ranks and rows, an ocean of people dressed in white robes and high-peaked white cowls: the mourners, the waiting funeral cortege for the last link with five thousand years of Chinese history and everything that had been Imperial China, the last eunuch, Sun Yaoting.

All the walls of all the temples and pagodas in the entire square seemed to have disappeared, sunk somewhere below the surface of the street, and if there was someone magnificent waiting there in all the formal robes of dukedom, Auden could not see him.

There were no voices in the square, only a sort of hum. Glancing quickly back over his shoulder to where the Chief Geomancer had the lead right-hand side of the teak coffin, Auden hissed urgently in English, "Which one is he? Where's the Duke? Which one is he?" and saw the Chief Geomancer's face, and *Oh, my God! He didn't know either!* and on top of the coffin was the open empty jade box and as the crowd pushed and shoved and pressed, someone close up must have seen there was nothing in it and then heard his tone, because the hum suddenly changed, became a gasp, and then, like something living, the entire crowd seemed to heave and press in even closer, and all the noises, at once, became like the sound of some sort of suddenly awaking and vengeful creature rising up from under the surface of the square itself.

At the back of the cortege, there was a crash as one of the geomancers dropped his section of the coffin in terror and it hit the ground a glancing blow before whoever it was next to him helped him get it back up. Staring at the crowd, seeing all the looks in the eyes as they changed, as they suddenly lit with anger, Auden was afraid to look around to see what had happened.

Then there was another crash as another of the geomancers, with a cry of fear, also let go, and then a scuffle, and then Spencer's voice ordered in Cantonese, "Pick it up! Don't let it fall! The Duke will be here! Hang onto it!" and then, as Auden turned to help, Spencer, standing a little way off from the end of the coffin and not touching it himself, yelled to him in English, "Phil! Don't touch it! We mustn't be seen to touch it! We're barbarians! We mustn't be seen to desecrate it! We're not part of it all anymore! It's China! It's got nothing to do with us anymore! It's all China now!"

It was, and any second as all the eyes peering out from under the cowls all around them turned bright with anger, China was going to crush them all like insects.

In the crowd near him, someone must have actually said something, because almost as if he tried to set up some sort of chant, Spencer intoned over and over in Cantonese, "The

Duke . . . The Duke Of Extended Sagehood . . . The Duke . . ." and then another of the geomancers must have panicked and Spencer roared at him in English hoping no one nearby spoke the language, "Get back! Get back or they'll realize we haven't got—" and as the translation went through the entire crowd like a knife, there was a roar and suddenly, pressed in hard by a solid wall of bodies, he could not get anything else out or even breathe.

It was the damned cowls all the mourners had on. At the front end of the crush, a full head taller than anyone else across the entire square, Auden couldn't see anything ahead for the damned white cowls.

Auden, the lone, defenseless, the different-colored face in what suddenly felt like a solid wall of Ku Klux Klansmen readying themselves to hang him from the nearest tree, yelled back over his shoulder to Spencer, "I can't see anyone! All I can see is—" and then, suddenly, as the crowd surged in, someone must have fallen or tripped and there was a break and he saw right across to the far side of the square.

Auden yelled, "It's the fucking Triads! I recognize that bastard Sammy Lee from the fucking Shanghai Bund gang! They're at the back shoving the people forward and—"

Then there was another break and he saw, across from them, more people, people from the 14–K, and then, milling in between them—and he could hardly believe for a moment he saw it there, then, in Hong Kong, still a month away from the takeover—soldiers in the uniform of the Chinese People's Liberation Army pushing and shoving and carrying guns.

And then, behind him, all the geomancers—not a single strong young man among them—all seemed to cry out in terror at once and then, as they dropped the coffin and it hit the ground with a splintering sound, there was a sound from

Spencer that Auden could not make out and he was in trouble, and as Auden himself caught a slashing blow from someone's fingernails in the crowd—an old woman with her face full of anger and hatred and disappointment—everything was wrong and ruined and no good and they had fucked it all up.

From somewhere on the ground, Spencer yelled in Cantonese, "The Duke Of Extended . . ." and then there was a cry of pain as someone must have kicked him, and then, as from all sides the whiteness of all the robes and cowls came in at him like a wave, Auden went down and all there was all around him were the screams and cries of pain from the geomancers, and, suddenly running out past his hand on the street in streams, lines of blood.

"Pick it up!" It was Spencer. Somehow, in the melee, he must have gotten to his feet. Spencer, screaming at the geomancers in English, roared as an order, *"Pick it up!* Pick it up! *Pick it up!"* but none of them did, and as Auden somehow got to his feet as well, all the geomancers were on the ground, cowered and balled up in the fetal position, and it was all over and there they were all going to die.

Suddenly, with a terrible feeling of sadness coming over him, not for himself, but for the poor, dead, ninety-five-year-old creature in the coffin with, like him, after this, nowhere to go, Auden yelled just once, for the record, "Here! In this place, it was the best time I ever had!"

He tried to turn to see the coffin to explain to the poor creature inside, "I'm sorry that I—" and then, Spencer, somehow back on his feet next to him and looking down a suddenly opened corridor in the wall of white, yelled, "The Duke! Which one of you is the Duke?" and then the corridor closed again and all he could see, glittering in the light, were knives and razors coming out everywhere and eyes flashing with hatred.

"Harry!" For an instant, as if in tableau, Auden saw Feiffer and O'Yee.

He saw them standing far off, halfway down the square, next to a man in a dark business suit.

He saw their faces and knew, like him, they could do nothing.

He saw the look of pain and horror in O'Yee's eyes, and for a moment, as the man looked directly at him, Auden had the urge to smile and wave before— And then, in his ears, Spencer roared, not to Feiffer or O'Yee because they could have no part of it, but to anyone, to the gods, to all the things he thought were right and should happen, "The Duke Of Extended Sagehood! The Yen Sheng Kung! Which one of you is he? *Which one of you is the Duke?"*

He didn't hear the two softly spoken words someone said from somewhere, but everyone else in the crowd did, and it stilled them into utter, absolute silence.

And then, as the crowd opened up around him like a huge white door swinging back to make him a great walkway down through it to where the coffin was, he said it, softly, again not raising his voice at all, for a second time.

Passing directly in front of Feiffer and, as he went by, taking the little paper-wrapped box from the man's hand before he even saw it was gone and holding it up for all the crowd to see, Colonel Kong of the Chinese People's Police and God alone only knew what else, said and left no shadow of doubt about it with his tone, *"I am,"* and, passing through the crowd, not as if he were dressed in an anonymous dark business suit, but in the long flowing robes of all the antiquity of his ancestors, came forward, and with the little box held high up above his head for everyone to see, stood by the fallen coffin on the ground and looked down at the open, empty jade box on its lid.

* * *

He was the Yen Sheng Kung: the Duke Of Extended Sagehood, the authentic lineal descendant of the greatest and wisest teacher and philosopher who had ever lived in the entire five thousand years of Chinese history, Master Kung—*Confucius.*

When he spoke, people listened.

When he asked a question, people knew he had already pondered it in every way it could be pondered, and had the simplest, the purest, the most moral and obvious and true answer to it there was to be had.

He asked a question now.

Now not raising his voice, but with his words audible in every stilled corner of the square as they were passed on in whispers, looking down at the open box on the coffin, Kong said slowly in Cantonese almost as if he merely said it to himself, as if it were nothing more than a casual, minor problem to be dealt with that day, "Well, who among you is the worthy one to represent all that China is and has been and will be by the act of placing this box on his coffin and restoring this poor man's body and soul back to intactness again? Which one of you, therefore, by that act, is the one who should have the mandate of heaven and the loyalty of all the people around you? Which one of you?"

He was a Communist: a Colonel in the Chinese People's Police. All around him were all the people he was going to have to deal with when he and his people finally and irrevocably took over, and behind them, slinking back out of his sight as his eyes roamed over them, were the Triads: all the people he was also going to have to deal with.

He looked down only for a moment at the geomancers still cowering on the ground—this time not out of fear of the crowd, but out of fear of him, and with a motion of his hand signaled them to get up, and maybe, as their faces filled with anxiety, in that moment, beckoned them away to irrelevancy and extinction.

Colonel Kong asked, "Well? Who?"

It was all—the takeover of the Colony of Hong Kong and the way it was going to be done and had to be done—all nothing more than a dress rehearsal for the larger issue, the final chapter in the history of modern China: the unification with the other China, with Taiwan.

It was a signal. It was a signal who the Chinese were, and had been in an unbroken line for five thousand years, and what—emperors and regimes, tyrants and despots and democracies, and all the other, brief, invented dreams and toy-anthill governments of men notwithstanding—what China would always be—its people.

Its people, one-quarter of all the human beings on the planet, were, like the eunuch, like Sun Yaoting, all born in what they believed was the greatest and wisest and most civilized nation that had ever existed, and then, like him, through circumstances and their own very numbers, condemned to poverty and struggle and nothingness.

Kong, telling them something they already knew, said still softly, "My ancestor began life as a tax collector. He collected the one-tenth of all the produce from the farmers that the emperor thought was equitable. He did this until the emperor decided that it would be more equitable for him to collect one-fifth, and then one-half and then four-fifths and then—finally—everything!" He paused for a moment. "Which of you wants only to collect from this good deed of yours only one-tenth? Or one-fifth? Or even one-half? Or nothing?"

He was untouchable. He feared no one, not even the people he worked for. Kong, speaking not for the Communists, but for China, said, "We intend to deal with the West. We intend to join our fellow man on this earth. Who among you wants no advantage from this good deed? Who among you, like my ancestor, signals that only good prevails? Who among you is *China?"*

It was an impossible situation. It was the sort of situation his ancestor, China's teacher, had dealt with every day.

"Who among you is not sure of himself? Who among you doubts all of his own actions, doubts that they are right, doubts his own motives, his own sincerity, his own *worth?* Who among you— Who among you if it comes to it—and it may—who among you *is prepared to do a good act and reap only personal sadness and pain from it—but do it nevertheless because it is the moral thing to do?"*

If anyone from the Triads spoke now, in a week or two they were going to be shot.

If anyone from his own people, the Communists, spoke now, in three weeks, having thrown him in prison as a traitor, they were going to have the entire island of Hong Kong and perhaps half of China itself rioting in the streets.

If he spoke himself and offered to return the box to its place on the top of the coffin, all it would mean was that everything he said was a lie and he too was nothing more than the emperor had been.

Kong said, answering his own question, "Who is what China is? *He* is!" and indicated no one. "Who is the good man of China? The honest man? The moral man? *He* is!" And again, indicated no one, and then, suddenly turning and pointing to him, did.

He was the authentic descendant of Confucius. What he said could not be disputed.

Going forward with the little box in his hand, Kong said, "I know this man! I know who he is and what he is."

It was not the final rite at the end of five thousand years of history, merely a continuation, a going-on in another form, merely a pause for resanctification.

It was the greatest honor that could ever be bestowed upon a living man, and politically, in the long view of another five thousand years, the wisest there could ever be.

Going forward directly to the man and handing him the little box that made everything whole again, Colonel Kong said softly to O'Yee, "Here. *You* do it."

18.

They stood there in the square, the five of them, watching for a long time, until finally the last of the white-robed mourners passed away out of sight down a side street towards the cemetery and they could no longer hear the sound of all the cymbals and drums and devotions and obsequies.

Lighting a cigarette, and then looking down at his hand to keep it steady, Feiffer said pleasantly in English, "Nice speech, Claude."

He had used to like smoking. Glancing down at the curling smoke, Claude said with a nod, "Hmm. Thanks. I thought it had a certain style myself." Standing a little to one side of him, he saw Auden mouth silently to Feiffer, *"Is he really the Duke Of—?"* and Feiffer nod back to him, *"Yes,"* and Auden mouth, *"Wow!"*

Claude said, "Tell me, Harry: what was in the box?"

It had cost everything he had. Feiffer, looking the man directly in the face, said as the last time he would ever answer that question, "Everything that was supposed to be in there. Everything that all these people here believed was important."

"I see." He smiled.

"Where's yours?"

"What?"

"Where's your box, Claude? The one you had in case—"

"Oh." O'Yee was standing farther off. For his own reasons, he could not bring himself to speak to anyone. Claude said a little louder, making sure he heard too, "Oh, my little box, the one I have in my pocket here? Oh. What is in that?" He took it out and it was not the same sort of box Feiffer had had at all, but bigger and rectangular, and heavier, covered in green baize. Clause asked, "This one here?"

"Yes."

Claude said suddenly very seriously, "Everything you ever wanted."

Claude said suddenly, totally out of character, "God knows how the hell I'm supposed to police this place with normal, hard-working, properly wired-up good Communist Chinese policemen with no imagination at all. God only knows! Personally, I don't think it can be done! Hong Bay isn't like anywhere else on earth. It doesn't need policing by cops! What it needs is policing by a goddamned *Confucian Harmony Squad!* What it needs is policing by a gang of complete and utter *lunatics!*"

It was a nice, pleasant day a little before evening, one month before the takeover.

It was a very pleasant day indeed, the nicest any one of them could remember for a very long time.

Opening the box that held four brand-new Special Administrative Region Hong Kong Police Detective badges and holding it out, Kong asked quietly, "It's in my gift. *Care to stay on with me here after the takeover and do it?*"